Presented To:

Sarah

From:

Lisa with
love

Date:

25.1.20

IN THE BLINK OF AN EYE

IN THE BLINK OF AN EYE

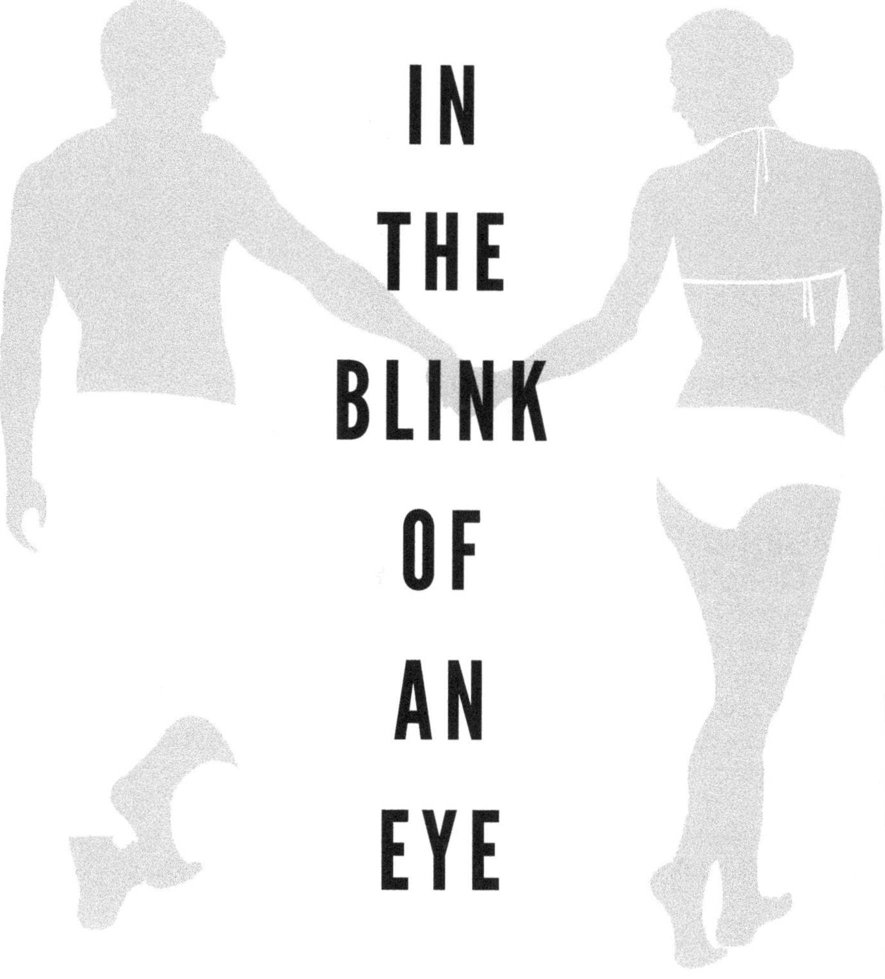

A NOVEL BY LISA LABON

Published By Open Scroll
Publications

Second Edition by:
Open Scroll Publications Ltd,
Kemp House, 160 City Road,
London, EC1V 2NX.
www.openscroll.co.uk

ISBN 978-1-9999856-1-5

The names and identifying details of some individuals mentioned in this book have been changed to protect their privacy.

A CIP catalogue record for this book is available from the British library.

Edited by Diane Wilkie. Email: dee.wilkie7@hotmail.co.uk

Cover design and Typeset by Open Scroll Publications Ltd.

Printed in Great Britain.

DEDICATION

This book is dedicated to my beloved mum and dad! Thank you both for bringing me into this world!

ACKNOWLEDGEMENTS

I would like to thank my husband Steve for seeing something in me all those years ago. Thank you for your words of encouragement that have helped me to become the woman I am today!

I would also like to thank my friends Chris Walker and Gwen Timms, for the love and support they gave me while I was writing this book. Thank you for believing in me even when I didn't believe in myself.

TO THE READER WITH LOVE

I have always had a passion for writing and find it a very good way of expressing my feelings. This has made me become very dedicated to my writing, and I get great satisfaction from it. This is my first novel and I have loved every minute of getting the story down on paper. It is the first of a trilogy and I am currently working on the second book. I have always wanted to write a book and feel so proud that I actually finished my first manuscript.

I have had to endure many hard times throughout my life and feel, that my experiences have helped me to accomplish my dream of being a writer and story teller. I like many people, like to forget my worries by getting engrossed in a good romantic book. I have a good imagination and find it easy to get so involved in the story that I find myself wishing that something that romantic, would happen to me. This was the thinking behind the story and why I wanted to share it with you.

I hope that you will feel the same way when you read 'In the blink of an eye,' as you get to know Danielle who is the main character of the book. We all wish for a happy ending to the story of our own lives, so I hope you will be able to relate to her so much that you come back for more, and also enjoy reading the second book coming soon!

Happy reading!

Lisa Labon

PROLOGUE

THE MIND IS A STRANGE THING. It has the ability to create a masterpiece out of just one thought, and the authority to shatter that creation with just one niggling seed of doubt. It has the power to hide our innermost secrets, and the audacity to remind us of them when we least expect it. When the night creeps in, our minds open up to a world full of dreams, offering a place of safety, and cushioning us from the damaging realities of life. Here, our worst fears can be transformed into visions of hope, and for just a short while, we are equipped with the capability of outsmarting those cruel hands of fate. Suffering and pain are non-existent in this place, where happy endings are as predictable as the dawning of a new day. Memories of death and loss are barred from entering this sanctuary, its mission to destroy, temporarily put on hold. 'Temporary,' however is the operative word, because eventually... you have to wake up!

"Where's Billy?" cried Danielle as she stood in front of an empty grave. Panicking, her eyes scanned the cemetery searching for her son, but he was nowhere to be seen. Knowing that he had to be there somewhere, she turned back to the vacant plot, and noticed a big vase of white Lilies sitting at the foot of the gravestone. Reaching down, she tried to touch the beautiful bouquet of unspoilt flowers, but as her hand neared the crisp white petals, they suddenly shrivelled up and disappeared.

"Danielle," the sound of the gentle wind whispered in her ear.

"He is not here…But, you are not to blame."

Disorientated, she withdrew her hand. Although she knew her heart was breaking, she didn't feel any physical pain, but for some strange reason, she felt at peace.

"Yes, he is!" she screamed, her tears beginning to flow.

"Billy, where are you?" she asked desperately. Then turning around, she saw him.

"There's my boy," she whispered into the air that had tried to convince her otherwise.

"There's my Billy." A big triumphant smile swept across her face, squashing her fears like the grass beneath her feet. Unable to move her legs, she cupped her hands around her mouth and shouted, "Billy, it's me."

To her disappointment however, Billy showed no signs of acknowledging her and kept on walking. Even though he didn't hear her voice, she was not deterred, and her smile widened.

My Billy's come home at last, she thought, as she watched

him walk past her only yards away, wearing his favourite blue and white roll necked jumper.

How tall and handsome you are...Oh how I have missed you. Tears were still streaming down her cheeks, only this time they were tears of joy. Finding her strength, she called him again and began to go towards him.

"Billy!" Now she was running.

"Billy," she cried coming up behind him.

"It's me, your mum." Billy stopped.

"Oh son, I am so glad you came home."

She stopped just inches away from him. Moving in slow motion, he turned around and looked at his mother. He stared at her for a few moments, and her heart felt as though it had stopped. Then as if by magic, a huge smile of recognition swept across his face. His gorgeous hazel eyes had the power to light up the heavens, and she had never seen him look so handsome. Suddenly, a deep sense of pride overwhelmed her.

"Oh darling, it has been so long... too long," she said holding out her arms. "I was afraid I would never see you again."

He fell into his mother's embrace. Finally, she was able to hold her son in her arms again. Squeezing him she said, "I never, ever want to let you go."

Billy stayed silent. But something deep down in Danielle's soul told her she had no other choice. Putting her head into his chest, she closed her eyes and breathed in the memory of her son.

"I love you so much," she said holding him tight, in the

hope that he would respond to her in the same way. Still, Billy stayed silent. A few moments passed them by.

"You are the only one who holds me like that," were the only words that came out of Billy's mouth as he held his mother tight. But then he pulled away. Aware that she would lose him at any moment, she tried her utmost to keep hold of her first-born son, but it was no use. Somehow, he had slipped out of her grasp. Fearing this would be the last time, she ever saw him, an excruciating pain tore through her heart.

"Where are you going?" she shouted confused, holding out her hand to him. She just couldn't understand why he wanted to leave.

"Please don't go," she begged, her voice now just a whisper, but he carried on walking. Her worst fears manifested themselves once again as she watched her son disappear out of her life. Then, in the blink of an eye, Billy was gone.

Helpless, alone, and now back in the arms of reality, Danielle woke up.

CHAPTER

ONE

Four years previously:

DANIELLE STOOD BEHIND THE bar watching the rain drops racing down the window. It was a typical English day. The wind was howling, and the customer's miserable faces all told the same story; they longed to be somewhere else. As she watched the water slide down the pane, she pondered how it was like a reflection of her own miserable life.

Every time the door opened, she hoped to see a smiling face. She didn't feel her usual happy self, especially as financially she felt worn down. She loved working at the Kings Head, but it barely paid the bills, so she felt it was time to look for something else. Taking a deep breath, she reminded herself that she was there to cheer up the customers, so she forced her worries to the back of her mind.

As the door opened, she put on a smile which became genuine as Matt rushed in soaking wet.

"Blimey it's raining cats and dogs out there," said Matt dripping water all over the floor.

“Two pints of the usual please Dan,” he asked pulling out a soggy packet of cigarettes from his pocket.

“I don’t believe it, I’ve just bought these.” His face was like thunder as he pulled out a stick of mush.

“You smoke too much anyway,” smirked Danielle as she pulled his first pint of beer.

“Mick is on his way in, so I will get a fag off him,” replied Matt childishly.

Knowing Mick was on his way in automatically cheered her up. She was always pleased to him. Having worked in the pub over the past year they had become good friends. The three of them often sat there moaning about their lives and putting the world to rights.

She placed Matt’s pint on the bar and proceeded to pull the next one, when the door opened, and Mick came hurtling in, cursing at the top of his voice.

“I don’t believe it. Some stupid idiot just nearly killed me,” he said his face red with rage causing everyone to stop talking and turn to look at him. He immediately became self-conscious as he realised with horror, that he had unintentionally become the centre of attention. As he blushed with embarrassment, he forgot how angry he felt. He smiled awkwardly at the onlookers as he walked over to the bar.

“I’ve just come from the travel agents where I picked up our tickets, and some moron just tried to knock me over. It’s not as if I’m a small bloke and he couldn’t see me! I thought I was a goner! I swear I could see the grim reaper laughing at me on the other side of the road,” he said picking up his glass and taking a big mouthful of his beer.

"Ah I needed that just to calm my nerves," he said to Matt.

Danielle took the money for the two drinks from Matt and walked over to the till listening to the two men talking behind her.

"So, we are all booked and ready to go then?" asked Matt smiling at his friend.

"Oh yes Matty boy! In three weeks, we will be sunning ourselves in beautiful Greece. I have spoken to Panos and it's all arranged," replied Mick smugly.

Their conversation caught Danielle's attention. "Are you two going away?" she asked curiously.

"Yes Dan, we are spending two glorious weeks in Skiathos with my mate Panos," replied Mick excitedly.

Danielle couldn't help but feel a pang of jealousy.

"It's alright for some," she said finding it hard to disguise the envy in her voice.

"Why don't you come with us Dan?" Matt suddenly piped up.

"You could do with the break. It would be good for you. What do you think?"

"Don't be silly how can I afford to go away? For one, I haven't got the money, and two I've got three children to think about," she laughed half-heartedly.

"I've thought about that and decided I can lend you the money, no strings attached, honest. You can pay me back whenever you can. As for the kids, I'm sure you can sort something out! Go on Dan, at least think about it, it would be great. You know it would."

Danielle smiled as she looked into Matt's big brown eyes.

She could not help feeling admiration and compassion for this kind man. The past year had been very difficult for them both. They shared a similar problem as both had ex partners whose mission in life, seemed to be to cause as much hurt and misery as possible! They were fortunately both survivors, and with each other's help they managed to get through the bad times. For a split second, Danielle was seriously tempted by Matt's offer, but she soon talked herself out of it. She knew it could never happen.

"I'm serious Dan it wouldn't be a problem. Please think about it," he said detecting the glimmer of temptation in her eyes. He had become very fond of her over the past twelve months, and during those times he had consoled her when she was feeling down. He had always felt helpless, as he watched her struggle to bring up three children on her own. This was heightened by all the major problems with her eldest son Billy, who was fourteen. The offer was his way of doing something nice and practical to ease her burden. She had earned a well-deserved break, and this holiday would be the perfect opportunity to make her life a little bit better, even if for only two weeks.

"I am very grateful Matt," she said putting her hand lightly on his arm. "But I can't." With that she turned away to serve another customer.

Matt looked to Mick for some support, but he was too busy chewing someone's ear off about his divorce and what a bitch his wife was being. Mick was Matt's best friend as well as his boss. They spent most of their time together, either at work or in the pub. Mick had his own car yard and Matt was his number one mechanic. They worked well together and had done so for the past five years. Mick trusted Matt one hundred per cent and this had set a strong foundation for their enduring friendship. They both enjoyed a beer every lunch time, at the Kings Head where they had gotten to know Danielle. They were both drawn to her bubbly personality and carefree attitude. At first neither of them realized just how difficult her life really was. It only became apparent as they got to know her well. This amazed them because she never gave anything away when she was working. This caused them to grow to admire her. She was a very popular member of staff with all of the customers, and the two men felt honoured to call her their friend. In spite of all their problems, the three of them still somehow managed to have a laugh together.

Danielle was absolutely devastated when her husband left her for another woman a year ago. She was forced to come to terms with having to bring up her children on her own. Somehow, she managed to pick up the pieces of her life and got herself a part time job at the Kings Head. Not only did it bring in some extra money, but it also kept her sane! For those few hours a day she could be herself, rather than just mum and dad to the kids. In the pub there was no bickering and squabbling, and just for a short while she felt she was still a part of the real world.

Billy was the eldest of her three children. His father leaving had a profound effect on him. Almost immediately, he developed a bad attitude and made his mother feel as if she could do nothing right. His bad behaviour not only affected her deeply, but also his younger siblings as well. He became very spiteful towards his younger sister and brother, and this was a huge concern for Danielle. Things got so bad that his conduct spilled over into his school life. She was constantly getting reports back from his school about him fighting and being a bully. The teachers were very sympathetic towards her because they knew the situation at home, but he was slowly getting out of control, and they were unsure of how to handle him.

She tried everything from talking to him like an adult, to punishing him by taking away his favourite things, but nothing seemed to work. When she asked him what was wrong, he just clammed up, not saying a word. This became very frustrating for her and she often lay awake worrying about his future. It broke her heart to see what was happening to her first-born son, and she wondered what would become of him. She loved him so much, but sometimes found herself hating him at the same time. She despised what he was doing to her, and especially what he was doing to himself.

His father was another matter. He didn't care at all as he was too wrapped up in his new family, which made her blood boil. She was convinced this was the reason behind Billy's behaviour. All she could do was hope he would soon come to terms with this big change in his young life and accept it. With these thoughts on her mind, she spent many nights crying herself to sleep. There were some good days when she felt as though things were getting back to normal at last and she could see the good boy she loved beneath all the anger, but those days were few and far between.

Fortunately, her other two children did not cause her any problems and she was thankful for that. Marie was twelve years old, an intelligent young lady who loved music and was always dancing around the house. Her presence was strongly felt, and she always brought a smile to her mother's face. She did of course have her moments because she could be very stubborn, but as a rule Danielle could cope with that.

Marie could see the affect Billy was having on their mother, and therefore always tried her best to please her. She had always been closer to her mum so when her father left, the impact on her was not as great, as it had been on her big brother. She had even tried talking to him, but he would not listen to her and just retaliated with his fists. It was as if he just wanted to hurt her. In the end she just tried her hardest to keep out of his way.

She did however love being around her younger brother Charlie and doted on him. She was four when he was born and was only too happy to help her mother with the new born baby. Her mum teased her about being his second mum. Now that he was old enough, she spent hours playing with him, leaving their mum to get on with other things around the house, and as far as she was concerned, Marie was a godsend.

Charlie was a very loving, good natured boy. He was eight years old and had inherited his mum's height and sense of humour. They were very close, especially as she knew she could take him anywhere and he was never any problem. He took his father's leaving quite hard in the beginning, and this manifested by him simultaneously becoming very clingy to Danielle. It did not take him long however to adapt to his new way of life. He didn't understand why his dad was no longer around, but he instinctively knew his mother's love was sufficient for him. He also loved his big sister deeply and got great pleasure from all the attention she gave him. He did not have much to do with Billy on the other hand, as he was always nasty to him and seemed to enjoy making him cry.

Charlie loved it when his mum's friend Matt came around to the house. It seemed like he always appeared when his mother was crying and upset, and always managed to make her laugh. He also made such a big fuss of him, and before long they soon developed a close bond.

Matt had a lot of time for Danielle and her children and enjoyed spending time with them. He could see the pain in Billy's eyes, which tugged at his heart strings. Ideally, he would have loved to have had a similar effect on Billy as he did on Charlie, but he sensed Billy was not about to let him into his world. Matt could not blame him for that, so respectfully kept his distance. It enraged him to think a father could cause so much heartache to his own son. He tried his best to assure Danielle that everything would be alright, but even he wasn't entirely convinced, so he promised to always be there for her, the way she was always there for him.

Matt was going through a separation from Jan his wife of twelve years. It was so difficult for him because he was still very much in love with her. He was also the proud father of two girls, and he did everything he could to provide a good life for his family. He worked hard and long, taking great pleasure in making them happy. It was worth it to see the smiling faces of his princesses. He hadn't noticed the distance developing between him and Jan, so when he came home one day to find his bags packed, the shock hit him like a ton of bricks.

"I need time to think," Jan explained. "I don't know what I want anymore. I need some space to sort out my head."

Her harsh unprovoked words rattled around his confused mind as she said, "I will be in touch with you soon."

The girls were at a friend's, so he didn't even get a chance to say goodbye to them. That was nearly ten months ago. He did finally manage to speak to Jan, but she refused to give him access to the children. He tried to reason with her but to no avail. She was adamant about her decision, insisting it was now in the hands of the courts.

He was gutted because she hadn't even had the decency to give him a proper explanation about her conduct. The thought that he would never see his lovely girls again, was absolute torture and ate him up inside!

If it had not been for his close friendship with Mick, and all the support he got from him, he was sure he would have ended his life there and then. The past ten months had been gut wrenching, but he was slowly but surely beginning to put the pieces of his life back together again. He knew it was still early days yet, but he finally found the strength to carry on. That's why he cherished time spent with Danielle and her children. It took his mind off his own troubles. He channelled most of his energy into work and helping her the best he could.

When Mick therefore asked him to go to Skiathos with him, the timing was perfect, and he simply jumped at the chance. A holiday was just what he needed! His only problem now was how to convince Danielle to go with them. He knew he had his work cut out but was willing to give it his best shot. He had the utmost respect for her and wanted nothing more than to give her a piece of happiness.

Similarly, Mick was at a very low point in his life too. His business was going well but his marriage was a disaster. His wife Tracey hardly spoke to him anymore, and when they did have a conversation it always ended up in an argument. This made going home unbearable. The only time he was happy these days was either at work or in the pub. He knew he drank a lot but convinced himself, he had it well under control. This was in spite of losing his licence through drink driving six months earlier. Of-course this was a big blow because now he had to rely on Matt to do all the driving around. After a few weeks however, he soon got used to not having a car. Through the stress of a court case and the problems at home, Mick went from nineteen stone down to fifteen! He had to admit though, he hadn't felt so good about himself for years! He began to quite like the man he saw in the mirror, because his weight loss gave him a boost of confidence. He decided to get a makeover, and even got his long hair cut and cropped close, to his head. (He had worn it shoulder length, from as far back as he could remember). Everyone commented on how his new look suited him so much better. Even the women noticed him now, and he revelled in all the newly found attention. This gave him an ego boost, but he was still painfully aware of the huge void in his life.

Although he loved the attention, it depressed him that it was not coming from the woman he loved. In fact Tracey still ignored him, which hurt him deeply. He missed her immensely, especially the closeness they once shared. The cuddles made him feel so wanted. Sometimes he even missed the arguing, because at least then he felt like he still existed. He longed for the long-lost wife who once loved him. He was just so grateful that he had his friends there to help him to cope.

Such a friend was Matt whom he loved like a brother, and always tried to help him whenever he could. That's how they came to work together. Matt was a very hard worker, and he was so grateful for Mick's support and offer of a job. He did not know what he would have done without him.

Mick watched his best friend nearly destroy himself when

Jan threw him out, so he did his best to keep him busy and take his mind off his suffering. It broke his heart to see Matt go from a strong confident happy go lucky person, to a downtrodden broken man. He therefore came up with the idea and began toying with the thought of them going away. He put the idea to Matt and when he agreed, he was over the moon. Almost immediately the flights were booked, and they were all set to fly off to Skiathos to enjoy the Greek sunshine.

This would be the sixth year Mick had been to Skiathos, as he adored the Greek island. He had spent the happiest times of his married life there, and both he and Tracey fell in love with the place. When they first arrived on the island, they were taken in by its beauty.

They had been due to stay at the Grand hotel, but things didn't work out. At the airport they were told there had been a mistake and they had been a double booking. Sheer horror went through them at the thought of having to sleep on the beach. In a panic, the representative who had been chosen to look after them, found them a hotel somewhere else. It was the last room left, and the couple breathed a sigh of relief.

They were driven by taxi up into the hills where they finally reached their destination, the Oasis Hotel. They could not believe their good fortune. To them it was pure paradise. It was a family run business and the now happy couple were treated like royalty, especially for the inconvenience, they had experienced.

Drawn in by the Greek way of life and the friendliness of the natives, they stayed in the Oasis every year afterwards. The host family made them feel so welcome and they became close personal friends. Mick struck up an even deeper friendship with the eldest son Panos over the years, and they became so close that Panos began to regard Mick as a brother, a high honour in Mick's eyes.

Matt had heard Mick talk about Panos and his family many times, and therefore looked forward to meeting them. He just hoped the next three weeks would hurry up and pass so that they could get the holiday underway. They discussed the possibility of Danielle coming with them and were delighted to be in agreement about it. The only problem now was persuading her to go. He picked up the phone and began dialling.

CHAPTER

TWO

THE NEXT DAY DANIELLE WENT to work in a very thoughtful mood. She kept thinking about Matt's generous offer and it was beginning to give her a headache. She was very tempted by the offer of a holiday, but soon convinced herself there was no way she could possibly go. The biggest obstacle was the fact that she felt she just could not leave her children for two whole weeks. It was bad enough leaving them for a few hours, which did not even happen very often. Bearing in mind how they already felt abandoned by one parent, she just couldn't do it to them because she felt guilty about that every day!

No Dan, get that stupid idea out of your head, she thought to herself. Her thoughts were rudely interrupted by the phone ringing.

"Hello, the Kings Head," she answered half-heartedly.

"H-hello Dan it's me. H-how are you?" stammered a nervous voice.

"Oh, Brad it's you. What do you want?" replied Danielle feeling quite agitated by the stuttering caller. There was an awkward silence which seemed to last for minutes.

"Well are you going to answer me? I'm really busy and don't have time to stand here chatting with you," she replied sharply. She scanned the room noting that there were only a few customers really, but she had no desire whatsoever to talk to Brad.

"I-I just w-wondered why you haven't returned any of my phone calls? I've left three messages on your answer phone, and I've been waiting for you to phone me all day." His voice quivered when he spoke.

More fool you then, she thought.

"I told you last week how I felt Brad, and nothing has changed. You were a lying cheat then, and in my opinion, you are no different now! Now leave me alone I am busy," she said beginning to lose her temper.

"Please Dan listen to me. I know what I did was wrong, but I love you and I will change, I promise… I don't want to lose you, I need you. Please give me one more chance to make it up to you, I am begging you."

The sickly tone of his voice made her skin crawl. She looked around the bar as one of the regulars looking rather restless, banged his glass on the bar. "I will be right with you Stuart," she said winking and then rolling her eyes at the thirsty man.

"Look Brad I have to go as there is a customer waiting. I will be at home later, but you will be wasting your breath."

With that she hung up the phone. She could have kicked herself for mentioning the last bit! Now he'll think I was inviting him round.

Why didn't I just hang up the phone when I heard his voice? I'm too soft, she thought, full of regret and annoyed with herself!

The last thing she needed was this hassle. She didn't want to speak to him, let alone see him. She made a mental note to text him later to tell him to forget about coming around after all. She wanted to ensure he got the message once and for all.

Previously she had met Brad in the Kings Head four months after her husband left. Her heart was still raw from the break up with her husband. She was at a low point in her life and still felt very vulnerable. They started talking one day and he seemed interested in what she had to say. He complimented her on how she looked, showing her the attention, she craved. Slowly they became friends and he found the courage to ask her out on a date. Flattered by his charm, she agreed. They went to a restaurant and spent all night in deep conversation telling each other about their lives. He told her all about the bad marriage he was in, and how unhappy he was at home. He apparently had four children and they were the only reason he stayed with his wife. She questioned him about why he didn't just leave. He explained that he and his wife had come to an amicable decision to stay in the same house for the sake of the children. He soon convinced her he that he was telling the truth.

They began to see each other regularly, and she felt at last her life was getting back on track. He made her feel special, a feeling she thought had long gone, and always told her how he loved being in her company. Before long they spent most evenings together although he eventually had to go home, except at weekends when he stayed over. She didn't mind this arrangement as she was content not to get too involved, as she still found it hard to trust a man. He was unperturbed by her friendship with Matt and did not feel threatened, by the closeness the two friends shared, which was an added bonus.

For months everything ran smoothly, and all things considered, she was at last content with her life. Just as she was lulled into a false sense of security, things suddenly started to go wrong with Brad. He began to make excuses about being unable to see her after work, and it always seemed to have something to do with his children. He had parents evening, or he had to take them shopping for shoes, or his boys were playing football. There was always something.

Initially she was sympathetic; he was after all, their father and they were his first priority.

She became suspicious and began to wonder what was going on however, when he began to make the same excuses repeatedly. What made matters worse was that people told her that they had seen him in another pub, when he had told her he was at home with his kids. She confronted and questioned him, but he always managed to talk his way out of anything until she believed him time and time again. She became very fond of him which unfortunately clouded her judgement. Many of her customers warned her that he would hurt her, but she would not listen.

Whenever they were together, he showered her with gifts, treating her like a princess, something her husband had never done. She therefore chose to ignore the rumours and the warning bells going off in her head, as she told herself they did not know him like she did, and that they were wrong about him.

Even Matt heard the rumours and tried his best to warn her about this man. He became frustrated when she would not listen because she was so obviously besotted by him. He just hoped one day she would open her eyes and see him for what he really was. That day came sooner than he had anticipated.

One evening Matt was feeling quite depressed, and since the Kings Head was not busy and nothing much was going on, he decided to go to another pub for a change. He phoned Mick and they arranged to meet up in a pub across town. Matt had heard a band was playing, so this gave him something to look forward to. It took him ten minutes to walk through the high street. He walked through the door and the sound of the guitar blaring out nearly knocked him sideways. He instantly recognised the band. They were well known in the area and this delighted him because the lead singer was an old friend from school. He strolled up to the bar and was pleased to see Mick was already there.

As Matt walked over to his friend, Mick turned around to face him looking extremely angry.

"What's the matter with you? You look like you're ready to punch someone," said Matt becoming quite worried at Mick's deadly expression.

"Look who's at the end of the bar," said Mick through clenched teeth. Both men peered intensely down the bar. The place was packed solid, and it took Matt a few moments to make out the figure ordering a drink.

"That's Brad isn't it? What's he doing here? Is Dan with him?" he asked as he'd noticed the man had picked up two drinks. The two men watched in silence as he took the drinks to a nearby table.

"I'm going to say hello to Dan," said Matt until Mick gripped hold of his arm pulling him back.

"Dan is not with him," he said firmly, taking a mouthful

of his drink.

"I haven't got a clue who is with him, but he has been all over her since I've been here."

They both watched in amazement as Brad put the drinks down and sat next to the mystery woman. When Matt saw him putting his arm around her and then kiss her full on the lips, he was seething with anger and had to bite down on his bottom lip to control himself.

"That bastard! Who does he think he is? I am going to kill him!" stated Matt clenching his fists ready for attack.

"Don't be silly mate," Mick chided. "We've got to think about this…Where's Dan?"

"At home I presume."

Matt nodded, his eyes never leaving the sordid couple.

"I'm going to phone her and get her down here, so she can see this for herself," said Mick getting his phone out to phone her.

Matt stood there his fists clenched tight, and it took all his willpower not to go over and smack Brad on the nose.

"Hello Dan, listen mate you are not going to like this," said Mick calmly as he proceeded to tell her what was going on.

Danielle had just put Charlie to bed when the phone rang. Marie was at the dinner table doing her homework and Billy was watching the telly. She listened intently to what Mick had to say, and when he mentioned Brad's name she froze.

"N-no Mick he can't be there because he's watching his son play football." She became more and more confused as he explained the grimy details, and a big knot evolved in her stomach. Mick's voice faded into the distance when she imagined Brad being with another girl.

"Dan, Danielle, are you alright? I am sorry babe, but you have got to get down here fast. He doesn't even know we are here, so you had better hurry."

"O-ok Mick I-I'll be right there," she said still in a daze as she hung up the phone. Her mind was racing, and she was desperately trying to absorb what had been said.

"Mum what's wrong?" asked Marie as she turned to her mother. She panicked because her mother's face that had gone a ghostly white.

"Oh n-nothing is wrong darling," Danielle replied unconvincingly.

"I need you two to keep an ear out for your brother because I have to go out." She quickly got her coat and kissed them goodbye.

"I won't be long I promise," she shouted walking out of the door.

Matt could not take his eyes off the couple as they laughed and joked together. He could feel the anger churning in his stomach like a swarm of bees trapped but frantically trying to escape.

At least now Danielle would see Brad for what he really is, he thought. He knew she would be devastated when she walked through the door, but she would soon get over it because both of her friends would be there for her.

He looked at his watch again; it felt like an eternity since Mick had spoken to her on the phone. Every time the door opened his heart missed a beat, expecting to see her. Brad was oblivious to his onlookers and carried on without a care in the world.

Danielle finally emerged through the door like a raging bull. On the way driving down in the car her mind spun. She could not believe Brad would do something like this to her. He was always telling her she was the most important thing in his life and how much he adored her. This scenario however was challenging that and providing proof that screamed loudly otherwise! When she pulled up and spotted his van parked outside, she knew he was in there, and that everything he had ever said was all a lie!

She burst through the pub door, pushing her way through the happy drinkers until she noticed Matt and Mick standing at the bar. They spotted her too and Matt pointed over to where Brad was sitting, without saying a word. She looked over and saw the couple sitting cosily in the corner. Taking a deep breath, she walked over to their table picking up a pint of beer from a nearby table on the way. Brad still oblivious to anything else, had no idea she was on her way over to him armed with a glass. He only realised something was wrong as he started dripping with the beer, that had been thrown in his face!

"What the hell do you think you're doing?" he asked confused about what was going on. His words instantly trailed off as he realised who was responsible for his soaking. He was literally stopped in his tracks and lost for words.

"You two timing son of a bitch!" she shouted at him before he had the chance to explain himself.

"How could you do this to me? Everyone was right about you! You're a no-good piece of filth. How could I have been so blind? Matt warned me so many times," she said pointing over to where Matt and Mick were standing.

"You were so busy with her you didn't even notice they were watching you. Don't ever come near me again, you hear?"

With that she turned around and walked towards the door.

Brad just stood there dripping wet, not sure what to do. He looked over helplessly at Matt who stared back at him, shrugged his shoulders, and smirked before following her out of the pub.

Mick brought another pint and took it over to the table she had picked up the drink from, apologised for the sudden disappearance of the gentleman's drink, and then left too.

Matt and Danielle leaned up against her car, his arm around her trying his best to console her. It had taken all her strength to hold back the tears when she confronted Brad's unfaithful act, but now she was away from the situation the tears were free to flow. She felt sick to her stomach, and all she wanted to do was go home. Matt offered to take her, but she declined explaining she really needed to be on her own.

He promised to phone her later just as Mick came out of the pub. The two of them watched with sympathy as she drove out of sight.

Driving home the tears streamed down her face as she wondered how on earth, she was going to tell her children. They had grown accustomed to having Brad around. Her heart sank knowing they were going to be so hurt and disappointed all over again. There and then she promised herself never to get involved with a man, ever again.

That was a week ago. Although the pain was easing slightly, hearing Brad's voice again, brought it all back again especially the old familiar feeling of being betrayed. She was busy daydreaming when Stuart banged his glass on the bar again bringing her back down to earth with a thud. She picked up his glass and began to pour out his drink, smiling apologetically.

"Are you having men troubles Dan?" he asked, his voice full of concern. He was a regular at the pub and it saddened him to see her looking so down. He noticed she didn't smile so much lately, which was unusual for her because she had always been happy and full of the joys of spring. To make matters worse, rumours flew round the pub about her break up with Brad. There was always some gossip going around about someone, and Stuart didn't usually take any notice. From her expression he knew they were obviously true, and he could not help feeling for her. He had wanted to tell her she was better off without him when it happened, but the timing had never been right.

"You could say that Stu," she said placing his drink down in front of him. "Men are nothing but trouble. I have had enough of the lying cheating toe rags. I am officially now a man free zone!"

He could hear the determination in her voice. "Well, all I can say Dan is it's his loss," he retorted. "You were too good for him in my opinion."

She watched him drink a mouthful of his beer. She had always liked Stuart and enjoyed talking to him. When they first met, she thought he came across as a bit of a snob, especially as he worked in the city running his own business, and she never saw him out of a suit. Once she however got to know him, she changed her initial opinion. She realized that he was a genuinely nice thoughtful guy, who she found out later was also having problems of his own.

"You know what you need Dan?" he said handing her the money for his drink. "You need a holiday just to get away for a couple of weeks to let your hair down."

She stopped and looked at him suspiciously. "Have you

been talking to Matt by any chance?" she said her eyes slanting together.

"He has asked me to go to Greece with him and Mick," she continued.

"Well Mick was the one who mentioned it. By what he said they are both very keen on you going with them. I think it's a good idea, as it will do you good. I am thinking of going too by the way," he replied, a smile forming across his face.

"What, you want to go with them?" she asked taken by surprise.

"Yes absolutely. My reason would be the same as yours. Just to get away from life for a couple of weeks to recharge my batteries. I think we both deserve it. Just think about it, Brad does not exist in Greece. He can't bother you three thousand miles away."

His statement was food for thought and he did have a good point, but she had to be realistic.

"Think about it, Dan you know it makes sense." Those were his last words on the subject, before he picked up his drink and went and sat down with his elderly mother.

She felt bewildered as she watched him walk away. The thought of Stuart being on holiday with Mick and Matt amused her, and she couldn't help but wonder what he had in common with her two close friends. Their hands were permanently black from working on cars, they could both drink for England, and every other word that came out of their mouths was a swear word.

How will they ever be able to hold a conversation let alone spend two weeks together? she thought smiling to herself.

She did agree that he needed to get away, based on what

he had told her about the bad time he was having at home, over the last few months especially as his wife was filing for divorce. This was something he never imagined would happen to him because they had spent many happy years together. She had given him three wonderful boys who had been raised in a calm and healthy environment. He was such a very proud father, as all three were now at university and he could not have wished for a happier life.

Suddenly a year ago his dreams were shattered when he noticed his wife's extreme mood swings. After a while they were then punctuated by verbal outbursts! They were few and far between at first and she always apologised soon afterwards, blaming stress from work. Of- course Stuart was sympathetic and very understanding because he knew how hard she worked. As time went on the outbursts became more frequent until they went too far, as they were now accompanied by violence!

It was so obvious that there was something terribly wrong, so he tried to convince her to seek medical help, but she flatly refused. Instead she turned it around accusing him of being the reason for it all, and the one to blame! He felt worn down by her attitude towards him, and it got to the point where she did not even want to be anywhere near him. The gulf between them grew more and more each day!

To cope with the way things were going, he plunged himself into his work, spending most of his time there. One day however the final blow came. She declared she was filing for a divorce and wanted him out of the family home.

He never imagined the woman he loved dearly could scare him, but she did. As he stood by his front door with his bags packed beside him ready to leave, he looked at her and realized he no longer recognised her. Her face was contorted with hate causing her veins to protrude on her forehead. He searched her face frantically to see even a trace of his lovely wife, but it appeared she no longer existed.

The woman in front of him screamed abuse at him as he picked up his belongings, and he walked out of the door for the last time. He could hear the most awful obscenities being hurled at him as he turned and walked to his car, and they went through his heart like a hot knife. Tears flowed freely now down his distraught face and it took all of his strength not to look back.

He finally had to come to terms with the fact that his marriage was over. He reluctantly moved in with his mother and began to piece together what was left of his life. He kept in regular contact with his sons and put his heart and soul into his business. It was this that kept him sane.

He had only just begun to drink in the Kings Head and had done so a couple of times before his separation. It was convenient for him as it was only a stone's throw from his mother's house. He had always liked the friendly atmosphere, so was pleased it had now become his local. He went there routinely most evenings after work for a couple of drinks to help him unwind from his gruelling day.

On the rare occasions that he took a day off, he liked to treat his mother to lunch, because the food there was well known in the area. Danielle always welcomed him with a friendly smile, and he found himself talking with her often. He liked that he could talk openly to her as she was a good listener. Their talks became quite topical at times and he respected her opinions, even if he didn't always agree with her views.

As time went on, he got to know the regulars well and began to thoroughly enjoy his pint or two after work. It was during this time that he had spoken to Mick a couple of times in passing. He was pleasantly surprised to find out he was a mechanic, especially as he needed one. He was having issues with his car so explained the problem to him. Mick was happy to oblige, so they arranged a date to meet. Mick did an excellent job of detecting what was wrong and then fixing it, and Stuart assured him he would definitely use him again.

Stuart liked Mick because he was a very funny man. Whenever they saw one another at the bar, they always made a point of saying hello. When he heard that he and Matt were going away, he took the chance and asked half-heartedly if he could tag along. He had been thinking about going away for a while, but nothing had materialized, and it had remained only a thought till now. When Mick therefore replied, "the more the merrier," he was over the moon to at last have something to look forward to. He just hoped Danielle would be able to come too, as this would be the icing on the cake.

He watched her go around and clear the empty glasses that were on the tables. She caught his eye and he smiled. "Don't forget what I said Dan," he reminded her. She nodded and carried on with her work. Looking at the clock she was pleasantly surprised at the time.

Not long now, nearly time to go, she thought.

CHAPTER

THREE

DANIELLE LEFT WORK AT THREE o'clock, got into her car to begin her usual journey to school to pick up Charlie. His school day finished at twenty past and if there wasn't any traffic, she would make it on time. Pulling up outside the gates she watched the children come pouring out. She got out of the car and could not help noticing all the dads that were picking up their children. It seemed so long ago since Charlie came running out into his father's arms, and she felt a twinge in her heart and a lump form in her throat remembering those happy times. *We were happy once,* she thought. She had almost forgotten how happy those times had been. All the good memories had somehow been wiped out by the bad ones, and her mind had been invaded by betrayal and pain. She wondered if she could ever be happy again. Could there be someone out there who could make her feel loved and wanted? She felt like such a failure, because it seemed as if everything she touched seemed to just crumble in her hands.

She sighed at the thought of being on her own for the rest of her life. All she had ever wanted and craved from a young age, was to be happy and to be able to receive and return love and understanding with someone special.

She thought about Brad, and how much he had hurt her. She could not think for the life of her why men treated her so badly. She soon convinced herself that the only explanation was that there must be something wrong with her. *I must give out an invisible signal that only the wrong type of men can detect,* she thought miserably. These thoughts and feelings suddenly began to depress her especially as she suddenly remembered the conversation she and Brad had earlier on that day. She had completely forgotten to text him to tell him not to bother coming over. She could have kicked herself for her absent mindedness. She put her hand in her bag searching for her mobile phone, when she was interrupted by Charlie coming up behind her and pinching her bottom.

"Hey who is that pinching me?" she asked spinning around quickly forgetting what she was about to do.

"Hi there, little man, have you had a good day?" she asked tickling his sides. Charlie nodded and ran to the car. Once in the car, he spent the journey home telling her about his day. He had won first prize for spelling, and proudly showed off his sticker on his sweatshirt. She was overwhelmed with pride as she listened to her son, and all negative earlier thoughts were pushed safely to the back of her mind.

Back home Charlie ran upstairs to get out of his school uniform. In a matter of minutes, he was changed and out to play in the garden. As she was in the middle of preparing the dinner, the phone rang. It was her mum Christine.

"Hello mum are you alright?" She had a very good relationship with her mother Christine and they were like sisters. Her mum had been her rock and kept her going in the most difficult times. She had proven to be the only person she could rely on. She loved her grandchildren and spoilt them rotten. She also had the utmost respect for her daughter for bringing up the children single-handedly. She did whatever she could to lighten her load. She had been there on numerous occasions when dealing with Billy was particularly difficult and getting Danielle down. She was very tuned in and sympathetic to her daughter's anguish.

Of the three, Billy was her favourite, and for some reason he seemed to listen to her. She adored both Marie and Charlie, but the bond they shared was with their mother, unlike Billy, who doted on his grandmother.

"Danielle I'll be round shortly if that's ok, as I have got some information Marie needs for school."

"OK I'll put the kettle on. Marie will be home soon. See you in a minute."

She hung up the phone and filled the kettle with water. She could hear Charlie talking to himself outside which made her smile. She was washing up the cups when the phone rang again, this time it was her sister in-law Louise.

"Hello Lou," she said drying her hands.

"Alright Dan, I need to speak to you. Can I come over, it's important," Louise said eagerly.

"Of-course you can. Is everything alright? You sound like you are about to give birth," Danielle asked suspiciously.

"Y-yes everything is fine. I will explain when I get there. See you soon."

By the time Danielle hung up she was left looking at the receiver wondering what was going on. She replaced the hand set and walked back into the kitchen. *I haven't been this popular in a long time*, she thought.

It was rare for her sister in-law to come around on the spur of the moment, and this gave her some cause for concern. The kettle was boiling when there was a knock at the door. She answered it, still bewildered by Louise's call, and opened the door to let her mother in.

"Hello, my darling," said Christine kissing her daughter on the cheek and handing her a carrier bag.

"I have brought some biscuits for my cup of tea and there are some sweets in there too for the children."

Danielle took the bag of goodies from her mother and looked inside. Christine walked into the front room where she was confronted by an over excited Charlie.

"Hello sweetheart," she said as he jumped up into her arms, giving her a big kiss. Danielle went into the kitchen to make the drinks.

"Lou is on her way over mum. Apparently, she has something important to tell me and she sounded so excited," shouted Danielle into the front room. "Do you know anything about it?"

"No, she hasn't mentioned anything to me," replied Christine laughing at Charlie pulling funny faces.

"Well she will be here soon," said Danielle walking in with two mugs of tea. She handed one to her mother as there was a knock at the door.

"That was quick," said Danielle as she looked out of the window to find Louise standing at the front door. She opened the door and Louise came rushing in.

"Slow down Lou or you will give yourself a heart attack."

Her face was bright red from her promptness and they both walked into the front room. She sat down to catch her breath and Danielle looked at her mother and shrugged her shoulders.

"I got a phone call from Matt last night," explained Louise excitedly as she tried to catch her breath. "He mentioned the holiday to Skiathos..." Her voice trailed off as she hesitated.

"Yes, he and Mick are going away. So?" asked Danielle failing to see any relevance.

"He also said he invited you, but you refused," continued Lou.

"What holiday? You didn't mention any holiday to me," Christine interrupted putting her cup down on the table.

"That is because there was nothing to mention as there is no holiday for me. I can't just get up and go away. What about my kids?" replied Danielle flatly, unaware that Marie had walked into the room.

"Are we going on holiday mum?" asked Marie excitedly.

"No darling we are not," replied Danielle sternly. The excitement soon disappeared from Marie's face and she threw her bag down on the floor.

"Well that's just it, Dan. I have spoken to Tony and we both agree it's just what you need. I know things have been tough for you lately and you deserve a break, so we will look after the children for you. Dan, this means you can go," Louise said trying unsuccessfully to contain her enthusiasm.

"What! You would do that for me?" asked Danielle in total disbelief. Suddenly she felt the need to sit down, as she was completely overwhelmed by Louise's kindness, tears immediately welling up in her eyes.

"If it would help, Billy can come and stay with me. I could do with the company and it would do him the world of good," offered Christine as she sat down next to her daughter, putting a reassuring arm around her shoulders. "I don't mind sweetheart. Lou is right. It will do you good to get away for two weeks in the lovely sunshine. I know what I would do." Danielle could not contain her tears anymore as they began to flow freely.

Still teary-eyed she asked, "Well Marie what do you think? How do you feel about spending two weeks with Auntie Louise and Uncle Tony, as they spoil you rotten?"

Marie thought for a moment. She had never spent so long without her mum before, and this made her feel anxious. Eventually however a small smile escaped her lips at the thought of being spoilt by her favourite aunt and uncle, and this overruled her doubts. The smile soon turned into a grin and she nodded her head in approval.

"I think I can put up with that for two weeks," Marie replied cheekily.

"Well, that's sorted then. Now you can phone Matt and tell him you can go. He will be over the moon," said Louise laughing, unable to control her joy. The big smile on her face was genuine as she got up and kissed Danielle on her tear stained face.

"What are you waiting for? Pick up the phone and put him out of his misery, he is waiting for your call as we speak," she added excitement written all over her face.

This unprovoked show of love touched Danielle. She felt

so proud to have such a supportive family, and very honoured they would do something like this for her. As she reached for her phone the tears welled up again, brought on by this act of kindness. Taking a deep breath, she punched in Matt's telephone number. The phone rang but seemed as though it was in the distance. She could not believe she was actually going to Skiathos. She had never been abroad before and the thought of going on a plane made her feel nervous. Her thoughts were interrupted by Matt's voice on the other end of the line.

"Hello Dan, I was just going to phone..."

"Matt the answer is yes! Yes, I will take you up on your offer. Lou and my mum are going to look after my children. I can come to Skiathos with you. Isn't that great?" she gushed. Her voice was so full of excitement she could hardly contain herself. Then there was a moment's silence.

"Matt, Matt, did you hear me? That is ok isn't it?" Sheer panic threatening to grip her as she waited for him to reply.

"Yes, yes, of course it is Dan. I am just taking it in. I can't believe you are coming with us and I'm so glad. As soon as I get off the phone with you, I'll phone Mick straight away and get him to book you on our flight as well. You will have the time of your life, promise. Oh, and before I go, can you tell Louise I owe her one. Speak to you soon, and don't worry we will look after you!"

When he hung up the phone she realised how quiet the room had become. She looked around and the two women were staring expectantly at her.

"I can't believe it, I am going on holiday!" she said, a huge smile spreading across her face. Her joy became infectious as the three women got up and danced happily around the room. They giggled hysterically like teenagers, filling the whole house with laughter. She could not remember when she had felt so happy. She felt so lucky to be a part of such an amazing family.

Christine and Louise left when Danielle started to dish up the dinner. Billy had football training after school and would be due home any minute now. He arrived home just as Marie and Charlie were about to start eating. Danielle took him to one side and explained she was going away in a few weeks. He was not pleased at first but when he found out he was staying at his Nan's, he quickly changed his tune and decided he liked the idea. He sat down and ate his dinner, and then all three of them went upstairs to clean their rooms.

Danielle was in the middle of washing up when there was a knock at the door. She wondered who it could be, and then it suddenly occurred to her that Brad was due to come around to see her. It had totally gone out of her mind to text him earlier because of all the excitement, and she was quite angry with herself for forgetting again. She dried her hands and walked to the front door, taking in a deep breath before opening it. She let him in and he went and sat down. He looked rather nervous and she couldn't help noticing his hands were shaking. She just stood there glaring at him without saying a word, waiting for him to speak first.

"Dan, all I can say is I am really sorry… I know I have made a terrible mistake and I realise that now. The past week has been terrible for me… I can't sleep, I can't eat and all I think about is you. I love and need you Danielle, please forgive me," he pleaded putting his head in his hands.

She looked at him and remembered the evening she caught

him with the other woman. All the hurt came flooding back and she was provoked by what he had done to her.

"There is no way I will forgive you Brad. All we had is gone because of you, and it makes me sick to the stomach just looking at you. I don't know how you can have the nerve to sit there and tell me you love me. You wouldn't know what love was if it bit you on your bum. All you care about is yourself. We are finished, do you hear me finished! I never want to see you again."

Brad looked her in the eye pleading for some sign of forgiveness, but all he saw reflected was hatred.

"Dan, please don't be hasty, I love you so much," he said a single tear rolling down his face.

"Save your pathetic tears for someone who cares because I don't," she said angrily. As her harsh words cut through him, it felt like they were ripping out his heart.

"But..." Brad said out of desperation.

"There are no buts about it. All I want is you out of my house and out of my life. Oh, and before you hear it from someone else, I am going away with Matt and Mick for two weeks. Now does that convince you I am being serious?" she asked marching towards the front door.

"So that's it then is it?" asked Brad flatly conceding defeat as he looked hopelessly at the floor.

"Yes. Goodbye Brad." He hesitated for a moment hoping for a different response, a change of heart, anything. When he got none, he reluctantly walked past her and out of the door.

Danielle slammed it shut and leant against the wall. She was proud of herself for putting him straight, and relieved to have found the courage to tell him exactly how she felt. If it wasn't for her going away, she didn't think she would have had the strength to finally put an end to their relationship. She took a deep breath of victory and looked up to find Marie sitting at the top of the stairs.

"Are you alright mum?" asked Marie feeling concerned for her mother.

"Yes, yes, my darling I am fine," Danielle replied smiling. "Now go and finish your room." She suddenly realised she did feel alright and knew then another chapter of her life had been closed.

Matt took great pleasure in telling Mick the good news. Mick then managed to book a seat on the plane next to them the next morning. By lunchtime the three friends were busy discussing their holiday. They were all very excited and felt like little children going on an adventure. It was still raining outside, but none of them cared, after all in three weeks-time, they knew they would be sitting on the beach taking in the glorious Greek sunshine.

Danielle hadn't felt so good in such a long time, and all the regulars were genuinely happy for her. Her smile lit up the room taking their mind off the miserable day outside. She floated around the bar without a care in the world but resented the fact that she still had to work. All she wanted to do was sit down and plan her holiday. She told herself however that the busier she was, the quicker the time would go. She stole every spare moment to speak to her two closest friends as they chatted excitedly about their trip. It was in-fact the talk of the bar.

In the middle of their conversation they all looked at the door at the same time as Stuart walked in with a big grin on his face. They watched him walk over and were surprised to see him in a pair of jeans and a t-shirt.

"What are you doing here this time of the day? Skiving off, are we? That's the joy of being your own boss," said Mick quickly glancing at Matt with a smug look on his face.

"Well sort of Mick," replied Stuart. "I have just come back from the travel agents and I have booked myself on the same flight as you guys."

All three of them looked at each other speechless, thrown not only by what he was wearing but also by what he had said.

"That is OK isn't it, Mick?" asked Stuart. "We did discuss this the other day," Stuart continued, the smile slipping from his face as he suddenly began to panic. Mick had completely forgotten about their earlier conversation so turned to Matt for a response.

"I don't mind him coming Mick as long as he doesn't mind our drunken jaunts. I just hope you will be able to keep up with us," Matt replied smiling.

"Well then Stu it looks like you're coming with us. The four of us are going to have a brilliant time," said Mick, putting his arm around him. "Welcome aboard the Skiathos express."

"What do you mean the four of us?" asked Stuart.

"Does that mean you're coming too Dan?" he asked, the smile reappearing on his face.

"Yes, it does Stuart, but I am a bit worried about the drunken bit," replied Danielle turning to Matt.

"Don't worry, we'll look after you," reassured Mick and Matt winked at her.

"Well this is cause for a celebration. Three beers please Dan and one for you of course." Danielle obliged, and they picked up their glasses.

"Here is to us and a great holiday. Skiathos here we come," they all cheered merrily.

God help everyone in Skiathos, the same thought going through all their minds.

CHAPTER

FOUR

PANOS STEPPED OUT OF THE shower, dried himself off, slipped on his boxer shorts and went out on to the balcony. It was six thirty in the morning and the sun felt warm on his face. The sky was blue and there was not a cloud in the sky.

The hotel was due to open in three weeks and he, his brother and father had the annual task of getting the hotel ready for its guests. Most of the rooms had been repainted and only a few remained to be done. He looked down at the gardens and saw Kosta the handy man already at work on the flower beds. Looking across the calm deep blue sea made him so grateful to be living on such a beautiful island.

Situated in the hills, the hotel had an incredible view and it still took his breath away to this day. Tiny uninhabited islands rose out of the sea like green sea monsters, and he dreamt of opening his own hotel on the largest of them one day. His father had brought his family to the island fifteen years ago with the dream of opening up his own hotel.

Through lots of hard work, his dream finally became a reality. They all worked extremely hard, putting their hearts and soul into the business. The hours were long and gruelling, the work load was heavy and at times it felt too much to cope with. His father however always held on to hope, which fed his determination to succeed.

He and his younger brother Yannis helped out after school, but their father was insistent it did not interfere with their school work because it was important, they had a good education. They were both fortunate to have inherited their father's drive so this was not a problem. They were a close family unit pulling together through the bad times. It had finally paid off because after seven painstaking years, they had built up a thriving business. It was a family run hotel, with only Kosta and a handful of maids who were employed from outside the family. Their mother ran the kitchen, keeping the maids in check, and her husband and sons ensured that the hotel was kept to the highest standard.

As the years passed Panos finished school, and then worked closely with his father. He had the ability to pick things up quickly, and it wasn't long before his father handed over majority of the work load to him. As he was the eldest brother it was only right that he was subsequently promoted to hotel manager where he thrived. He loved his work and the responsibility that came with it. He enjoyed meeting new people every year and felt especially proud when many of the guests came back annually. He got to know them and made many friends from all over the world. He grew particularly close to one man. This English man appeared on the island the first year that the hotel opened, with his wife.

The first time he met Mick he instinctively knew he would

bring a lot of joy into his life. He was right because Mick proved to be a caring, lovely, jovial man. Panos loved it when he stayed at the hotel because he always made him laugh. He made an extra special effort to ensure the couple had the best time when they were around. Over the years their friendship blossomed, and both men made a point of keeping in touch with one another during the months that they were apart.

Panos stood looking out over the sea and smiled as he reminisced over the good times he had shared with the couple. But his smile soon faded when he remembered the apparent troubles that had recently occurred between Mick and his wife. As they spoke on the phone Mick confided in him regarding all that was going on in the marriage. He also explained that due to their differences Tracey would not be accompanying him this year. He however reassured Panos that he needn't worry because, he would not be alone and would be bringing three friends with him. Panos could detect the pain in Mick's voice as he listened to his friend speaking, and his heart truly went out to the couple. He was really looking forward to seeing his friend again but thought it would seem strange that Tracey wouldn't be with him.

Mick also explained that his three friends needed to get away from it all and Panos was very happy to oblige. Any friend of Mick's was a friend of his, and he would be more than happy to make their stay a pleasant one. He was surprised to find out that one of the guests was female, nonetheless he planned to welcome her with an open mind and heart. All he knew was that her name was Danielle and she was having a few problems at home. Mick added that she was a dear friend who needed some serious cheering up.

That's typical of you Michael, he thought to himself smiling.

"You are always thinking about other people," remarked Panos.

Mick and his friends were the first guests of the season, apart from one other couple. Panos did all he could to arrange everything to be perfect for them. He felt a twinge of excitement as he imagined Mick already being at the hotel. This happy thought helped to push Mick and Tracey's sad predicament to the back of his mind, as he got himself dressed to join his family for breakfast.

When he reached the restaurant, his mother was already serving up the food, and his father and brother were in deep conversation. He sat down next to his brother and joined in with the discussion about their plans for the day. They were all pleased to be right on schedule.

"So Yannis, when is Anna due to arrive?" Panos asked his younger sibling whilst tucking into his hearty breakfast.

"She will be here on Friday in the evening sometime. I cannot wait to see her," Yannis answered, a big smile erupting across his face.

Panos studied his brother's face and could detect a twinkle in his eyes when he spoke. Yannis and Anna were due to get married in the autumn, and he couldn't help feeling slightly envious when Yannis continued to talk about his plans for the wedding, pure joy evident in his voice. This took Panos back to a year ago when he had been planning his own wedding. He could feel a big knot in his stomach as he remembered that happy time, and a pang of pain stung his heart. These feelings surprised him because he thought they had been buried a long time ago, but listening to Yannis, reopened up a wound, full of hurt and betrayal.

Sophia had been a close friend of the family. Her father

was raised in the same village as his father had been, so they were like brothers. From the moment he laid his eyes on Sophia he fell in love with her. Even though they were young he vowed one day she would become his wife.

When his family moved away, they made a point of keeping in touch. Sophia found it difficult to cope without him at first, but soon made a new life for herself when she started university. They eventually lost touch with each other, but she was always at the back of his mind. Although he was busy with his studies and building up the hotel filled his time, he still held on to the hope that one day she would come back into his life again.

Then just over a year ago her family came to stay at the hotel, bringing Sophia with them. She was all grown up and he thought she was even more beautiful than he remembered. The love they felt for each other was reignited from the start, and both families were overwhelmed when they announced their engagement. Her family went back to the mainland leaving their daughter to adjust to her new life.

For the first couple of months they lived in bliss. They were always by each other's side, but as the hotel became busier their time together soon became limited. Before long most of his day was spent pleasing and dealing with the guests, while she spent most of her time in the kitchen helping his mother. She felt forcibly separated from her fiancé and began to feel very lonely.

Her time spent at university away from her family had given her a new lease of life, and she felt she had been freed from her father's old-fashioned ways. He had always insisted the man should earn the money and the woman should be in the kitchen feeding the family. She discovered her independence at college, so being at the hotel stifled her. She felt her freedom had been taken away, and the more time spent without Panos, the more she was convinced she had made a huge mistake. She did love him deeply but felt it wasn't working or what she wanted. Eventually she knew she had to go her own way. She was an educated girl and did not want to spend the rest of her life in the kitchen as her mother and mother in-law had. She made up her mind and decided that when the time was right, she was going to break the news to him that she was leaving. The right time never came.

One night without telling anyone, she sneaked out and left him and his family to start a new life on her own. She wrote him a letter explaining her reasons for going and put it under his door. She knew he would be devastated but felt it was the only way to move forward.

When the news got out about her disappearance, both families were in shock. She had left no forwarding address and her family had no success in tracking her down. Her father was in complete despair and her mother spent two weeks crying.

"How could she bring such dishonour to their family?" they asked. As far as her father was concerned, she was a disgrace and he never wanted to see her again.

Panos remembered vividly the fateful morning he found her letter. It was like it happened just yesterday. The pain she had forced upon him had slowly eased, but the legacy of mistrust she left behind still dominated his heart. He threw himself into his work, in a real effort to forget, putting all his energy into making the hotel the best it could be.

Eventually, slowly he began living again. He had his pick of all the girls he met who stayed at the hotel, but he only ever used them for sex. There was never a short supply of beautiful girls on the island, and he enjoyed the convenience of these short-term affairs. He never wanted to have a serious relationship again, and resented Sophia for making him feel that way. He vowed never to let another lady back into his heart, and it would have to be someone extra special to convince him otherwise.

He tucked thoughts of Sophia safely away and finished his breakfast. They had a lot to finish off that morning and he was eager to start as soon as he had finished his coffee. He had some work to catch up on in the office whilst his father and Yannis finished painting the rooms.

He had a mid-morning appointment with Cassia from the tour company, so he needed to get what he could done as soon as possible.

He was due to meet her at her office to discuss the annual agenda. Cassia's father owned the company and it was the only one Panos felt he could trust. They had come to an amicable business arrangement as many of his hotel guests booked their holiday through her company. He liked Cassia and had the utmost respect for her judgement. It was a fairly new company and with their collaboration, they had the perfect ingredients for success. Their families had become close friends, so he decided he would take her out for lunch.

At eleven o'clock Panos had managed to get through his work at the office. When he told his father where he was going, his father pulled him to one side.

"Cassia is a very nice Greek girl, Panos and she could make you a very happy man," he said looking into his son's eyes.

"You are not getting any younger and it concerns me you

haven't got a good woman to take care of you."

He had purposely turned a blind eye to his son's wild ways up until now, because he knew it was all because Sophia had hurt him. He did feel it was now time for him to have some stability in his life. He knew Cassia's father well and had a lot of respect for him, and he would have been proud to have her as his daughter in-law.

"I know you mean well papa, but Cassia and I are just friends. I do not want to settle down yet. Please be supportive of my decision," he said taking hold of his father's hand.

"Papa now I must go."

His father brushed his hand away muttering something under his breath and then walked briskly away. Panos knew he had made his father angry, but he could not help the way he felt. Leaving the hotel, he drove the short journey into the town.

His father's disapproval bothered him because they were close, and it played on his mind, but he was adamant he did not want to get involved with Cassia or any other girl he knew. He had made many friends on the island over the years and had earned great respect from the locals. Because of his family's wealth they were greatly admired. Everybody knew who they were, and nobody seemed to have the courage to dare cross them. Having plenty of friends was enough for him, so a stable relationship was out of the question at this time.

He met Cassia at the appointed time and they spent an hour talking about business. He had on many occasions asked her to join him for lunch in a restaurant that was owned by Nicos a close friend of his, but she always declined. He spoke constantly about his single friend, in the hope she would give in and finally agree to meet him, but he was unsuccessful in persuading her. She was happy with her life, she said using this as an excuse. She apparently did not need the complications of a relationship. It had become a standing joke between them, but he never gave up.

Today would be no different, he thought, but he asked her anyway for the hundredth time. He was pleasantly surprised when she agreed this time! A big cheeky smile erupted across his face. Feeling pleased with himself after the meeting, they strolled down the high street towards the harbour.

Nicos arrived on the island around the same time as Panos and he too came to Skiathos with his family to seek their fortune. Nico's father dreamed of opening a restaurant, and started one from scratch, managing to build up a popular Taverna for the locals and holiday makers. When the two young men met, they got talking one morning in the supermarket and found they had a lot in common. They were both intelligent, enthusiastic, strong willed business men with strong family ties, and this was a good foundation for their friendship. The two families fitted in well together and many nights were spent in each other's company. They grew very close, both regarding the other as a brother.

When Panos walked into the restaurant he was pleased Nicos was there to greet him. Nicos was always happy to see him and welcomed him with open arms. They embraced and then Nicos turned his attention to Cassia as he smiled at her.

"Panos you must introduce me to this lovely lady," he said boldly looking deep into her eyes.

"Nicos, I would like you to meet Cassia." Panos knew his friend well and knew he would be taken by his attractive companion.

"The pleasure is all mine my friend," replied Nicos, his eyes still transfixed on hers. He gently took her hand and kissed it. Cassia blushed quickly looking away. Nicos led them over to a table by the window, pulled out a chair for her and handed them a menu.

"I will send over some complementary drinks and then I will join you," he said kissing her hand again. His heart literally skipped a beat as he walked away.

Prior to this meeting, Panos had mentioned his good, looking lady friend many times, and even though Nicos had never met her he knew he would like her. After all, when it came to the ladies Panos was an expert. When he therefore described Cassia to him, he took Panno's word that she was an incredible woman. Nico's trust in his friend's assessment was proven to be one hundred per cent correct! When his eyes fell on her, he had a good feeling that his day was going to be a good one!

The thought had crossed his mind why on earth Panos had let this woman slip through his fingers, and he was genuinely surprised he showed no romantic interest in Cassia at all. Nicos soon gave up trying to work out his unpredictable friend and was just grateful this exquisite creature was available.

She sure is a beauty, he thought to himself as he ordered their drinks, feeling very confident in himself.

"I think he likes you," said Panos smiling cheekily.

Cassia watched Nicos walk away from their table and had to admit she liked him too. He was very handsome, incredibly charming and just the way Panos had described him.

Once upon a time she had hoped Panos would show some interest in her, (That was why she kept turning down his invitations, to meet Nicos before now) but he showed no obvious signs. She soon realised it was not going to happen. Besides it was common knowledge throughout the female community that he had a reputation with the ladies, and he did not want to settle down. So now after finally meeting Nicos, she decided to focus all her attention on his tall strong handsome friend.

When the food arrived Nicos decided to take his break, so he could join them. They talked and ate their meal, and Cassia felt at ease as she listened to her new friend Nicos. He went out of his way to shower her with compliments, attempting to make her feel really special. His efforts were effective as he had her hanging on his every word.

Panos just sat there quietly taking it all in, listening to his friend and smiled at his charming ways. He was glad that his powers of persuasion had finally worked, because he had instinctively known all along that Cassia would absolutely adore his charismatic friend. Suddenly they had nearly eaten all their food and things had gone quiet, so he took the opportunity to tell Nicos about his coming guests.

"My friend Michael from England is coming to stay in a few weeks. You remember him don't you Nicos?" asked Panos.

"Oh yes, how could I forget such a funny man? He will have to come down with his wife for a meal."

Panos explained he would not be coming with his wife because they were having matrimonial problems, but that he would not be alone. "He's apparently bringing three friends with him, one of them is a woman."

Nicos was sorry to hear this, and his heart went out to Mick and was dismayed by this bad news because he remembered they were such a lovely couple.

"Well, he can bring his friends along too. I would love to see him again. What is this girl like?" Nicos asked inquisitively.

"He didn't say much, only that it was her first time abroad, and that she is also having problems at home."

"She isn't single then?" asked Cassia. She was very attracted to Nicos and did not need any competition, especially from an English girl.

"I am not interested even if she is," replied Panos bluntly.

"She is probably fat and ugly anyway."

They all laughed and carried on with their meal, soon forgetting about the girl who would be accompanying Mick in three weeks.

Once they finished their meal, Panos realised he had to get back to the hotel. They said their goodbyes and Nicos asked to see Cassia again. She nodded saying she would love to and gave him her phone number. He reassured her he would be phoning her very soon, taking her hand to gently kiss it. Panos was happy for them both and made his feelings felt. Pride oozed out of every pore for being the instigator of this union, and he looked forward to seeing them again as a couple. He relished knowing that he had played cupid and loved the silly look on Nico's face. Love was definitely in the air and he was so pleased for his friend.

His father's voice came into his thoughts without warning and played with his heart. "You are not getting any younger and it concerns me you haven't got a good Greek woman to take care of you."

Just for a moment he thought maybe his father was right.

No! Panos thought. *Love might be all right for Nicos but it certainly isn't for me,* his trail of thought continued.

He shuddered when Sophia entered his mind, quickly disarming the thoughts before they had a chance to get the better of him. He chose to think of something else, when he turned to Cassia. Her beautiful olive skin glowed and he had never seen her looking so happy. Pride won over the battle of his will and he was satisfied with the outcome of his afternoon. The meeting had gone well, and Cassia had come up with some brilliant ideas. He was not only proud to have her as a business associate but also as a friend. She was an asset in both areas and he was grateful to have her in his life. He walked her back to her office, now filled with joyful thoughts, when she thanked him for introducing her to Nicos. He kissed her on both cheeks, promising to call her soon. Then he got in his car and drove happily back to the hotel.

The weeks soon turned into days and before he knew it the hotel was ready for opening. Mick and his friends were due to arrive the day after next, and Panos could not wait to see his crazy friend again. Mick had promised to phone him that evening to confirm the flight details. Panos told him he would pick them up from the airport. It was usually Kosta's job to do the airport run, but as it was an exceptional guest, Panos chose to drive down there himself. He made sure Kosta cleaned the mini bus, so it was ready for its first journey of the season. His inspection of the bus was more than satisfactory and now everything was ready for his new guests.

He received the call when he was in his office. It was nine o'clock Greek time.

"Hello, Panos my friend. How the devil are you?"

Panos could hear music in the background and smiled. He could detect a slight slurring in the caller's voice so presumed he was in the pub.

"Ah Michael, I am very well thankyou and how are you my friend?" he replied mimicking a bad English accent.

"It's Mick," retorted Mick, agitated by Panno's continued use of his full name.

"Why do you insist on calling me that?" This was the only thing that bothered him about his friend. It reminded him of being teased at school.

"Mick is, what you say, a sissy's name. So, are you a sissy Michael?" Panos loved to wind him up; it was so easy to do.

"So Panos is a manly name? I think not," retaliated Mick.

"I don't know any men with a poofy name like that!"

They both laughed, any tension dissipated, and Mick proceeded to give him the details of his flight.

They were due to leave Gatwick at seven o'clock in the morning, so they would be landing in Skiathos at around one o'clock Greek time. Panos assured him he would be there to meet them. This pleased Mick because he could not wait to see his Greek friend again. They spoke for a few more minutes then said goodbye. Panos wished him a safe journey and hung up the phone.

Mick placed the phone on the bar and looked at the time. The other three were due to arrive any minute, so he took the initiative and ordered their drinks. Things were no better at home so the quicker their time for departure out of the United Kingdom came, the better.

He had just walked out on Tracey in the middle of an argument. She had been going on about his drinking again, blaming their marriage break up on him yet again.

How dare she blame me? She is the one who wants a divorce.

Typical! he thought looking at the pint in his hand.

"I don't have a problem," he said under his breath. "She doesn't know what she's talking about."

He was taking a big swig of his beer when the three friends walked through the door. Matt picked Danielle up from her house and they met up with Stuart as they arrived at the pub. Excitement was written all over their faces as they made plans for their departure.

Mick's thoughts of Tracey soon disappeared from his mind when he told them, about the conversation he'd had with Panos. Danielle and Matt were eager to meet this Greek man Mick had spoken about so often. Danielle imagined him to be an old, grey pot-bellied man! She couldn't help smiling at the image she had conjured up in her mind. Mick noticed her face was glowing, and he couldn't wait for Panos to meet her. He had intentionally failed to mention Panno's good looks, so just left it to her own imagination. He had also deliberately kept her attractiveness from Panos. He was really looking forward to their first meeting and was going to enjoy showing off his good looking, friends.

Stuart was going to make his own way to the airport so arranged to meet them all there. Matt's first port of call was to pick up Danielle, and then they planned to meet Mick at his house. The atmosphere was a happy one as they planned their getaway.

Matt had also noticed the look on her face. He had not seen her so happy in a long time and felt proud it was down to him. She looked so gorgeous and he looked forward to spending lots of time with her. He watched her and as she spoke and soon realised, he wanted to be more than just friends. His feelings for her did not surprise him, and although they had been steadily growing, he had managed to ignore them, up till now. Looking at the happiness radiating from her smile brought these emotions to the surface. He knew he had to control them, so convinced himself a deeper relationship was out of the question. A couple of drinks later she asked Matt to take her home. Christine was watching the children and she did not want to leave them any longer than she had to.

When she arrived home all three children were tucked up in bed. Christine explained that everything had been all right and Billy was looking forward to staying with his Nan. She left soon afterwards, and Danielle was left to gather her thoughts for the following day. She had promised to take them all to Pizza Hut for tea. She felt both excited and sad about leaving them, so her last day spent with them was going to be a special one.

Matt phoned her the following day to finalise the details. As they were booked on an early flight, he told her to be ready for three o'clock. He and Mick went to work as usual. Mick had a few loose ends to tie up, which kept him busy for most of the day, and Stuart had last minute arrangements to sort out, so all four friends were occupied on their last day in the United Kingdom.

Marie and Charlie were the first to be dropped off at their Aunt and Uncle's house. Charlie became very tearful as his mother kissed and hugged him goodbye. Seeing his tear stained face tugged at Danielle's heart strings. She was overcome with guilt and the feelings were so strong she felt she should cancel her trip. Louise reassured her she would take good care of them and that she had nothing to worry about. Eventually she managed to drag herself away, fighting to hold back her own tears. Thankfully Billy seemed very calm as she drove to her mother's house. She couldn't help noticing his face showed no sign of anger, and his usual frown had disappeared. This hurt her severely because she knew it was because he was going to stay with his Nan. He had only spoken a couple of words in the car and his tone towards her was a happy one, for a change. She wondered if he was going to miss her and hoped that one day, they could be close again.

Christine greeted her grandson with a big cuddle, and Danielle felt a twinge of jealousy as she watched her son run into his grandmother's arms. Christine had to remind him to give his mother a kiss goodbye. He obliged, and as he did so Danielle squeezed him tight. She told him to behave himself, and then without saying a word, he took his bag into the house. Christine could see the hurt in her daughter's eyes, so gave her a hug.

"You have a great time sweetheart and don't worry. Billy will be all right," said Christine placing a fifty pound, note in her hand.

Danielle could not speak because she was afraid it would give her tears a reason to escape. The two women held each other for a few moments, said their goodbyes and Danielle returned home.

She walked through the front door feeling very apprehensive. The house was so quiet that it was deafening. Shutting the door behind her she stood still. Her mind went straight to Billy and his quick departure which hurt her deeply. Her heart ached for his love and she began to cry. She walked into the kitchen, her tears now free to flow, when the phone began to ring. She wiped her eyes, took a deep breath and picked up the receiver.

"Mum, I'm sorry."

The voice on the other end surprised her and it took a few moments for her to recognise that it was Billy.

"I love you mum and I hope you have a good time. I'm going to miss you so much."

Billy's voice trembled when he spoke, and he began to sob. "I will be good I promise."

"I know my darling and I love you too with all of my heart. I will be back before you know it."

They spoke until he had stopped crying and said goodbye properly this time. It was like a big weight had been lifted off her shoulders, and just hearing his voice made her feel much better.

Her thoughts went back on to her holiday, and she welcomed the excitement that now returned. She started running a bath, got undressed and lay down on her bed. A smile spread across her face as she wondered what the next two weeks were going to bring. She imagined being on the soft white sand, soaking up the glorious Greek sunshine. It was hard to believe, that this time tomorrow she would be in Skiathos.

Billy's loving words swam around her head, and butterflies danced in her stomach when she realised, she felt extremely good. Her bath was ready now, so she got up and went into the bathroom, singing Madonna's 'Holiday,' at the top of her voice.

CHAPTER

FIVE

PANOS WOKE UP TO THE SOUND of a cockerel crowing outside his window. He looked at the clock beside his bed, it was six o'clock. He got out of bed opened the shutters and to his disappointment it was cloudy. The wind was howling as he watched the leaves blow into the pool.

Not a good day for my friend to arrive, he thought. It was not unusual for this time of year, and he was confident the sun would soon break through the clouds. Getting himself showered and dressed, he felt a wave of excitement bubble up in his stomach because the day had finally come for his friend to arrive.

Matt arrived at Danielle's at three o'clock and was surprised she was ready to go. They took the short drive to Mick's house to find that he was not. He was frantically looking around for the tickets he thought he left on the kitchen table. He cursed Tracey at the top of his voice.

It must have been her who moved them, he thought.

This is the sort of thing she would do just to annoy me.

He began to panic and looked at the time, as he realised the taxi would be there in ten minutes! He double checked all the places he was most likely to have put them, but they were nowhere to be found. He sat down at the table putting his head in his hands. Racking his brains, he tried to remember back to when he had them last, and desperately tried to retrace his steps. His mind drew a blank, because he had been so drunk the previous night, and his head was beginning to ache, with the effort.

The only place left to look was the garage, and he knew they couldn't be out there, but he decided to look anyway out of desperation. He got up to get his coat and put his hand in the pocket. Instead of pulling out his keys, he pulled out a white envelope! He breathed a sigh of relief when he realised, he had at last found the tickets. He felt his face go bright red with embarrassment. He suddenly remembered putting them in there for safe keeping and could have kicked himself, for being so stupid.

The taxi soon arrived and all three of them put their suitcases into the boot of the car. It was pouring with rain and freezing cold, but this did not bother them, because in a few hours they would be basking in the Greek sunshine. They got into the car and began their journey to the airport, chatting like excited teenagers, quickly putting themselves in the holiday mood. Once they arrived at the airport, they paid the driver and quickly checked in. Then they went to the bar to meet Stuart. The airport was full of happy holiday makers who were escaping from the rotten English weather.

The next time I'm here I will have a lovely tan, Danielle thought looking at all the cheerful faces around her. She wanted to pinch herself because she felt that she was in a wonderful dream.

Matt was the first to spot Stuart. He was sitting at the bar with a pint of beer in front of him looking into space. Danielle thought he was acting strange, because he didn't seem to be with it. Matt called his name three times before he finally acknowledged they were even there.

"Are you alright Stuart?" asked Matt concerned.

Stuart just looked at him with a vacant look on his face.

"Stuart. Are you OK?" repeated Matt. Eventually a look of recognition swept across his face.

"H-hello Matt. I was in a world of my own. I'm glad that you have made it," he replied as the corners of his mouth lifted.

They sat talking and laughing and soon the thought of Stuart's strange behaviour soon slipped from their minds. All their cares and worries left as they waited patiently to board the plane.

When it was time, they got on the plane and found their seats. Danielle sat next to the window with Matt, while Mick sat behind them. Stuart couldn't believe his luck and was relieved to be sitting one seat along from Mick. As the engines started, she turned around to talk to Matt and noticed his expression had changed dramatically. He had gone as white as a sheet.

"Are you all right Matt? You look terrible," she said becoming quite concerned by the quick change in his appearance.

"I will be once this plane is off the ground. Take off always has this effect on me," he confessed.

"Don't worry I will all right in a minute," he explained noticing the distress on her face. She could not help but worry, it looked like he had seen a ghost. She patted his knee and a slight smile formed in the corners of his mouth as he gripped hold of the arm rest. She turned around to look at Stuart to find him studying the magazine the airline supplied. She realised he was looking at the flight plan but couldn't help noticing his hands were shaking. She soon put this down to nerves. She was surprised she did not feel nervous herself, considering it was her first time on a plane. She could feel the butterflies in her tummy, but this was due to the excitement of her first adventure abroad.

She looked over at Mick who was also engrossed in the same magazine, staring at a gorgeous tanned model half naked on a beach. She was advertising a well-known brand of perfume. Danielle could not work out the connection between the woman, the beach and what it had to do with perfume. But she could see how it caught Mick's roaming eye.

In your dreams, she thought to herself.

"Hey Dan, is that what you look like in a bikini?" asked Mick, his eyes firmly focused on the beautiful woman.

"Yes, in my dreams," she replied mockingly.

"Don't put yourself down Dan I bet you look better than that," Matt intervened. She just laughed.

"I wished I did look like that. Then I would be jetting off all over the world earning loads of money."

Matt just looked at her and tutted. To him she was the most beautiful lady he knew. Her attitude towards herself frustrated him because she had no self-confidence. She didn't have a clue how lovely she actually was. He watched her as she looked out of the window and the same longing for her started to bubble in his heart.

If only she knew how I felt about her, he thought.

He was too scared however to reveal these feelings, because he didn't want to ruin their friendship. He was soon reminded of his nervousness when the plane began to make its way down the runway.

The take off part of the journey was a success. Danielle noticed the colour was gradually returning to Matt's cheeks and they all sat back and enjoyed the flight. She spent most of the time looking out of the window and couldn't get over how high above the ground they were. The view was incredible, and she felt like an excited child again.

The flight was four hours long and Mick and Stuart spent most of it asleep. When they were approaching the end of their journey an announcement from the captain filled the plane. He explained they were just coming over the island but unfortunately the weather was not good. The low cloud had restricted the view, but he promised it would be better the following day.

Danielle looked out of the window and could just make out the tiny island below. She felt quite disappointed with the forecast, hoping the captain's prediction about the following day was right. They finally came in to land and the colour drained from Matt's face again. They landed with a bump, the sound of the brakes on the tarmac was deafening, but they landed safely.

The airport was tiny compared to Gatwick and the four friends waited patiently for their cases. The whole area was full of holiday makers who were not deterred by the weather.

They made their way eagerly from the airport and Mick searched the waiting cars for Panos. To his disappointment he was nowhere to be seen. Fortunately, Mick remembered the Taverna across the road, so suggested they wait there for their host. He phoned the hotel to find out what was keeping Panos. He spoke to Yannis and was told Panos was on his way to collect them.

Danielle could not believe the weather. There was a drizzle in the air and it was windy. It was like being back in England and all of her fantasies of being on a sun drenched, beach disappeared. Mick sensed her frustration and felt guilty about the dreadful weather. He had never been so early in the season before. He had boasted about the weather being so hot and they would go home with a glorious tan, but now here he was watching the trees bend in the wind and found it hard to believe he was on the same island. He decided to go up to the barman and ask him for the coming forecast and was relieved, the plane's captain had been right; the sun would be out tomorrow. Their morale soon returned but the flight had taken its toll on Danielle. She felt extremely tired from the early start and was in need of a nice hot shower.

Panos looked at his watch. He was running late so ran over to the mini bus and was pleased to find it was ready. He jumped into the driver's seat and made the short journey down to the airport. Rain was scarce on the island, so he had to be extra careful going down the hill to the main road. A picture of Mick came into his mind and a big smile beamed across his face. He felt anticipation rise up from his stomach and hoped he would get on with Mick's close friends.

Approaching the airport, he noticed no one was there and for a few moments he was baffled. Then he remembered the

Taverna. He knew Mick well and was sure this would be the place to find him. He looked over to the bar and made out four people sitting there, but he did not recognise any of them. He parked the bus and walked over anyway to take a look. When he got closer to the Taverna he spotted a familiar face. The face belonged to Mick, but the body wasn't how he remembered it! Mick studied the man walking towards them and soon realised to his relief it was Panos. A big grin swept over his face when Panos got nearer. He extended his hand to greet his Greek friend.

"Michael it's so good to see you! I didn't recognise you. You have lost so much weight! You are looking so good my friend," he exclaimed as he shook his hand enthusiastically, and eyed him up and down.

"And your hair is so short. You look like a different man," he concluded putting his hand on Mick's head.

"Easy Panos don't mess up the hair, it's cost me a fortune to look this good."

They all laughed and Panos turned to the other three. He nodded at the two men shaking their hands when he was introduced, then he came to Danielle.

"Panos this is my good friend Danielle."

Mick studied his face when he took hold of her hand. Panos was quite taken aback because she was nothing like he had imagined her to be. There standing in front of him was a beautiful lady. Taking her hand, he gently kissed it. The feel of her soft skin on his lips surprised him, sending an unfamiliar sensation flowing through his body.

"Hello Danielle. It is good to meet you," he said softly looking into her eyes.

She too was pleasantly surprised by the sight of this handsome man. From the way Mick had described him, she was expecting someone in his fifties! She looked at him and realised that he must be closer to her own age. He looked like a young George Michael dressed in a black leather jacket, a white shirt, and black trousers. His short hair was dark, and he wore a goatee beard which complimented his handsome face. For a split second when she looked into his dark brown eyes something happened and changed within her. She could feel the colour rush to her cheeks, so quickly she let go of his hand, forcing her eyes away from his.

Matt rolled his eyes and felt a bit uneasy around this man. He felt he had a sickly charm about him and he felt slightly threatened by his presence. He was also surprised by his good looks especially as he had also imagined him to be a lot older. He concluded that he felt very wary of this man.

It was not lost on him that wherever Danielle went, men looked at her because she was a very attractive girl. He usually felt proud to be in her company but Panos had provoked a different feeling, a feeling he could not put his finger on, and therefore one he did not like!

Panos rushed over to the mini bus and opened the back door. He took hold of Mick's case and put it in the back, doing the same with Stuart's. Then he noticed Matt was carrying Danielle's. They were both laughing together, and he wondered if they were here as a couple. He felt confused because Mick had said she was single.

Well you're a lucky man, he thought to himself.

He could not get over how pretty she was. They travelled up to the hotel and Mick was busy telling Panos about his life with Tracey.

He could not help but feel sorry, about Mick's obviously difficult situation especially because of the pain he saw prominent in Mick's eyes.

Danielle, Matt, and Stuart were joking around in the back, and every time Danielle laughed, Panos felt compelled to look at her through the rear view mirror. Her face lit up when she smiled, and he found it hard to concentrate on the road and on Mick's conversation. Matt's uneasiness soon relented because Danielle showed no signs of interest towards their Greek host. To his relief, she seemed to be happy in his company. Danielle felt really relaxed. The few glasses of vodka she had consumed on the plane calmed her nerves, but as they drove up to the hotel the butterflies slowly returned.

Panos pulled into the driveway and stopped the bus. They all got out and were presented with a magnificent hotel. He helped them with their luggage and led them up the steps to the main entrance. Danielle had never seen anything like it, and as they walked into the lobby it opened out into the main room. There were marble floors with cream sofas scattered around. The lush green plants placed next to them, made it feel very homely. She gazed around the room and felt in complete awe of its uncomplicated beauty. To the right was a big oak counter which she presumed was the reception desk, and across the room was an impressive wooden bar. She was overwhelmed by the cleanliness of the hotel and felt she could stay here forever.

A young man appeared from another room and Mick embraced him the same way he had Panos. He introduced him as Yannis Panos's younger brother. He looked completely different to his brother and she would never have guessed, they were related. Yannis was shorter than his older sibling, had dark blonde hair and was not blessed with his brother's looks. She thought it strange that two brothers could be so unlike one another. She thought of her own children. All three of them looked similar. They were like peas in a pod especially the boys, and everyone commented on how much they looked like their mother. This made her feel extremely proud and her heart suddenly ached for them. This was the first time she had thought about them since getting on the plane. She wondered what they were doing and if her sister in-law and mother were coping.

They would not believe this place, she thought, taking in the pristine Hotel. This incredible sight over ruled her feelings of guilt, and she couldn't wait to tell them all about it. Her mother would be green with envy.

Panos soon distracted her when he led them up to their rooms. Mick, Matt, and Danielle shared one room and Stuart's room was next door. Panos unlocked the door and put the key on the dressing table.

"I will be downstairs in the bar if you need me. Make yourselves at home," he said smiling as he left them to unpack. She could not help noticing his lovely smile. It was so warm, and his voice was so gently spoken that it intrigued her. She smiled to herself.

He is good looking, she thought as he shut the door behind himself. She threw herself on to the bed.

"I don't believe I am actually here!" she shrieked turning over on to her belly pounding her fists on the mattress.

"What a wonderful, wonderful hotel! They must be worth a fortune!"

She stopped and looked at the two men staring at her.

"Thank you, thank you and thank you for being the loveliest people I know. This is great!" she said almost crying. She got up off the bed and kissed them both on the cheek.

"So, you like it here then Dan?" asked Mick sarcastically.

"You wait until the sun comes out then you will cry," he teased.

She kissed them both again whilst scanning the room for a home for her clothes.

Matt informed them he was having a shower before he unpacked and disappeared into the bathroom. Mick left his case on the bed and went next door to speak to Stuart. He was dying for a beer. It had been almost an hour since his last one and he felt as if his throat had been cut. Since Danielle and Matt were going to be a while, he decided to ask Stuart to join him at the bar. Stuart told him he would be ten minutes, so Mick walked back into the room, sat down on his bed and watched Danielle flitter around the room. Three minutes passed, and he began to get rather agitated. He looked at his watch again, giving Stuart another three minutes.

Stuart was very pleased with the accommodation. He had been all around the world and had spent many nights in a hotel. This was by far one of the finest he had visited. He was glad he had a room to himself because he did like his own space. He was a very tidy person and was no different when he was away. Impressed with the cleanliness of the room he felt right at home. It suddenly dawned on him that this was as close as he was going to get to feeling at home, as his wife would not let him anywhere near his own. He struggled to come to terms with the fact, that he had lost his wife. It would have been easier if she had had an affair, then he could fight for his place in her heart, but when he was up against something he could not physically see, that had manifested itself in her mind, he felt helpless. His heart ached because of his loss and the previous years now seemed so pointless. Tears stung the back of his eyes as he forced himself to let her go. He had to remind himself why he was here in Skiathos. It was to start again, only this time on his own.

Suddenly he heard Danielle laughing from next door and this made him smile. She was an inspiration to him, so he soon put the thoughts of his previous life to the back of his mind. He heard Mick say he would meet the other two in the bar and opened the door. He quickly put on his jacket and proceeded to open his door just as Mick was about to knock.

"Easy Bert you almost gave me a heart attack!" said Mick jumping up into the air clutching his chest.

"Me ol' ticker isn't what it used to be," he continued.

Stuart could not apologise enough. Once Mick caught his breath, he reassured him he was all right, claiming they were wasting serious drinking time, and swiftly made their way to the bar.

Panos was in the reception area talking on the phone. He noticed the two men walking down the steps and mimed he would be two minutes. Mick signalled back an OK sign and sat on the bar stool anxiously waiting for his drink.

They watched Panos speaking in Greek and he seemed to be getting rather angry. He slammed the receiver down shouting something at Yannis, who was walking from the bar to the restaurant. He then threw his arms up in the air as Yannis answered him and walked over to the bar muttering under his breath.

"Blimey Panos, you don't sound very happy. Have you

got a problem?" asked Mick surprised by his friend's sudden outburst.

"No nothing that cannot be sorted out my friend. Stupid people, they cannot get anything right," replied Panos angrily walking behind the bar.

Mick was taken aback by his Greek friend's manner. He had never seen him so angry before. He almost felt too frightened to ask for a beer. "Err… can I have two beers please Panos?" he asked reluctantly.

"Of course, I will be happy to oblige my thirsty English friend."

Mick suddenly felt very relieved when a big smile swept across Panos's face as he prepared the drinks.

"You had me worried then. I thought you were going to hit someone," Mick said eyeing up his drink being poured.

"I do not hit anyone Michael," Panos laughed. "It is just that some people do not know how to do their job. That makes me angry yes, but to hit someone no." Panos's tone soon softened when he placed Mick's long, awaited beer on the bar.

"Where are your other two friends?" he asked not remembering Matt's name.

"Matt is unpacking, and Dan is taking a shower. They will be down soon," answered Mick taking a big swig of his drink.

"Ah, that's just what the doctor ordered." The cold fizzy liquid felt like honey as it went down his parched throat.

"What has the doctor got to do with it?" Panos asked confused at Mick's statement. Mick tried to explain, but soon gave up because he was getting nowhere fast.

"You English are very strange. I will never understand your crazy language," said Panos putting his hands up in the air again.

"Easy Bert not so much of the strange if you don't mind!"

Mick had a way of making people laugh with the things he came out with. Panos just shook his head in amazement and smiled.

Stuart asked him about the island and the best places to go. He was fascinated by different cultures and how they differed from his own. He knew Greece and the Greek islands were saturated with history, and he wanted to absorb as much of its heritage as he could. Panos answered his questions with pride. He loved his country and was always willing to oblige any historical queries. Mick on the other hand thought the conversation was rather boring because he had heard it all before. He did not care about its history, as long as the sun was shining, and the booze was flowing, that was the making of a good holiday as far as he was concerned! He looked at his watch and became quite agitated. *Come on Matt,* he thought to himself, taking a mouthful of his beer. He heard his stomach rumble and suddenly realised he was starving. The other two men however just carried on chatting happily.

Suddenly the faint sound of footsteps could be heard in the distance. When they got louder all three men turned around to see Danielle walk into the room. Her shoulder length auburn hair bounced loosely around her face and all traces of tiredness from the journey had disappeared. Panos watched her walk up to the bar and was stunned by the sight of this English lady.

"At last! I thought you had fallen down the plughole," said Mick as he finished off the last drop of his beer.

"What are you having Dan?" he asked.

When she replied, Panos felt a strange feeling rush through his body. Her big green eyes sparkled like precious jewels and her smile radiated a warm glow across her face. As he looked at her, he could not put his finger on what exactly he felt, because it was something unfamiliar to him, and this unnerved him. Staring at her, he realised she was the most beautiful lady he had seen in a long time.

"Panos," Mick repeated for the third time. "Can I have three pints and a vodka and tonic for Danielle please?"

Panos could hear Mick's voice but it seemed so distant, and he didn't respond at first. He was totally unaware that Mick was even talking to him. Danielle turned to Panos concerned by the delay, and when her eyes met his he suddenly realised Mick's question was aimed at him. The blood rushed to his cheeks, quickly bringing him to his senses. He turned to Mick just in time to hear the repeated question. She was oblivious to Panos's stare, but Mick noticed the glint in his eye and smirked. He had deliberately failed to mention to his friend that she was so attractive and the look in Panos's eyes said it all. He loved provoking certain reactions in people. It was like a game to him, and he felt extremely proud to have such a pretty friend. He loved showing her off, even though she was unaware of his intentions.

Panos took a deep breath to calm himself down and began to pour the drinks. His reaction towards her had taken him totally by surprise. There was something about her eyes that enchanted him, and he couldn't help wondering what it was about her that made him feel this way.

Eventually Matt entered the bar and sat next to Danielle. The four reunited friends drank their drinks and planned to go into town to get something to eat. Panos watched them closely and was disappointed they were not eating at the hotel. He noticed how close Matt and Danielle were and couldn't help feeling a little envious. By the way they joked together he presumed they were obviously a couple. He smiled at Matt's fortune and the feelings that crept up on him quickly disappeared temporarily.

He ordered them a taxi at Mick's request. When it arrived, he saw them off, said goodbye and went about his usual routine. The four friends were like teenagers again and they giggled all the way into town. The taxi pulled up by the harbour and Mick paid the fare.

Danielle got out of the car and looked at the small boats bobbing about in the sea. She could hardly believe she was three thousand miles away from home. Matt interrupted her thoughts by putting his arm in hers and he escorted her to the nearest restaurant. They caught up with the other two and went into a quaint Taverna. The sound of Greek music filled the air as they walked in, and a very friendly native showed them to a table. The place was filled with happy people eating their meals and she noticed they were all Greek. She felt slightly nervous when the waiter handed her a menu, but to her relief it was written in English. Mick took the liberty of ordering the drinks as she searched the menu to find something she liked. She was a novice when it came to foreign foods, so when she spotted spaghetti bolognaise, she felt relieved to find something she was familiar with.

The drinks were soon served, and Mick proposed a toast.

"Here is to Skiathos and to all our problems being left behind in England! Here is to us!"

They all raised their glasses and cheered simultaneously. The food soon arrived, accompanied by what looked like a shot of vodka. The waiter informed them it was complimentary and from their host team welcoming them to the island. Danielle looked over to Mick puzzled. He picked up his glass and drank it down in one gulp and watched their faces as they waited patiently for his approval. He shuddered, shaking his head from side to side, like a wet dog trying to dry itself.

"Ahh! Hit the spot," he said leaving them in suspense for a few more minutes.

"Well, what is it?" Matt asked impatiently.

"It's ouzo, a traditional Greek drink. You're obliged to drink it otherwise they'll get offended. It's OK, it tastes like Pernod."

Danielle sniffed the contents of her glass and smelt the familiar smell of aniseed. She emptied the clear liquid in to her mouth and swallowed. The potent liquid burnt her throat as it went down, nearly choking her. Her eyes watered and as if by magic, a warm relaxing feeling sailed through her body.

"This is good stuff," she said putting her empty glass down. It was quickly replaced by another one. After a few more 'ouzos,' and a good meal, the four merry friends decided to head back to the hotel. They paid for their food and went to find a taxi.

Back at the hotel Panos was busy cleaning the bar. The other guests who had dined in the hotel had now retired to their rooms. Wiping down the bar he felt restless but didn't know why, which bugged him. Simultaneously a picture of Danielle appeared in his mind. He thought of her surprising beauty and smiled when he remembered the original picture, he had painted of her. *I couldn't have been more wrong,* he thought.

His thoughts turned to Mick and how much he had changed since his last visit. He still couldn't get over the change in him and he was grateful it was only Mick's appearance that was different. He was still the funny man he had grown to love, causing him to laugh out loud. He was brought out of his thoughts when he heard a car pull up outside. He listened carefully, when he heard the familiar sound of laughter which got louder. He smiled as the four friends walked back into the hotel. They were heading for the bar when Mick tripped up the step and landed on the marble floor.

"Bloody Greek steps! They are everywhere, they are so bloody dangerous!" he shouted picking himself up from the floor.

Danielle was feeling quite drunk and was nearly crying with laughter.

"Sorry Panos we seem to be a bit inebr... inebr.....oops I mean pissed. They did insist on plying us with lots of ouzo, and of course we couldn't say no... It seems to have affected my ability to walk though," Mick exclaimed, dragging himself on to a bar stool.

"I think we should have a night cap. Panos, if you don't mind," he continued.

They all agreed so Panos began to pour the drinks. Stuart tried to sit on a stool but found this a hard task to carry out. He too ended up in a heap on the floor. His second attempt also failed but he managed to get himself on to the nearest settee, so decided to stay there.

The vodka mixed with ouzo filled Danielle with confidence and removed her inhibitions. She sat down and was able to speak to Panos at the bar, surprised that her usual shyness had miraculously disappeared. She even asked him about Greek men because she was intrigued to know about what his attitude was towards women. She explained her thoughts on the matter and it ended in quite a heated discussion. She had surprised him with her views and he tried desperately to put her right. At this point Matt intervened in the middle of their conversation. His timing couldn't have been more wrong. Panos felt frustrated because he was just beginning to get his point across, and the unwelcome interruption really upset him. He was enjoying the difference of opinions they were sharing, so feeling disappointed, he left them to carry on the conversation.

Mick joined Stuart on the sofa and both men had trouble focusing on each other. Panos watched the four drunken friends and laughed.

They are going to regret this in the morning, he thought to himself.

He felt strangely frustrated with Matt for interrupting his conversation with Danielle. He had enjoyed talking to her even though her speech was a bit slurred. He was even more attracted to her now because of what she was saying. A woman had not made him feel this way for a long time, it made a nice change to have a decent conversation, he thought to himself. After two more drinks all four of them were now sitting on the sofa giggling uncontrollably. The whole room was alight, with laughter and it was a brilliant end to their first day on the island.

Danielle opened her eyes to find Panos pulling the covers over her. She quickly shut them and waited until he had left the room. She tried desperately to remember how she came to be put to bed by a complete stranger! The last thing she did remember was talking to him at the bar, and her heart stopped when she recalled their conversation. She could have died of embarrassment.

How did I get so drunk? she thought. She kept her eyes firmly shut until she heard him leave. Then she anxiously felt below the covers to see if she was dressed, and to her relief she was still fully clothed.

"Matt, Mick...are you in here?" Danielle whispered into the darkness. She was met by silence and it suddenly dawned on her she was alone. She tried to get out of bed but found she couldn't. Her head was banging so she lay back down. Tears stung the back of her eyes. She had never felt so humiliated. Then she was overcome by a wave of nausea. She rushed to the toilet and was violently sick. After five more minutes of vomiting she managed to drag herself back into bed. Her head was still aching, and her stomach was sore when she finally drifted off into a lonely sleep.

CHAPTER

SIX

DANIELLE WOKE UP TO FIND THE room filled with daylight. The sun shining through the balcony window made her eyes smart, bringing the reality of the previous night back into her mind. She couldn't believe how drunk she had been.

I felt alright when I was talking to Panos, she thought to herself. The now familiar feeling of embarrassment came back, when she realised, he had put her to bed and she hid her head back under the covers. She was disgusted with herself for being so drunk. She had not even been there for twenty-four hours and had already made a fool of herself.

I will never be able to show my face downstairs again, she thought, feeling the blood rush to her cheeks.

I wish I was at home! Her head was still aching, and she felt sick to the stomach; she could have cried with shame.

"Dan, are you alright, mate?" She poked her head out of the covers to find Matt looking at her with one eye closed, looking just how she felt.

"No, I'm not," she whispered. "I can't believe I got so drunk! Anyway, what happened to you? And why did Panos have to put me to bed?" she asked cringing inside.

"The night is a bit of a blur. The last thing I remember was feeling really ill and having to go outside for some air. When I came back, he said you had gone to bed...Ooh my head!" replied Matt rubbing his head.

"I am never going downstairs and I don't want to see Panos ever again. What must he think of me?" she said putting her head back under the covers.

"Don't be silly Dan. I bet he sees drunken people all of the time. It's what happens when people go on holiday, they get drunk. Come on honey you weren't that bad," he said desperately trying to console her. "Besides you can't hide under there all day."

He leant over to her bed and began to rub her back. Danielle poked her head back out and looked at him sheepishly.

He does have a point, she thought to herself. Then the corners of her mouth began to lift up and she forced herself to smile.

"What a fool I have made of myself," she said now laughing.

"No, you haven't," he reassured her giving her a big cuddle.

"Come on. Have a nice shower, it will make you feel better. Then we can enjoy the sunshine," he said looking out of the window.

Danielle looked at him and smiled back. He always managed to make her feel better. He never judged her, and this was why she cherished his friendship so much. He always seemed to know the right thing to say, even if it was an exaggeration.

"Thanks Matt, you are a good friend," she said sitting up.

Looking into his blood shot eyes she smiled. Matt returned

the gesture and his heart rate quickened. His feelings for her began to resurface, bringing with them the desire to be more than just friends. He found it hard to control this sudden rush of emotions. Even in her drunkenness he adored her. He wanted to tell her there and then, but his heart wouldn't let him. The thought of revealing this truth scared the living daylights out of him. He knew she had feelings for him because they were so close, but she had never shown any signs of wanting a deeper, more intimate relationship. He soon convinced himself that this was out of the question and soon dismissed these insane thoughts.

Mick soon woke up feeling dreadful. "Ooh my head, it feels like a bomb has gone off in my brain," he said sluggishly. He sat up and looked at Matt with one eye closed.

"I have got to stop this drinking lark, it's bad for my health! What happened last night? It's all a blur."

Danielle laughed at him but couldn't help feeling sympathetic towards him. His hung-over state reminded her of her own, so taking Matt's advice she headed for the bathroom.

Matt shared his recollection of the previous night and Mick was not surprised. It was the same old story only this time it was told in a new location. Mick shut his eyes and his heart sank. He could feel his hands shaking, which was not unusual, but now his insides were doing the same. This strange sensation unnerved him.

It's as if it is trying to take over my body, he thought.

He was overcome by a terrible fear when a loud voice in his head said, "You drink too much!" Then the image of Tracey's face appeared in his mind. Those four dreaded words rang through his head again, but his wife's lips did not move. Now he was confused, he didn't know if it was Tracey's constant nagging that haunted him or if it was the voice of his conscience. Suddenly he panicked. He hated the thought of either one and tried desperately, to find a reasonable excuse for his shakiness. Then the answer came, and he smiled. *It's because of the water,* he thought smugly. *Greek water is different from the water back home.*

His fear soon subsided, and he was pleased to feel calm again. His quick thinking helped to restrain his thoughts from going down an unnecessary road, and he was so thankful for this comforting revelation.

Thirty minutes later the three friends entered the restaurant. Danielle walked in reluctantly, scanning the room for any sign of Panos but to her relief he was nowhere to be seen. Stuart was already sitting at a table drinking a cup of coffee, so the three friends went over to join him. She felt on edge and hoped Panos didn't show his face. He didn't. They sat quietly nursing their hangovers and ate their continental breakfast. After the meal they felt much better so decided to take the mini bus into town. Mick was keen to show them the familiar sights and they were all relieved the sun was now shining beautifully.

Matt had to go back to the room to get his money, so Mick told him to meet them out on the terrace. He led Danielle and Stuart out through the French windows. When she stepped out, she was not prepared for the sight that awaited her, and the glorious view which took her breath away. The sky was blue, not a cloud to be seen, and the warmth of the sun brushed against her skin, welcoming her to this wonderful place. The sea was as blue as the sky, reflecting the tranquillity she felt inside. She walked over to the edge, looked down and was confronted with the bluest pool she had ever seen. Sun loungers were placed neatly around the edge, and the water sparkled like crystal. Closing her eyes, she took a deep breath. The atmosphere was idyllic, and she could not imagine a better place on earth; it was perfect!

As she was lost in the moment, a weird feeling suddenly swept over her. It was a feeling of deja vu, as if she had been here before. She opened her eyes and the feeling disappeared. She was taken aback by this strange sensation, it just didn't make sense. It was almost like she knew what was going to happen next, as if the moment had been played before somehow.

I must be crazy, she thought, and dismissed her notions as being silly.

"It sure is a beautiful sight," said Mick quietly walking up beside her. She just nodded, taken in by her surroundings. Stuart was standing the other side of her and he was also admiring the incredible view. He felt so at peace with himself. He hadn't felt this way in a long time and was so pleased to be in this gorgeous place. They stood quietly waiting for Matt in the mid-morning sun, completely overwhelmed by this lovely place. The minutes soon passed and before long Matt walked up behind them.

"The bus is leaving in ten minutes," said Matt boldly. "I have just seen Panos and he will be driving the bus down into town."

Danielle turned to him, thinking about how content he looked. She had not seen him look this way before and was touched by his infectious smile. She smiled back at him until she suddenly realised what he had just said, especially the bit about, Panos driving them into town! A wave of terror gripped hold of her, when the vision of the night before, invaded her mind.

"Don't worry Dan, he will be ok," Matt said noticing

the horror on her face. "Don't forget what I said earlier. He probably sees drunken girls all of the time, it's all part of his job," he continued with a comforting arm placed reassuringly around her.

"I know, but how many girls has he had to put to bed!" Out of the blue she laughed. "I must have looked so pathetic. I bet he won't want to speak to me now."

Good at least I won't have to look into his eyes again, she thought to herself.

"That's better Dan. It's good to see you smiling again. Don't worry about it, we're on holiday. He has probably got better things to think about," said Matt squeezing her shoulder. The three friends began to make their way towards the bus.

Matt couldn't have been more wrong! Panos was eagerly waiting by the bus! He had been unable to get Danielle out of his mind. The vision of her lying on her bed was vivid in his mind. There was just something about this girl that intrigued him. The fact that she had been drunk made absolutely no difference whatsoever. He felt a niggling feeling inside, when he envisioned her, a strange feeling that was alien to him. He had enjoyed talking to her, listening to her views, and he really wanted to get to know her better. He was even more determined now that she had mentioned she and Matt were just friends. He was impatient for their next encounter.

When he heard them coming from the pool area, he slid open the side door of the mini bus. He put a big welcoming smile on his face when they emerged, but it soon disappeared when he saw Matt's arm around Danielle's shoulder. Overcome with disappointment as the four of them came towards him, he had to take a deep breath to control himself. He smiled half-heartedly to try and hide these unwanted feelings.

Mick was the first to get on the bus. Panos shook his hand as he got on and then exchanged pleasantries with Stuart and Matt who got on behind him. The moment he had been waiting for arrived and he tried to make eye contact with Danielle, but she was too ashamed to even look at him as she felt so awkward. She quickly walked past him and tried to get as far away from him as possible. Her heart was beating fast and she could feel the blood rushing up to her face, as she resisted the urge to run to the back of the bus.

He sensed her embarrassment and was desperate to let her know she needn't have worried about the events of the night before. The way she reacted towards him, prompted his disappointment and the moment was lost. He had no choice but to shut the door, get in the driver's seat and proceed the drive into the town.

On the way Mick had full control of the conversation. The drunken events of the night before were soon forgotten because he had them all laughing at his silly ways. Panos kept glancing in the rear-view mirror at Danielle. He was pleased to see her smiling and stole every moment he could to look at her. He kept telling himself not to bother, but he just couldn't help himself. He wanted to catch her eye to reassure her it was ok, and tried a few times, but she kept looking away and she wouldn't meet his gaze. She had noticed that he kept looking at her, but she could not face seeing him. The memory of her humiliation was still raw in her mind, so when she caught his eye she had to look away.

She made herself remember Matt's encouraging words from earlier and forced herself to look out of the window instead. The view was amazing. The island's beauty stirred up an excitement in her stomach and the realisation took her breath away. *This sure is the place where dreams are made,* she thought to herself as a smile played on her lips. Feeling in tune with her surroundings, she could hardly believe she was actually here.

Her thoughts were suddenly interrupted by a roar of laughter. Mick had yet again said something funny that made the men laugh themselves to tears. She laughed even though she didn't know why, and realised she felt better, and was able to push her earlier feelings to one side.

The bus stopped at the top of the high street. As they got off the bus Panos wished them all a good day. Danielle was the last to get out and he held out his hand to help her off. She found that she had no choice but to respond to his kind gesture, to avoid appearing rude! As he helped her down, a spark of electricity seemed to ignite between them when their hands touched. They both felt it and she couldn't help looking into his soft brown eyes. Her heart seemed to melt as he smiled at her, and she smiled back uncontrollably. No words were said or necessary and she shyly looked away, aware of something strange occurring, but was unsure of exactly what it was.

She again had a feeling of de-ja-vu.

What is happening here? she thought to herself quickly pulling her hand away. The other three men were making their way down the high street, totally oblivious to what was going on between her and Panos.

"Come on Dan!" shouted Matt realising she was still by the bus.

"I'm starving," he complained.

She took the opportunity to escape from the awkwardness of Panos's stare and ran down the street to rejoin her friends. He told them the bus would be there at two o'clock if they wanted a lift back. Without even looking back Mick put his hand up in the air, answering for all of them as Panos drove back to the hotel.

There were far more people in the town, many of them tourists, and Danielle breathed in the friendly atmosphere. They walked past the small shops and made their way towards the harbour. Mick was dying for a beer as usual, so he suggested they went to a Taverna he knew of. Matt was surprised at how friendly and welcoming the natives were. Everyone said good morning and the waiters went out of their way to make them feel comfortable.

They ordered their drinks and the three men reminisced about the night before. Danielle's thoughts were elsewhere. Panos was at the fore front of her mind and she was thinking about what had happened by the bus.

He is very handsome, she thought to herself as she picked apart everything that had passed between them so far.

She soon however convinced herself that he was just being friendly. *He is most probably like that with all the girls he meets,* she thought to herself, not wanting to get her hopes up. She knew what Greek men were like because she had seen the film Shirley Valentine!

She thought back to the night before and was reminded of the conversation she had with him. She had made her views very clear and could feel the blood rush to her face again. She soon dismissed this unwanted feeling and pushed him to the back of her mind. Their drinks came, and she concentrated on looking out across the sea. She still found it hard to believe she was really there and was totally captivated by the island. Once again, she had the same familiar feeling which flared through her body. This time the sensation was so strong it sent shivers down her spine, and the cold chill made her shudder. It really felt like she had been here before. She shook her head and the feeling passed.

Hearing Mick say her name helped her to get her mind back on joining their conversation. Stuart paid the bill this time and the four friends took a slow stroll back to meet the bus. All She wanted to do now was chill out by the pool, and all were happy to comply. By the time they walked up to the top of the high street it was two o'clock.

The mini bus was already there. Danielle focused on the driver and was disappointed to see Kosta in the driver's seat. He couldn't speak very good English but always managed to get his point across. Mick had a lot of time for this man. Even though there was a language barrier, they always managed to have a laugh together, especially as he was game for anything. Each year Mick had visited the hotel Kosta had managed to throw him in the pool. Mick was determined this time it was Kosta who was going to end up in the pool. He had tried in the past but had always failed.

This year is going to be my year, even if it's the last thing I do, thought Mick smiling to himself.

Kosta was very full of himself and took great pleasure in boasting about his sexual conquests with women. He would make the shape of a woman with his hands saying, "shaggy, shaggy" whilst thrusting his pelvis to and fro. This always made Mick laugh because it seemed to be the only English word Kosta knew perfectly. They got closer to the bus and Kosta got out and opened the door. As Mick got on, Kosta began play fighting with him. Mick quickly retaliated by digging him in the ribs. "Kosta, this time you are going in the pool. I will throw you in with your clothes on," he teased.

"No! No Mick in pool again. Kosta strong! Mick Splash!" replied Kosta gently slapping Mick across the face.

"No not this time, my friend," Mick replied, slapping him back. Their laughter brought their play fight to a halt and they all followed Mick onto the bus. They travelled up the hill and Mick couldn't help noticing his friend's awestruck faces. *I knew they would love it here,* he thought smiling cheekily. Feeling so proud to have made his friends happy, pride oozed out of his every pore.

The sun was very warm now and Danielle was looking forward to lounging by the pool. When they got to the top of the hill the magnificent hotel stole the view. It stood out on its own and Danielle agreed it lived up to its name sake. The bus reached its destination and they all got out and made their way to their rooms to get changed. She went into the bathroom and put her pink bikini on. She hoped she did not look too fat and wrapped a sarong around her waist. She came out to find Matt and Mick ready and eager to get down to the pool, so she quickly grabbed a towel and put it in her bag.

"Blimey, Dan you do look like that girl in the magazine, only a lot whiter," said Mick laughing. He didn't realise she had such a good figure, for someone who had three children. Matt was also surprised.

She went bright red and rushed out the room muttering something under her breath.

She rushed past Yannis and Panos who were now at the bar. All Panos could see was a pink object fly past him and moments later Mick and Matt appeared too.

"What's wrong with Danielle?" asked Panos curious about why she was upset.

"Nothing, I just embarrassed her a bit," replied Mick confused by her hasty departure.

"A bit?" exclaimed Matt sarcastically. "The poor girl ran out as red as a beetroot!" he continued feeling very protective over her.

"I am going to make sure she's OK. Get me a beer and get Dan a glass of wine, that's the least you can do for her."

He felt quite agitated at Mick's insensitivity towards Danielle, and quickly disappeared out onto the terrace.

"Blimey, I only said how good she looked," said Mick turning to Panos helplessly.

"It was a compliment. That girl is so sensitive, but I will apologise to her when I see her. I don't know, women!"

He threw his hands up into the air and proceeded to order their drinks.

"So, Michael how are you my friend?" asked Panos suddenly aware that Mick was now alone. He took this opportunity to find out more about Danielle as he began to pour Mick's beer.

"How are you enjoying your holiday so far?" he began.

Mick thought for a minute taken aback by the question and suddenly realised he was missing his wife; it was the first time he had thought about her. He felt quite angry that Panos had asked, because he had been fine up until that point. Just as suddenly a feeling of guilt consumed him.

"Err, yes I am having a great time Panos," he replied quickly composing himself.

Panos handed him his drink and he took a big gulp. As the liquid flowed down his throat, he put his thoughts of Tracey to the back of his mind.

"Yes, its brilliant being with my mates, there are no arguments and I am being told what to do," he said smiling.

"You must be pleased you've got special friends around you. That's good. Matt is a great support for you, no?"

"Yes, he's like my little brother. We have grown close over the years and he is a damned good mechanic."

Mick took another mouthful of his beer and began to share about Matt's domestic troubles. "He has to come to terms with being on his own too. It's so sad, as he really misses his Mrs," said Mick laughing at his play on words.

"So, Matt and Danielle are not together then? As a couple I mean?" Panos asked flippantly trying to hide his interest in her.

"No, my friend they are not. I know he has a soft spot for her and can be quite protective of her at times, but no they are not together. I think he would like them to be more, but I know Dan just wants him as a friend..."

Mick paused suspicious of Panos's inquisitiveness. "What's with all the questions Panos? You haven't got a soft spot for her, have you?" asked Mick smirking. He couldn't help noticing Panos was blushing.

"I saw the way you looked at her when you first met her. She is a very good looking, woman. You wait until you see her in her bikini. She will knock your socks off!"

Confusion swept across Panos's face. "Knock my socks off?" he questioned laughing out loud.

"You will understand me when you see her," replied Mick cheekily patting Panos's hand.

Panos continued with the drinks order and felt very pleased at Mick's answer to his question, smiling to himself. Soon Stuart joined them at the bar. Panos put on his serious face and the two men began talking.

Matt walked down to the pool and over to Danielle. She

was laying on her front reading a book.

"Are you all right, Dan? Don't take any notice of Mick. Sometimes he doesn't know when to keep his big mouth shut," he said lying down on the sun lounger beside her.

She didn't answer but put her book down and turned on her back. Matt hadn't realised she wasn't wearing a bikini top until she turned over. He was absolutely stunned. He couldn't help eyeing up her lovely body, but had to quickly look away, frightened to take in the gorgeous sight of his friend beside him.

"Oh, Matt this is the life. I could stay here forever," she said closing her eyes, letting the sun's rays gently caress her skin.

He was speechless as the vision of her invaded his mind. He hadn't realised just how lovely she really was, and it took all his mental strength not to look at her. For the first and only time, he felt sorry for Brad who had let this beautiful lady slip through his fingers. He forced himself to look up into the clear blue sky.

Brad you really are a jerk, he thought, feeling quite angry.

He suddenly realised he was falling in love with her and felt the familiar aching in his heart. He really wanted to tell her how he felt but, had to force himself not too. He was so scared that she did not share the same feelings about him. He could not handle any more rejection so once again, he swallowed his insane thoughts.

"Where is Mick with our drinks?" he said sitting up looking around to see if he could see him. To his relief Mick and Stuart were walking over to them carrying a tray. Mick's eyes nearly popped out of his head when he took one look at Danielle's half nakedness. He nearly said something again but the stern look that Matt gave him, made him think twice. For once he kept his mouth tightly shut.

The four companions spent the afternoon chatting and soaking up the sun. They had the poolside to themselves and knew they had to make the most of it because other guests would be arriving later. Mick wondered if there would be any single women arriving, and the same thought went through Stuart's mind.

Matt kept thinking about Danielle and found it very hard to concentrate on anything else. The more beer he drank the bolder he became. In the end he decided to take the plunge and when the time was right, he was going to confront her with his feelings. She on the other hand was oblivious to what he was thinking, and every now and again Panos would come into her mind. Raising her hand slightly she looked at it. In her mind she could still feel the electricity she had felt when he touched it. *I'm just crazy,* she thought, telling herself again that he was just being friendly. Quickly putting her hand back down she felt a bit silly.

After a lazy afternoon of relaxing they went back to their rooms to freshen up for dinner. Once ready they went into town for their meal. They decided to try a different restaurant this time. They enjoyed their food and after a couple of hours they went back to the hotel for a few drinks.

Danielle was determined to put herself to bed this time, so kept herself reasonably sober. Panos was busy with the new guests who kept him away from the bar, but he watched her from a distance. She looked so lovely and he was disappointed he could not talk to her. There will be another time he reassured himself, after all it's only the beginning of her holiday.

Stuart was getting very drunk and by the end of the night was bouncing off everything that was in his way. He finally fell on one of the settees and stayed there, unable to get up. Danielle thought her sides were going to split from laughter.

Tonight, would be his night for making a complete fool of himself, she thought to herself smiling.

The next couple of days were spent pretty much in the same way. They went sightseeing in the morning and spend the afternoons by the pool. Danielle had never laughed so much, because there was never a dull moment with Mick around. Panos was desperate to talk to her privately, but never managed to get her on her own, because Matt was always guaranteed to be a few steps behind her. This was starting to really annoy him and get on his nerves! It didn't help that every time he saw her, his feelings for her grew stronger.

CHAPTER

SEVEN

IT WAS SUNDAY AFTERNOON AND the four friends were sitting in their usual spot around the pool. The hotel had become busier now because more guests had arrived, and the poolside was full of couples. Mick was disappointed there were no single girls visiting the hotel. Thinking back to all the years he had visited with Tracey, the hotel seemed to be teeming with young single females. It was just his luck that now he was single, there was not one of them in sight. He looked at his watch. It was two forty-five. *Only fifteen minutes to go and then the grand prix will be on*,he thought.

He was passionate about formula one racing, and had never missed a race at home, so he was determined it would be no different while he was away. Panos shared the same passion for racing and promised him they would watch it together in the bar. Mick followed the Ferrari team. His favourite driver was Michael Schumacher. Panos was a fan of the McLaren team and David Coultard was his favourite driver. They thought they would make the race a bit more exciting by deciding to wage a bet on it.

Matt nodded, picking up his towel as he stood up. He was not as fanatical as Mick when it came to motor racing, but he had to admit he did enjoy watching them race.

"Stu, what about you mate, are you coming up with us?" asked Mick as he walked towards the hotel.

"I'm not into motor racing, so I'll stay here and keep Danielle company, if it's all the same to you Mick," replied Stuart with his eyes closed.

"OK suit yourself," replied Mick flippantly, walking away.

Danielle had no interest in motor racing and would rather soak up the glorious sunshine any day. She loved the peace and quiet and was enjoying the serenity of her surroundings. The sun felt warm against her skin making its mark, turning her a golden brown healthy, colour. She felt really content, and that nothing could spoil this wonderful feeling.

"Dan, I am going to get a drink, do you want one?" Stuart suddenly asked, interrupting her thoughts. She looked at him and couldn't help feeling sorry for this skinny man. The sun had made him very pink, especially on his balding head. She could tell he was trying hard to fit in, but he was so different from the other two. She looked at him and smiled.

"Yes, please Stu. Can you get me a bottle of water? Thank you."Then she closed her eyes and went back to her thoughts.

Stuart got up and proceeded to the bar. When he walked into the lounge the bar was left unattended. His eyes looked down to the end of the room where Panos was sitting, talking to Mick.

"Yes please, Panos," he shouted across the room. Panos looked up from his conversation, saw Stuart waiting at the bar and scurried over to serve him. He obliged Stuart his drinks, and then noticed his very pink head.

"You should be very careful in the sun Stuart," he said feeling anxious for this man.

"You really should be wearing a hat my friend. You have to protect your head." He couldn't help being genuinely concerned. Stuart just nodded. He listened to Panos's advice and made a mental note to buy one later. Until then he decided to stay in the shade.

It suddenly then dawned on Panos that Danielle was outside alone.

"Stuart, can I ask you something please?" he said quietly. Stuart just looked at him suspiciously. He hesitated for a second and moved closer to Stuart so only he could hear. He quickly glanced over to where Mick and Matt were sitting, because he wanted to make sure their conversation was private. To his relief the other two men were engrossed in the TV.

"Do you think Danielle would go out for a meal with me?" he asked. His heart started to beat faster as his eyes darted over to Matt, hoping their conversation was not causing any suspicion.

"Stuart I really do like her, and seeing you were alone with her I thought you would ask her for me," he continued, handing him a glass. Stuart didn't answer straight away but thought for a minute. He really liked Danielle and did not want to be the one responsible for causing her any more heartache. He knew what these Mediterranean men were like when it came to women and did not want her to get hurt. He had noticed the way Panos looked at her and had caught her looking at him too, a few times, but did not want this man to just use her. He started to shake his head, but as if reading his mind Panos took hold of his arm.

"I don't just want to sleep with her Stuart. I really like her, and she fascinates me. I can't get her out of my mind! I really want to get to know the beautiful lady…"

He paused, appealing to him as he looked straight into his eyes.

"I do not just like her looks. I like her voice, the way she walks, the way she laughs. Everything about her is so incredible. Please believe my sincerity," he concluded, his eyes pleading with Stuart's.

Stuart was surprised when he found himself actually believing him.

"OK Panos I will ask her, but please do not do anything to hurt her! She has been through enough this past year," he replied sternly.

Panos shook his head and the biggest smile beamed across his face. He took his hand away when Mick shouted over that the race was about to start.

"Oh, thank you Stuart," he said and scurried back over to join Mick and Matt.

Stuart walked back to Danielle who was lying on her front reading a book. She was so engrossed in the story she was unaware of his presence. He put her drink down on the table and sat on a lounger next to her.

"Is that a good book Dan?" he said, not meaning to startle her.

"Blimey Stuart, you scared the life out of me! You shouldn't creep up on people like that!" Her voice was raised, and she had to catch her breath.

"You took your time. I didn't think you were into formula

one," she said sitting up. Then she grabbed the bottle and poured herself a glass of water.

"I'm not. I was just talking to Panos..." he said watching her gulping down her drink.

"He seems a very nice man, don't you think?" he continued waiting, eager for her to reply.

"Ah I needed that," Danielle said drinking down the last drop. "The sun is so dehydrating. Of-course it has nothing to do with all the alcohol I have consumed," she laughed sarcastically.

She wiped her mouth and hesitated. *What a strange thing for him to ask,* she suddenly thought suspiciously.

"Yes, I suppose he is," she finally answered.

"Well, he thinks you are quite lovely Dan and he wants to know if you'll go out for something to eat with him." He waited for her reaction.

She was shocked by Panos's request and this was evident by the expression on her face. Then she smiled.

"Are you serious Stuart, he actually asked you to ask me?" she said feeling quite flattered.

"I am serious Dan, that's why I was so long. From what he was saying he seems quite besotted with you."

"Oh." She was totally lost for words. Then drawn by an invisible force they both looked at the terrace to find Panos standing there looking down at them. He stood there for a few moments and then quickly disappeared back into the hotel.

"I think he wants to know your answer," he said surprised to have seen him standing there. Why else would he be standing there?

You must be eager, he thought to himself.

"Well Dan," he continued smiling. "What's your answer?"

Danielle was taken aback by his proposal. *Maybe he wasn't just being friendly after all*, she thought.

She was reminded of their encounter at the mini bus and her heart skipped a beat when the memory of his touch came flooding back.

I do think he is very attractive, she thought to herself. *I don't suppose it would hurt just to have a meal with him, just this once.*

Suddenly Matt entered her mind. She had wondered a few times whether his feelings for her were deeper than he had let on. She couldn't help feeling obligated to him because he had paid for her holiday. Her feelings for him were purely platonic and she hoped she had not done anything to encourage him to feel otherwise. She did not want to hurt his feelings. At the same time, she convinced herself that going out for a meal with Panos would only be the one time, and that what Matt didn't know, couldn't hurt him. Deciding to share her views with Stuart, to her surprise he agreed with her.

"Dan you are a free agent honey and you can do anything you want to. You are going to pay Matt back when you can as it was a loan. He knows that," he encouraged her.

"Stuart you are absolutely right," she said as a wave of confidence flowed through her body. "So yes, you can tell Panos I would love to go out with him."

She lay back and thought about this gorgeous Greek man who actually wanted to spend time with her. She spent the rest of the afternoon with Panos at the fore front of her mind.

Stuart's head was starting to throb, so he gathered his things together, and told her he was going for a lie down for a while. She assured him it was a good idea. They agreed to meet in the bar later and he assured her he would pass on her answer to Panos.

When he left the poolside, Panos once again stole her thoughts and she tried to figure out why he would want to go out with her. She told herself just to play it cool. After all it would only be this once. She could not help but smile to herself and realised she felt extremely happy. *This is going to be a holiday to remember,* she thought grinning from ear to ear.

Mick's voice echoed in the distance and she guessed Schumacher must be winning. She didn't understand what all the fuss was about. She knew they had money on the race but didn't know how much and she really didn't care. She was just happy lying there soaking up the wonderful sunshine thinking about Panos. She loved being on the island and couldn't imagine being anywhere else.

Matt was getting into the race and had to admit it was very exciting. He had seen Stuart talking to Panos earlier and hadn't taken much notice but when he turned around again the two men were now in deep conversation.

"I wonder what those two are talking about. They suddenly seem very friendly," he said to Mick inquisitively.

"They are probably talking about something cultural. I know what Panos is like when he gets going and Stu is the same. Believe me mate you don't want to get involved, it's so boring," said Mick putting his hand over his mouth faking a yawn.

"If the conversation doesn't involve women or cars then I don't want to know. Go on Schumacher!" Mick's eyes never left the screen. Matt laughed and got back into to the race.

"So, Stuart, the lovely Danielle said yes?" he asked almost

in disbelief. "That has made me a very happy man! Thank you my friend," he continued self-assuredly. Stuart just nodded.

"This is where I get off Panos. The rest is up to you. I am going up to have a lie down. Can you please tell Mick I will meet him down here later?" His head was throbbing badly, and it was starting to make him feel sick. He put this condition down to lack of sleep because the late nights had really taken its toll on his ageing body. Panos had noticed that he looked very queasy. He comforted Stuart by telling him a good sleep was all he needed, and he would wake up feeling much better. He said he would pass on the message to Mick, thanked him again and watched him walk away.

The room was a lot busier now. Guests had come in from their day in the Greek sunshine and they were all thirsty from their travels. Panos was literally rushed off his feet. He loved talking to different people and loved to see them happy, and always made a conscious effort to make his guests feel welcome. When they were happy, he was happy, but today it wasn't these particular guests that made him smile. They congratulated him on his exquisite hotel, but this wasn't the reason why he wanted to sing out loud.

Then he saw her. Out of the corner of his eye he spotted her and was stopped in his tracks when she walked past him. Her skin was kissed by the sun and her green eyes shone like priceless gems as she glanced at him. He caught her eye and smiled but she looked shyly away. She was the reason why he wanted to sing, this beautiful English girl who had entered into his life.

She couldn't help looking at him as she walked over to where Mick and Matt were sitting. His face was beaming, and she couldn't help wondering if she was the one responsible for his smile.

"Yes, I know she is a looker Panos, but I am parched," the guest from northern England complained getting quite restless because he had been kept waiting.

"Oh, I am so sorry sir, here is your drink," Panos said going red in the face. He couldn't believe he had let himself be side tracked from his work. He was renowned for his professionalism but somehow this lady had made him forget himself. This was not like him. No other woman had affected him like this, and it was all very new to him. He realised he would have to be very conscious of how he was with the guests from now on. This was a completely new experience for him, and the feelings on the one hand really annoyed him, because he was so used to being in control of everything.

What is this woman doing to me? he thought. He took a deep breath to compose himself and carried on serving his guests.

Danielle sat down next to Mick. His face was stern because Schumacher was losing. "It's only a race Mick, don't look so serious mate," she said jokingly.

"It's only a race?" he asked jumping down her throat. "I have got a hundred quid on this race," he continued.

She was taken aback by his tone. The serious expression was still on his face and she thought he was going to burst out crying.

"More fool you then. You've got more money than sense," she replied calmly. "I have got no sympathy for you Mick. Gambling is a mug's game."

"Well I wouldn't expect you to understand, being a woman!" he retorted, the tone of his voice staying deadly serious.

"Now, now people. Let's not let this get out of hand," intervened Matt quickly.

"Well, what does she know?" muttered Mick under his breath.

Mick is right, she thought. *I do not understand, and I never will.*

Looking over to the bar she noticed that Panos was busy serving and she couldn't help smiling to herself. He looked so handsome in his uniform. He caught her glance and her heart somersaulted when he winked at her. She could feel the flutter of butterflies in her stomach and felt like a teenager again. She was reminded of her first love and was surprised she could feel the same way again. She looked at her watch. *The race should have finished by now,* she thought to herself. She was beginning to feel very tired and wanted to go and have a lie down. She wanted to be wide awake for her outing with Panos. She did wonder how she could do this without having to tell Matt. She soon decided to play it by ear because she was too tired to think. The joy of sharing a room with two snorting pigs was really starting to get to her. She couldn't wait any longer so made her excuses.

"Do you want me to come with you Dan?" asked Matt. "It's near the end of the race and I don't mind."

"No, it's OK I just want some time by myself. I would be OK if it wasn't for you two snoring all night," she said half-jokingly.

"I don't know what you mean Dan? I don't snore," Mick butted in feeling a little bit guilty for the way he had spoken to her earlier.

"That's the understatement of the century," she said picking up her bag and walking away. Mick rolled his eyes and quickly re-focused on the race.

Panos saw Danielle leave the lounge and looked around to see if anyone needed serving. To his relief no one was waiting, so he quickly left the bar. She walked up the first flight of steps and suddenly he appeared out of a side door, and her heart nearly stopped as he approached her. She froze on the spot when he started to speak.

"Hello Danielle. How are you today?" he asked softly, his big brown eyes twinkling.

"I- I am very tired so I am going to lie down for a while. H-how are you?" she asked nervously.

"I am very happy since you have come to my hotel." He was still smiling and took her hand which was shaking because he had taken her by surprise.

"You are shaking, are you cold?" he asked anxiously. She could feel the blood rushing to her cheeks, and shook her head looking down at the floor.

"N-no, I have not been getting much sleep," her voice quivered.

He put his hand under her chin and gently lifted up her face. Then it happened again, a spark of electricity as their hands touched. He looked deep into her green eyes and was once again astounded by their beauty. As he did so he felt something stirring deep within and his heart began to beat faster in his chest. They stood there looking at each other, but not saying a word for what seemed like an eternity. The same unfamiliar longing swept over both of them, as they both had the same thought, *What is this person doing to me?*

She was completely spellbound by this man holding her face.

"We will see each other later OK?" Panos asked breaking the silence, a warm smile still dominating his face. She just nodded, unable to speak. He pulled her hand up and gently kissed it.

"I look forward to it beautiful Danielle." With that he went back through the door from which he came.

Danielle just stood there motionless. She watched as the door closed behind him and was overcome by various feelings. She tried to take in what had just happened, but he had provoked a reaction she was not prepared for. There was an instant attraction between them, she knew, but wasn't quite sure whether she liked this feeling that came from deep within her. *What is this man doing to me?* she thought as emotions that had been lost a long time suddenly resurfaced. A huge smile escaped from her lips and she began a slow walk up to her room.

She walked into her room, closed the door and leaning against it, she closed her eyes. The vision of Panos was prominent in her mind and she felt like she was floating on cloud nine. She walked over to the bed and lay down. Closing her eyes her mind began to race. After a few minutes she drifted off into a very peaceful sleep, until she was disturbed when Mick walked into the room slamming the door behind him.

"Dan are you asleep, mate?" he bellowed, startling her.

"I was Mick," she answered in a sleepy voice. "Where's the fire?" she asked putting her head under the covers.

"Sorry Dan but you have been up here for a while now. I need to get in the shower and get changed for dinner... Matt is on his way up," he stated cheerfully.

"I take it you won the race seeing as you are so happy," she said sitting up rubbing her eyes.

"Na the McLaren's team won so I had to cough up the cash. What's a hundred quid anyway between friends?" he replied, looking for his towel.

"You've changed your tune. I thought you would have the right hump," she said confused by his happy attitude.

"It is only money after all Dan," Mick replied brashly.

He found his towel and went into the bathroom. Danielle just laughed.

He did act flash when it came to money. He liked the fact he gained a lot of respect because of his wealth, but Danielle and Matt could see that many people took advantage of him. On many occasions he would buy the whole pub a drink. He was a very generous man, which caused him to get a lot of attention. They both wondered whether these people would still be his friends if he was flat broke. As his friends, they had warned him many times, but he seemed oblivious to their concerns.

Danielle reached over for a carton of orange juice. She was pouring herself a drink when Matt walked through the door.

"Are you alright Dan? Do you feel better after your sleep?" he asked, making a bee line for her. Even though she looked like she had just woken up, to him she still looked pretty. She was getting a gorgeous tan and was literally glowing. She drank her drink and nodded. As Panos invaded her mind again, she got up and walked out onto the balcony, oblivious that Matt was still talking to her, and in fact had followed her out. He sat down next to her but soon realised she wasn't listening to him and felt quite hurt by her apparent ignorance.

"Dan, are you OK? I've been talking to you for the past five minutes and you haven't heard a word I've said. What's wrong babe?" He asked looking at her. Her eyes were closed, and he thought she could not have looked more beautiful. She showed no signs of responding as his eyes fixed on her.

This isn't like her, he thought. Suddenly he had an overwhelming urge to tell her exactly how he felt about her.

"Dan!" Matt raised his voice to get some sort of response out of her.

"Are you OK?" His tone did not change. This seemed to work as she opened her eyes and looked at him.

"What!"she snapped, agitated by him for disturbing her thoughts.

"Oh, it doesn't matter," he exclaimed hurt by her reaction towards him. He turned from her when she shut her eyes again and looked out to sea.

She has never spoken to me like that before, he thought, and a tear began to form in the corner of his eyes. He racked his brains to think if he had done something to upset her. He could not think of anything because he had spent most of the afternoon with Mick watching the Grand Prix. He was so confused.

She was so happy earlier, what possibly could have happened to drastically change her mood? The previous confidence he felt soon became a faint memory.

When she managed to tear her mind away from thoughts of Panos, she was consumed by a wave of guilt because of the way she had spoken to him.

"I am so sorry Matt," she said looking at him. "I have just got something on my mind that's all. I shouldn't have snapped at you like that," she said reassuringly patting his leg.

"Oh- OK mate, no harm done eh?" He wondered what she could possibly have on her mind to make her act this way.

"I am here if you need to talk," he said kindly.

Maybe she is thinking about her children, he soon convinced himself.

They were disturbed when Mick wandered out with a towel around his waist cursing at the top of his voice.

"Bloody Greek steps! Why do they have the stupid little things? They're everywhere and I have just banged my toe. It really hurt!" he cried out. Then he sat down to look at his injured toe.

"Alright mate you don't have to shout, the whole island can hear you," said Matt trying not to laugh.

"Well it hurt. Bloody Greeks!" said Mick lowering his voice.

She thought about the many times he had walked in and out of the bathroom and laughed. "I am sure you will live you, big pansy," she commented as she got up.

"I am getting in the shower," she said still laughing. "Do you want mummy to go and smack the naughty step for you, little boy," she teased.

Mick picked up his sandal and threw it at her, narrowly missing her leg. "I am glad you think it's funny," he replied sulkily, still rubbing his little toe.

She got her towel and walked into the bathroom (minding the step). Untying her sarong, she took off her bikini and began to wash her face. Catching a glimpse of herself in the mirror, she was shocked hardly recognising the face staring back at her! Her skin was a golden brown making her eyes shine a deep emerald green. Usually she didn't like looking at herself because she hated the way she looked, but she couldn't help staring back at herself in the mirror. People said how attractive she was, but she could not see it herself. Being able to accept compliments, was not her strong point, because she always suspected that there must be an ulterior motive behind the remarks she got!

Surprisingly, she actually liked who she saw in the mirror now. She stepped back and looked at her tanned body. Even this she liked. She studied herself closely and a wave of confidence filled her being.

"What is happening to me?" she whispered to herself. She touched her brown silky skin and for the first time in her life she actually felt beautiful. The familiar feeling came back flooding her thoroughly. It was as if she had been here before. For just a split second it all seemed to make sense, the reason for her being here and the emotions she was feeling. Just as quickly as it came it passed, and she was totally in awe of what was happening to her.

She got into the shower and let the warm water sprinkle over her body. *He thinks I am beautiful*, she thought smiling to herself as he entered her mind once again. She could feel excitement rising up from the pit of her stomach at the thought of spending some time with him that evening. Her thoughts were rudely interrupted by the sound of Matt's voice.

"Dan, are you going to be long babe? I need to get in the shower!" She had lost all track of time captured by these strange mystical feelings.

"I'm nearly ready," she replied getting out of the shower.

She dried herself off and wondered what she was going to wear. Feeling sixteen again, she wanted to look good for Panos. Suddenly she knew exactly what she was going to wear. She threw on her pyjamas and came out of the bathroom brushing past Matt.

Mick was already dressed. He got his walkman out of his suitcase and was attaching the speakers. "Do you fancy listening to a bit of Celine Dion?" he asked. She was one of his favourite female singers.

"I don't mind Mick," she replied. "How's your toe?" she asked as she laughed because she just couldn't help herself.

Mick chose to ignore her sarcastic remark and pressed play. She did not take any notice of the song playing and began hunting for her special black dress. She found it and placed it neatly on the bed. Then she got her makeup and began to skilfully apply some mascara.

Mick poured himself a large vodka and orange. He took it out onto the balcony wondering why she even bothered putting makeup on as she did not need it. He had given up on the ways of women because it was all a mystery to him.

He thought about Tracey and wondered what she was doing back home. Was she coping without him? He hoped she wasn't. Even though they had their arguments he did miss her. It felt strange being here in this special place without her, going to the same places they had been to together. He picked up his glass and took a big swig of his drink. Then he started to sing along to Celine's song Because You Loved Me.

Danielle didn't take much notice of the lyrics that came out of the walkman. She could hear Celine's amazing voice blaring out, but she was oblivious to the words. She could hear Mick trying to sing and the shower running, but all she could think about was Panos. She could not get this man out of her mind. She had never experienced anything like this before, even though she had been married for eleven years. Her head was whirling. She liked this feeling but decided to be realistic and not get caught up in her emotions as it was just a meal. Once again, she convinced herself Panos was just being friendly and nothing else.

She finished off her makeup by putting on a touch of lipstick and picked up her dress. At that point Matt emerged from the bathroom fully dressed so she went in to get changed. He poured himself a vodka and orange and joined Mick on the balcony. He sat down to wait for her and looked around into Stuart's balcony.

"There is no sign of Stuart! Mick, I hope he's ok! His balcony door is closed," he said concerned, but Mick was too engrossed in the song.

"Mick," he said shaking Mick's leg. "It doesn't look like Stuart's in his room."

"Err. What? Oh, he's probably already down at the bar waiting for us," Mick replied half-heartedly.

"Well what do you think boys?" Danielle appeared at the door looking a million dollars in her short, figure hugging black dress. They were both speechless as they stared at their stunning friend. Matt thought she looked absolutely gorgeous, and the black material made her skin look even browner.

"Well, what are you waiting for? Let's get this show on the road," she said heading towards the door. Both men quickly finished their drinks and followed her out. Mick started to say something rude, but matt nudged him in the ribs warning him not to. It was very rare for Matt to be speechless but watching her walk in that very sexy dress took his breath away. When all three of them entered the bar the sense of pride overwhelmed the two men as every person turned to look around at their gorgeous friend.

Sheer disappointment filled Danielle when Yannis was the only person present at the bar. She really wanted to ask where Panos was but had to stop herself. Yannis looked at Danielle and was taken aback by this lovely English girl. Panos had confided in his younger brother and Yannis had encouraged him to go with his heart. Yannis knew what his brother was like with the ladies, because he watched him with them. They had never spoken about them however because Panos had never felt the need as they were only ever casual affairs.

He did however tell Yannis that he felt this lady was somehow different. Going by how she looked tonight he understood what his brother had meant. He knew Panos would be so proud to have her on his arm. Yannis had always felt a twinge of jealousy towards his brother because the girls would always flock to him, but after he had met his future wife these feelings had soon subsided.

"Panos apologises for his absence but something has come up," Yannis explained. "He will see you later," he continued smiling as he took a quick glance at her. She returned a smile understanding his message. Then Yannis took their order and passed on the message Stuart had relayed to Panos earlier about meeting them in the bar for dinner.

"That's strange," exclaimed Matt.

"He didn't look like he was in his room. We just assumed

he was down here already."

Matt was puzzled. Yannis just shook his head and carried on pouring their drinks.

"He is just probably catching up on his sleep. It has been a pretty boozy few days," Mick piped up.

"He will show up tomorrow as right as rain, you just wait and see." All Mick was interested in was getting his beer. He was sure Matt was making a fuss over nothing. In the end Matt had to agree with Mick and hoped he was right.

Mick asked Yannis to order them a cab to arrive in twenty minutes. Picking up their drinks they went and sat down with Danielle, explaining the situation regarding Stuart. She was reminded of how he had looked earlier and agreed he must have needed a good sleep.

The taxi arrived on time and the three friends went to town to eat. They got out at the harbour and walked past the boats, which they all agreed, must be worth a fortune! They chatted about what they would do if they won the lottery. Matt said he would buy a big boat just like these ones and treat his good friends to a round the world trip.

Danielle wanted to buy a big house on the island because her mother and children would love it here. It was no surprise when Mick said he would buy a bar, so he could get drunk all the time and forget about his then ex-wife. They all laughed at their fantasies and soon found themselves at a quaint fish restaurant in the town square. They all enjoyed their meals and each other's company, and soon forgot about their absent friend. She could not believe how much alcohol she had consumed over the past few days. Mick assured her that was what holidays were all about and she laughed. "I'm not complaining and am enjoying every minute of my holiday."

Along with the alcohol and the feelings that Panos had provoked, she felt she could conquer the world. She started to feel guilty again about the way she had treated Matt earlier and kept apologising to him.

"It's alright mate. I'm just glad that whatever was on your mind earlier is not now, and that you are happy again." He loved to see her smile and enjoyed the attention she got from everyone looking at her. The natives were especially taken by her and many times they commented on her lovely looks. Even a lady from England came over to her and complimented her on her dress and how stunning she looked. He was so proud to be in her company. He wished he could tell her how he really felt about her, but he found it impossible to get the words out.

At first all the attention she received embarrassed her, but after a few drinks she felt flattered. She went to the toilet and Matt took this opportunity to confide in Mick about his feelings for her. Mick felt touched by Matt's honesty but told him bluntly, that he did not think she shared the same feelings for him. Looking at his face though he soon regretted his comment and tried to soften it by adding he could of course be wrong. He felt guilty for hurting his best friend's feelings but knew deep down he was right the first time. But this time kept his views to himself. Matt loved Mick for his frankness and was pleased to think he could still have a chance with her. He decided his feelings for her were driving him mad and wanted to know once and for all. He decided there and then that when the time was right, he was going to tell her just how he felt.

Danielle couldn't wait to get back to the hotel. She didn't explain why but Matt thought it would be a chance to get some time alone with her. He felt very brave because of the alcohol in his system and thought tonight would be the night to proclaim his undying love for her.

Butterflies danced around in her stomach as they made their way to the taxi rank laughing and joking around. Mick never once mentioned his bad toe. Once again, they arrived at the hotel still laughing. Many guests frequented the lounge and to Danielle's delight Panos was back behind the bar. He had been called away earlier and was disappointed he had missed her before she had gone to town. He made sure he was back in plenty of time to be there when she returned. He felt agitated while he waited patiently for her arrival. Every time a car pulled up, he felt like he was walking on the edge and his heart would leap. He kept hoping it was her, but sheer disappointment consumed him when other guests appeared instead.

He was pleased the hotel was busy because this made the time he waited go quicker. He heard a car pull up and waited in anticipation. His heart began beating faster by the second and to his relief a familiar voice could be heard. Mick's laughter filled the room when he walked up the front steps. The three friends appeared, and they began walking towards him.

There she is, my beautiful Danielle has returned, he thought to himself. He took one look at her and had the overwhelming urge to pick her up and run away with her. She looked so beautiful. He could not take his eyes off her as she got closer to him. He just wanted to take her in his arms and hold her.

"What is it about this woman?" he asked himself for the millionth time. "Why has she come into my life, and why is she having this effect on me?"

He found it so hard to contain himself. She was like a magnet pulling him towards her. Yannis had mentioned how beautiful she looked, but no one could have described how beautiful, or prepare him for this picture of perfection walking his way.

Mick and Matt were oblivious to his stares when they reached the bar. Mick was too involved in telling Matt a joke who was intently listening to him. Danielle was not listening to the jokes because she was focused on Panos. He looked extremely gorgeous in a crisp pale blue polo shirt and Armani jeans. She thought her heart was going to jump out of her chest as it was beating so fast, and the butterflies in her tummy were now having a party.

"Can I have my drink now?" a German guest asked for the fifth time. Panos could hear the man's voice but it seemed so distant. Then he realised the German man was talking to him. *She has managed to do it again,* he thought. He had been so distracted by her, his professionalism had taken a back seat.

"I am so sorry sir," he said blushing as he eventually handed him his drink. The man walked away, and he looked up to see Danielle standing in front of him. His cheeks were still red, and as he smiled at her, they went a deeper scarlet. When their eyes met there was undeniable chemistry that seemed to fly between them.

Matt burst out laughing when Mick reached the punch line and was nearly brought to tears.

"Hello Panos, my good friend. How are you on this fantastic night? I must say you look very dapper in your designer wear," Mick said mimicking a posh English accent. Regrettably Panos had to tear his eyes away from Danielle to reply.

"Why, Michael, I am very well, thank you. You cannot hide your jealousy my friend because you cannot afford to buy clothes of this style and quality," he mimicked back, pointing to his clothes his face returning to its original shade of white.

"Panos, my son how wrong you are, I wear clothes like that to work. They are peasants clothes my friend, for peasants I say," he replied throwing his hands up in the air emphatically. Both men started laughing.

Danielle was relieved Mick had interrupted their eye contact. She could so easily have gotten lost in his deep brown eyes. This made her feel a little afraid. Usually she liked to be in control but when he looked at her, she felt all her strength evaporate. During such moments she tried to look away from him, anxious about what he was doing to her, but he seemed to project an invisible force, that just overpowered her. She felt helpless whenever he held her gaze. *This is so crazy! How can this man, who I hardly know, have such an overpowering influence on me?* she thought to herself. She was totally shaken by this man.

"Panos, can you do the honours and get my friends and I a drink please?" asked Mick politely. Danielle pulled herself away from the bar and went and sat down. Matt said he wanted a beer and ordered Danielle's drink too as he followed her over to the settee and sat down. It annoyed Panos because Matt seemed to be acting as if he was her boyfriend.

"Yes, of course, Mick," Panos replied seriously. He was so preoccupied by Danielle he had almost forgotten he needed to speak to them urgently because something very important had come up regarding their friend Stuart.

"Michael, I must speak to you all privately, concerning your friend Stuart," he said in a low voice as he looked around the room.

"Go and sit down and I will bring your drinks over shortly," he said trying to reassure Mick as he noticed a bewildered look on Mick's face. "Go, I will explain in a minute."

Mick was concerned he was going over without his drink, but by the tone of Panos's voice he realised he must have something very serious to say. He went and sat down opposite Matt. Danielle couldn't help noticing the troubled look on Mick's face.

"What's wrong Mick? You look worried, and where are our drinks?" She too was becoming concerned because Mick never came away from the bar without a drink. He proceeded to tell them what Panos had said, and for the first time they all sat in silence. They waited patiently for Panos to come over, wondering what he could possibly have to tell them. Mick had a horrible feeling in the pit of his stomach and tapped his foot on the chair leg. Matt picked up a magazine and flicked through the pages to break the monotony. Danielle felt both glad and disappointed she would not be going out with Panos. She looked over to him and he smiled. Panos noticed Matt's attention was elsewhere, so jerked his head back to summon her over. She understood and got up to go over to him.

"I'm just going over to speak to Panos to find out how long he is going to be. The suspense is killing me. I won't be a minute." She didn't even wait for a response and walked over to the bar. Suspicion flashed across Matt's eyes as he watched her walk away and he could not take his eyes off her. Panos could feel his heart rise into his throat when she glamorously walked towards him. He could see Matt's eyes were transfixed on her, so was very careful not to let his feelings for her show in his face, he smiled graciously at her when she stood in front of him.

"I am so sorry Danielle for tonight. I really want to get to know you. I cannot get you out of my mind!" He could have kicked himself for letting his feelings escape.

"And we will go out tomorrow if that is alright?" he said quietly.

She wanted to tell him she had the same feelings, but she couldn't risk letting him know. Then he looked longingly into her green eyes. She looked down at the bar aware of what his eyes were saying. He felt a wave of sadness as he looked at her shiny auburn hair. He wanted to touch her so badly, but he could feel Matt's eyes boring into him.

"You are so beautiful little Danielle, so beautiful."

She looked up and smiled, enthralled by his kind words.

"That's better. I will be over in a minute and I will explain. Do not worry it will be sorted out."

She smiled, trusting his words, and nodded bashfully.

"OK, Panos." She smiled again and walked back over to the table.

Matt quickly looked back at the magazine. A pang of jealousy had gripped hold of him when she was talking to Panos, even though he couldn't hear the conversation.

"What did he say Dan?" he asked as she sat down.

"Not much," she lied. "He just said he will be over in a minute to explain," she replied quickly, hoping he would believe her.

Mick looked at his watch. They had been waiting for fifteen minutes now. He was thirsty and was in dire need for his beer. Panos had noticed the friends were sitting in silence. He wanted as much privacy as possible and waited until most of the guests had gone up to their rooms. Only a handful of them were left in the bar so he poured three drinks and finally walked over to their table. He put the drinks down on the table and sat down next to Mick.

"It's about time Panos," Mick said picking up his drink gulping down half of its contents.

"So, what is this about Stuart?"

"Stuart has left the hotel!" Panos didn't want to beat around the bush so just came out with it. Mick spat a mouthful of drink across the table.

"Left the hotel?" exclaimed Danielle.

"But why did he leave? What did he say to you Panos?"

Her eyes pleaded with his, because she felt so confused.

"What are you saying Panos? Are you having a joke with us?" Mick asked wiping his mouth dry.

"No Michael, I am deadly serious. When you left to go into town, he came down from his room with his bags packed and told me he was leaving. He just said he was not happy here. He paid his bill then left in a taxi."

Panos looked across the room and saw the German guest waiting at the bar. "I will be back shortly," he said frustrated by the interruption and got up to serve him.

"I don't understand. I was talking to him earlier and he seemed happy enough. He had a headache but that was all," said Danielle putting her head in her hands, trying to figure out what reason there could be for Stuart to leave so suddenly, without saying anything to anyone.

"I thought something was wrong when his balcony door was shut," said Matt starting to regret not knocking on his door to see if he was alright. *Maybe I could have talked to him*, he thought regretfully.

Danielle looked over at Panos and watched him walk from the bar over to the reception desk. He picked up the phone and began to talk into it. The three friends sat in disbelief. Panos came off the phone and walked back over to them. He had written something on a piece of paper which he held in his hand.

"Your friend Stuart has gone to the hotel San Remo which is near the harbour, and got himself a room there," stated Panos.

"I will go and see him. Panos please book a taxi for me. I need to talk to him and find out what we have done wrong," said Danielle getting up, her voice full of concern.

"Why didn't he say something to me?" she asked no one in particular, somehow feeling responsible for his behaviour.

"He did get totally drunk last night. I needed a pisshead's phrase book to understand what he was saying," said Mick being his usual sensitive self.

Danielle looked at him with disgust.

"I was just saying," he said sensing that Danielle was not happy with what he had said.

"He has probably got the hump over something really silly. You watch, he will be back tomorrow, you mark my words."

They hoped that for once, Mick was right. They would

have to wait until tomorrow.

"Well who wants another drink? You had me worried for a minute then Panos," Mick said relieved that perhaps it wasn't too serious.

"Panos most probably wants to go to bed Mick, it's late," Danielle remarked. She was upset her night had ended the way it had, and she was really worried about Stuart.

"Nah, he don't mind us having one more, do you me ol' mate," Mick said making his way over to the bar. Panos obliged nodding as he walked over to the bar to pour the drinks.

Matt went off to the toilet so Panos looked straight at Danielle. As she looked back at him, he winked. She felt a tingle go through her bones and goose bumps appeared on her skin. She had to admit she really did like him.

He gave Mick his last drink and he started to sing as he washed down the bar. He walked across the room still singing. He had a spring in his step and went to fetch some dirty glasses from the tables. Mick noticed this was very strange behaviour. He had never seen him act this way before and was struck by his Greek friend's quick change of mood.

"I say Panos, me ol' mate, what are you so happy about all of a sudden? Slow down son you are beginning to scare me," Mick said beginning to laugh.

"Hey Uncle Michael," Panos replied childishly looking at his watch, "Isn't it past your bed time ol' man?" he teased.

"Why you little..." Mick ran up behind him and went to grab his waist, but he was too slow. Panos turned around and grabbed him. Then he picked him up and threw him onto the floor.

"Uncle Michael is too slow for strong Panos."

Mick got up and brushed himself down. Nothing was hurt except his ego. "You can laugh my friend, but you will be sorry!" he shouted out looking flustered.

Danielle laughed so much that tears streamed down her face. Mick sat down next to her agitated by her reaction.

"You're supposed to be on my side Dan. He could have really hurt me!" He hadn't realised how strong Panos was, and this surprised him.

"Mick, you are such a girl," Danielle retaliated as Panos came over and patted him on the back.

"Danielle is right. I will call you Michelle from now on," he laughed. Danielle thought she was going to fall off her chair from laughter. Then Mick began to see the funny side and smiled.

"Don't worry Panos I will get you back my friend."

Mick suddenly felt very drunk. All of the excitement had made the drink go to his head.

Right on cue Matt came back into the bar. "I don't know about you two, but I am ready for my bed, I am shattered," said Matt yawning, drinking the last mouthful of his drink. "Are you two coming?"

"OK mate, I am right behind you. Are you ready Dan?" asked Mick at the same time he stumbled over to the stairs.

"I will be up in a minute. I am just going to finish my drink. Just leave the door unlocked I won't be long." She felt very nervous at the thought of being left alone with Panos, but she didn't want to leave him. Mick was two minutes behind Matt, his mind preoccupied with thinking of ways to get Panos back.

Danielle walked over to the bar and watched Panos washing up the last few dirty glasses. They seemed so far behind the times here, she thought to herself. She had a glass washer in the Kings Head and it made life so much easier. Alone at last, her heart began to pound, and the butterflies had returned.

Panos finished drying the last glass, dried his hands and started to sing. "Beautiful Danielle, she is so beautiful my Danielle, I am so glad she has come to stay. Beautiful Danielle she is so beautiful my Danielle, I don't ever want her to go away."

She was mesmerised by his lovely voice and felt she must be dreaming. He came from behind the bar and brushed past her, sending chills down her spine. The static atmosphere surrounded them, and he sat down next to her. They sat in silence for a few moments. Her mind began to race, as she desperately tried to think of what to say.

"So, Danielle, do you like my hotel?" asked Panos finally breaking the static silence.

"Y-yes, it is a beautiful place. It is a credit to you and your family," she replied afraid to look at him. Her whole body was shaking so she took a mouthful of her drink to try and calm her nerves. Panos could detect her nervousness and just wanted to hold her in his arms. It took all of his mental and physical strength to keep his emotions under control. He picked up his cigarettes and offered her one. She nodded as he pulled two out from the packet and lit them both, handing one to her. She thanked him, taking in a deep breath.

Maybe this will help me calm down, she thought.

"So Panos, what really happened with Stuart?" she asked

sensing he hadn't revealed the whole truth earlier. She looked down and stared at the bar.

"I did not want to say this in front of Michael, but Stuart was very scared when he left," he said taking a drag of his cigarette.

"What could he possibly be frightened of, we're his friends." She looked up in complete disbelief. Her mind was spinning, and she could not think of a plausible explanation.

"He told me that he had heard Matt and Mick talking through the wall. Apparently, they were planning to throw him over the balcony when they had the chance. He said he feared for his life so wanted to leave. I know it sounds bizarre, but he looked so frightened. He was shaking and smoking very heavily," he continued.

"He said what! But that's ridiculous, they would never do that! He must have misheard them." She could not believe what she was hearing.

"Why would he make such an accusation, I don't understand?" She put her hand over her mouth in total shock. Then she had a thought and started to laugh.

"He is having a joke with us, isn't he Panos? Where is he hiding?" She looked into his eyes, searching for a response to confirm her suspicions, but he shook his head.

"This isn't a joke, is it? You are being serious, aren't you?" she said as her heart sank.

"I am sorry, but it is no joke. Don't worry, you will go and see him tomorrow and sort it out. I know he will talk to you." He put his hand on hers and his warm touch seemed to calm her.

"OK, Panos, I will speak to him and bring him back."

He looked at her and admired the sincerity in her voice. Once again silence fell upon them.

"So, beautiful Danielle, tomorrow I will take you somewhere very special," he said gently stroking her arm.

"I want to know all about you. You are so different to all the other girls I have met. I can tell you are a very special lady."

"I bet you say that to all the girls," she replied awkwardly laughing. He was hurt by her blunt statement.

"No, you are wrong," he said abruptly, "I have never felt this way about another girl. I think about you constantly. When I wake up, when I go to sleep you are there." He pointed to his head.

"I do not know why I feel this way, but I do." He lifted up her face to look at her and sheer horror gripped her because she thought he was going to kiss her.

"Please believe me," he said looking deep into her eyes pleading for her to listen to him. "I do not lie." He quickly looked away, still caressing her arm.

She was filled with so many mixed emotions, her eyes still on him. Could he possibly be telling the truth? she wondered. She wanted to pull her arm away but found she couldn't. His touch was like a magnet willing her to stay.

"I do like you Panos," she admitted, "but you have got to see it from my point of view! This is all happening a bit fast, and I have only just met you. You must understand that I can't help wondering if this is just all too good to be true." She couldn't help the honesty that could be heard in her voice.

"I do understand pretty lady and I will prove to you that I am sincere."

He was relieved by her response. Usually he would have had no problem getting a woman into his bed by now, so he was feeling reassured that he was right about her, that she was different. He smiled at her. "You will see."

Her heart was pounding as he spoke and once again, she felt in awe of this gentleman.

"Michael tells me you are a good friend to him, and he needs that at this bad time," he said quickly changing the subject.

"Yes Matt, Michael and I, have become very close to one another over the last year. They have been very good to me too I must say!" Her eyes shining with pride when she spoke. She continued to explain what had happened to her over the past twelve months. Panos listened intently and his heart felt for her as she talked openly about Brad. He was intrigued by her integrity and wanted to know everything about her. As she continued, he could see the pain in her eyes. He found it so hard not to respond by holding her, but he did not want to scare her away, so he restrained himself. Her conversation was abruptly halted when the door leading to the rooms opened and a rather drunk Mick stumbled in.

"I was wondering where you had got to Dan. I need to get some orange juice, so I thought I would make sure you were alright," he said clumsily, making his way over to the bar.

Danielle quickly moved her hand away from Panos's but not before Mick had noticed the two of them cosily sitting together.

"Don't mind me, I'll just get my drink and I will leave you two love birds alone," he said smiling from ear to ear.

"That explains the singing, Panos, you sly ol' dog. I knew there was something happening between you two."

Then he put his arm around Danielle. "Don't worry, your secret's safe with me."

"We were talking about Stuart," she explained her face going bright red.

"Yeah OK, if you say so Dan," he said slurring his words looking over to Panos winking.

"No seriously, Stuart said something about you and Matt and that's why he has left the hotel."

Danielle continued to tell him what Panos had told her and the silly grin dropped from his face. He listened carefully and could not believe his ears. She finished by reassuring him she would speak to Stuart and clear up this whole misunderstanding.

What was this man on? he thought

Danielle got up and took hold of Mick's arm. "Come on you, let's go up and get some sleep. We can talk about it in the morning with Matt. Goodnight, Panos," she said smiling at him, leading Mick towards the stairs.

"Goodnight my ol' mate," Mick said, letting her take control.

"Goodnight," Panos replied calmly and watched them walk away.

The two friends walked into the hotel room in silence, both of their heads full of Stuart's ludicrous accusations. Matt was fast asleep snoring. Danielle went into the bathroom to get ready for bed. When she came out Mick was also fast asleep. She smiled and got into bed and closed her tired eyes. She tried to ignore the horrendous sound that was coming out of their mouths. It helped her to concentrate her mind on Panos and soon drifted off to sleep.

CHAPTER

EIGHT

AS SOON AS DANIELLE OPENED her eyes, she could feel the warm sun on her face as it beamed through the balcony door. The loud chirping of the grasshoppers could be heard outside; a sure sign of a hot day. Her first thought was of Panos and the short time they had spent alone together. Mick was still asleep, and she was surprised that Matt was already up and taking a shower. She looked at her watch and was amazed that it was half past ten. The water stopped and soon Matt appeared with only a towel around his waist. He smiled at her walking over to the wardrobe. The fresh smell of lynx shower gel followed him, filling the air with its refreshing scent.

"Good morning Dan, did you manage to get a good night's sleep?" he asked, walking back into the bathroom holding his clothes. It seemed he was in a particularly good mood this morning. Prompted by his question, she suddenly realised she had managed to get the best night's sleep of the holiday so far.

"Yes, I did Matt, yes I did," she replied, but then Stuart's accusations invaded her mind. She decided to wait until Mick got up before telling Matt what she had learned about Stuart. She quickly jumped into the shower and by the time she came out, she saw that Mick was awake and already busily telling him what Stuart had said. Matt just laughed.

"How can you possibly find it funny mate?" asked Mick stunned by his reaction.

"Well, we didn't say we wanted to kill him, did we? We therefore have nothing to worry about. He has probably caught too much sun and it's made him delirious. Don't worry about it! He's is no doubt regretting what he said as we speak. It's my guess he will be back with his tail between his legs before you know it."

"We tried to kill him? Please! What a plonker!" he laughed again, aware that all the guilt he had felt last night had disappeared.

Mick thought for a moment and guessed Matt was probably right. "Yes," he agreed, "he is a right plonker!"

Putting Stuart safely at the back of his mind, Mick was suddenly aware his head was banging, and he felt terrible. He scanned the room looking for the bottle of vodka, which was sitting on the chest of drawers. He got up and poured himself a drink. Danielle watched him in disgust as he took a long mouthful.

"Since when do you drink as soon as you get up?" she asked finding it hard to hide the distress in her voice. The thought of drinking this early in the morning made her want to heave!

"I don't normally, but all this stress with Stuart is not doing my nerves any good. Anyway, who do you think you are, my wife?" he asked defensively.

Matt looked at his friend and wondered what was happening to him. He had seen him drinking first thing on many occasions since all the arguing with Tracey had begun, and Mick always had plenty of excuses to back up his reasons. Matt had tried to talk to him about it, but Mick would just laugh it off and promise it would be the last time. Matt's heart ached to see his best friend doing this to himself. He just hoped he would soon come to his senses and get his life back on track.

"Right," Matt rubbed his hands together.

"Mick get dressed, I am starving so let's go down to the town and get some breakfast." Mick was reluctant, but he knew he needed to eat something, so forced himself out of bed to get showered.

"I won't be long," he said walking listlessly to the bathroom and taking his drink with him.

"So, Dan do you fancy going to the beach this afternoon?" asked Matt. "There is apparently a gorgeous beach not far from here. It's supposed to be quiet and breath taking too. I heard a couple talking about it yesterday." Matt was feeling very confident and had decided to tell Danielle just how he felt about her, as soon as the opportunity presented itself. It was now or never!

"OK but I need to see Stuart first if he hasn't already come back, that is." She hadn't realised he had meant just the two of them as her thoughts were solely on sorting out this mess.

"I will go and see him while you're having breakfast, I am not really hungry." She had lost her appetite after spending time with Panos. He was having a strange effect on her because she usually loved her food!

"I think you should just leave him and let him come looking for us. He probably feels a right fool now. Just give him time to think about what he's done. To tell you the truth Dan, I am quite annoyed with him and you should be too."

Danielle nodded in agreement with him, but she had a horrible feeling she would come to regret it.

All three of them went down to the lobby and were greeted by Yannis. The three men talked, and Danielle looked around the room for any sign of Panos, but he was nowhere to be seen. Then the now familiar sense of disappointment came over her as Mick ordered a taxi.

"Panos is sleeping. He had a very late night," Yannis stated, reading her mind.

She smiled at him and turned to look at Mick for a reaction, but there was none. He seemed to be unaware that he had walked in on both her and Panos, she felt relieved he did not seem to remember. She asked Yannis if he had seen Stuart and he just shook his head as he lifted up the receiver and began dialling. He informed them the car was on its way, so they sat out on the terrace to wait for their lift into town.

On the ride into town Matt monopolised the conversation. Mick and Danielle listened half-heartedly as they had other things on their minds. Mick was suffering from a hangover but still could not wait to get a beer. The vodka he had earlier had not had any effect on him, and he knew a long cold beer would do the trick. Danielle's mind was preoccupied with Panos, and this was starting to drive her mad. Matt noticed his friends were distant and guessed they were just thinking about Stuart, so tried to do his best to take their minds off him.

They reached their destination and walked along the high street to a restaurant which was run by an English couple. Hearing the familiar accent, Danielle decided to phone her mother while the two men ate their breakfast. She finished her coffee and left the table, explaining that she wouldn't be long. She was desperate to speak to her mum to find out if everyone was all right. Matt was still chatting, and Mick washed his food down with a pint of beer, relieved to find he was beginning to feel a lot better.

Danielle found a phone box nearby and dialled the number. A feeling of loss consumed her as the line just kept ringing. She hung up the receiver and swallowed hard, as tears stung her eyes. She hoped they were all alright and started to feel guilty because her thoughts had been dominated by Panos. She felt a longing in her heart to hold her babies, but quickly had to force these feelings away, otherwise she would have been a blubbering mess. She made a mental note to try again later from the hotel. When she got back to the restaurant the two men had finished their meal and were having a drink. It was now coming up to lunchtime, and Matt was eager to get to the beach to spend some time alone with Danielle. He had told Mick of his plans, and to his relief Mick was quite happy to spend the afternoon by the pool. He wanted to be at the hotel when Stuart decided to show his face. They paid the bill and made their way to the taxi rank.

They got back to the hotel and to Danielle's delight Panos was busy serving behind the bar. As she walked back into his life all his feelings for her came flooding back. Mick went straight to the bar and ordered himself a beer.

"Are you having a beer Matt before you two shoot off

down the beach?" Mick asked.

"No, thanks mate. I want to get down there as soon as possible, I really need to speak to Dan and get this over with," said Matt smiling and winking at his friend.

Panos overheard the conversation and wondered what Matt had to say to her. *Why didn't she want to stay at the hotel?* he thought, feeling both hurt and angry.

Why did she want to be alone with this man and not stay here with me? He looked at her suspiciously as she reached the bar. She smiled at him, but his expression did not change, although she looked deep into his eyes desperately searching for some kind of explanation. He left her grasping at straws as he turned and walked away, leaving her completely confused.

"Are you coming to get your things for the beach Dan?" asked Matt already halfway across the room.

"Oh-oh yes the beach." She had totally forgotten she had said she would go with him.

"Are you not coming with us Mick?" she asked as Mick picked up his full glass of beer.

"No, I am going to pass on this one and stay here with my mate Panos," he stated knowing Matt wanted to be alone with her.

"I will be there in a minute Matt, I want to get a drink to take with us first," she said. Matt continued walking up to the room.

"Panos, can I please have a bottle of water?" she said calmly. Panos went to the fridge and then forcefully placed the bottle on the bar, not even looking at her.

"Panos, are you OK?" she asked him half smiling, willing

for him to smile back at her.

"Yes!" he replied sternly, his lips tightly pressed together.

She picked up her drink and briskly walked away, hurt by the man's change of attitude towards her. She could not figure out what she had done wrong and went up to her room feeling quite puzzled.

"Why are you not going with them?" Panos asked Mick abruptly. Mick was shocked by the tone of his voice, but at that point the memory of seeing the two of them together the night before came flooding back. He remembered he had walked in on them. Suddenly Panos's hostility towards Danielle made sense.

"So, you like her then?" asked Mick sympathetically?

Panos just shrugged his shoulders.

"I am sorry Panos. I had forgotten about last night."

He suddenly felt guilty; because of his drunkenness he had totally forgotten what he had seen, and he had not warned Matt. Now he was going to tell her how he felt, and she liked Panos.

Matt is going to make a fool out of himself, he thought. *Why did I drink so much?*

"I thought she liked me too," Panos said, his tone still abrupt.

"She obviously wants to be with him!" he exclaimed.

"No Panos, you are wrong. She just wants to be friends with Matt. I know that for a fact, and by the look on her face last night she does like you. She wouldn't have said so if she didn't. I know what she is like. Believe me Panos, don't give up mate."

Panos's face softened and Mick could now see the disappointment in his expression.

"You really do like her, don't you?" In all the years Mick had known Panos, he had never seen that look on his face before.

"Michael," Panos paused and took a deep breath, wondering whether he should confide in this man about his unfamiliar feelings. In the end he swallowed his pride and continued.

"Michael, when she is away my heart is aching for her to return. She is in my head constantly, I think about her all the time and when I see her with Matt it makes me so angry. I want to be with her so much; I do not understand why she makes me feel this way. I am sorry, I know Matt is your friend, but I feel so jealous when he is around, sorry but that is how I feel, I cannot help it." Then he looked down ashamed of his words.

"I will talk to her if you want," Mick said genuinely concerned. He hadn't realised what an impact Danielle had on him. At that point they were interrupted when Matt and Danielle walked back into the room on their way to the beach.

"See you later," said Matt smugly as they walked out of the hotel.

Danielle did not say a word and did not even look at the two men standing at the bar as she departed. Panos's heart fell as he watched her walk away. He knew he should not have spoken to her the way he had, and quickly began to regret his actions. He would have to speak to her later and try to explain, and just hoped that she would listen.

Matt and Danielle walked down the steep hill to the main road. There was not a cloud in the sky and Matt took in the glorious scenery. Danielle's mind was full of thoughts for Panos. She could not find a reason for the change in his attitude towards her and was totally baffled by his hostility.

They crossed the busy road and made their way down to the beach. On the white sands there were only a few holidaymakers basking in the magnificent sunshine. They found a secluded spot and made themselves comfortable. Matt watched as Danielle applied sun tan lotion on her body. She was a deep golden brown and he could not help but feel admiration for her. He was so pleased that she was there with him. As she laid there, her beautiful body glistening in the sun, he knew this was the right time to tell her just how he felt about her.

"Dan, I am so glad you are here. In Skiathos I mean, not just here on the beach."

Oh great, he thought, *I have only just started talking and I am already babbling*. He took a deep breath and started again.

"You know I think the world of you, don't you?" he continued.

"And we have grown close over the past few months," he paused. Danielle's eyes were closed, and she wondered where this conversation was going.

"I know you have not had it easy and have been let down by men such as your ex-husband and Brad; I am so pleased you came to your senses with that man as he was no good for you." He was babbling again. Danielle listened and hoped he wasn't going to say what she thought he was going to say.

"What I am trying to say Dan is that I have fallen in love with you." There, he had said it. Now all he had to do was await her reaction.

She just laid there motionless, afraid to open her eyes.

"Dan, I want to take care of you and your children, and I know I can make you happy."

He looked at her willing her to respond. Her mind was racing, and she could not think straight. It was hard enough dealing with the confusion she felt about Panos. Now her best friend had put a spanner in the works. *What a mess,* she thought.

Her head was spinning, and she did not want to be in this situation. She did not want to hurt his feelings, but she had no other alternative. She had always had her suspicions but thought he understood that she just wanted to be his friend. *Why couldn't he keep his feelings to himself?* she lamented.

She was so confused. Eventually opening her eyes, she sat up and looked at him. She knew he had been deeply hurt by his wife because the pain was still visible in his eyes. She took a deep breath.

"Oh Matt, I think the world of you honestly I do," she said taking hold of his hand, which made him begin to smile.

"But only as a friend."

His smile very quickly faded.

"I am sorry, but I do not see a future for us." She could see his eyes filling up with tears as he withdrew his hand and quickly looked away.

"Matt, I cherish our friendship and would hate anything to damage that, but my feelings for you are purely based on friendship." She hated being so blunt with him, but it had to be said with no ambiguity.

He had to lie down because his worst fear had become a

reality. Why hadn't he just kept his mouth shut? He desperately tried to come to terms with his mistake, and the embarrassment he felt. The awkwardness of his honesty was apparent between them and they lay in silence for the next hour.

Matt finally got up to go for a swim. She felt so bad and hoped this would not spoil the rest of the holiday for him. When he was swimming, he thought about how stupid he had been and did not want to ruin the friendship they had. He knew she cared deeply for him, so soon came to terms with the way it had to be. His heart felt bruised, but he quickly covered his emotions over by forcing a smile on his face. As he walked back over to her, he decided to apologise for his misjudgement and tell her to forget what he had said. Danielle opened her eyes. She could see him walking towards her and was relieved to see him smiling. He told her his thoughts and she gave him a big hug.

"So, we are still friends then?" she said smiling.

"Yes forever," he replied. They both suddenly realised they were starving, so gathered up their things and began the long walk back to the hotel.

CHAPTER

NINE

PANOS SPENT THE AFTERNOON thinking about Danielle, his mind full of regret for his recent behaviour. He was angry with himself for allowing his frustration to get the better of him. His heart felt heavy with the longing for her to return, and he looked at his watch every five minutes, as he waited impatiently for her to get back. He couldn't wait to speak to her and apologise for his unforgivable behaviour. He tried to take his mind off her and think about something else but found it impossible, as every minute seemed like an eternity. Finally, she walked into the hotel and as she caught his glance he smiled, his heart beginning to pound when she smiled back. She said something to Matt who continued up to their room, then she walked towards him.

When she reached the bar, her smile had faded. She ordered herself a drink and Panos obliged, not knowing what to say. He had rehearsed an apology all afternoon, word for word but now she stood in front of him, his mind went blank.

She picked up her drink, politely thanking him and turned to walk away. He quickly took hold of her hand before she could leave.

"D-Danielle I need to speak to you please," he said softly.

"I need to talk about this morning and the way I behaved. My actions were unforgivable, I am so sorry." He searched her eyes for some sign of reconciliation, but they were emotionless.

"Panos I am sorry, but I really don't understand. Why would you be like that towards me? What did I do wrong? This has been going through my head all day. Please explain it to me." Her voice had softened slightly as she waited patiently for his reply.

Panos took his hand away and looked down at the bar. He did not want to tell her the reason because he was a proud man and jealousy was a sure sign of weakness. Every time he saw her with Matt, a gut-wrenching feeling consumed him, which he was finding increasingly hard to control. He didn't know how to explain this to her, because he didn't want her to think badly of him! But these feelings could not be helped, and he suddenly realised that since she had come into his life, he was losing control of his emotions.

"Look Panos I can see I am wasting my time here. You are just the same as any other man I have met."

He felt extremely hurt by her words. They cut into his heart like a knife. Then she began to walk away.

"No please, Danielle don't walk away. I am not like those other men, like you say I am."

She stood still and looked at him, aware of the hurt in his eyes, and she could not help feeling compassion for him.

"Please, please, believe how sorry I am," he pleaded. Then he quickly looked around as Mick walked in from the terrace.

"I will talk to you later tonight, ok?" She nodded as Mick got closer to them.

"Would you like a beer Michael?" Panos asked, getting a glass ready to pour Mick's drink.

"Yes please, my good man, and one for the lady," Mick said.

He scanned the room looking for his friend and asked Danielle, "Where is Matt?"

Danielle explained he had gone up to the room to be by himself for a while. Mick guessed it had not gone well for him down at the beach. He wasn't surprised, but at least now he knew she only wanted to be his friend. His heart went out to his friend and he decided to leave him alone for a while before going to see if he was alright. He knew that he was a tough man and was confident he would soon get over his disappointment.

"I have been talking to a nice couple from Birmingham, and they said they saw Stuart in the town earlier," said Mick. Danielle's ears pricked up at the mention of Stuart's name. With everything that had gone on all day she hadn't given him a thought, and guilt began to raise its ugly head.

"They said he was swaying all over the place and was obviously drunk. Apparently, they tried to talk to him, but he just ignored them." Mick laughed when the vision of a drunken man entered his head.

"Mick, it's not funny, he must be in a right state."

Her voice was stern but full of sympathy for Stuart, and she was very concerned about his state of mind.

Panos noticed the worry in her face and his heart went out to this considerate lady. The longing he felt for her was triggered by her concern, and he just wanted to hold her. He was reminded of how he had treated her earlier and felt terrible for the way he had acted. He wished he could have controlled his jealousy, but it had appeared furiously, like the wash left by passing ships upon the beach. Now these feelings had vanished, and he just wanted to protect this amazing woman.

"You just don't know what has happened to the poor man. He must be feeling really bad," Danielle said. She could feel tears beginning to sting her eyes and she gulped them down to stop them escaping.

"I am sorry Dan. I don't want to upset you. We will go to town soon and find him, so you can talk to him, ok?" said Mick trying to reassure her as he put his arms around her shoulders. Panos wished he could do the same, but he chose to walk away instead. He left the two friends and went over to reception, where a couple were waiting patiently for their room key.

Danielle was consoled by Mick's suggestion and felt a little bit better. She was pleased to know she could see Stuart as soon as they had changed. Mick finished his drink and told her he wanted to go up and talk to Matt. He advised her to stay and talk to Panos. She glanced at him puzzled, wondering what he meant.

"Dan, please talk to Panos. He is really sorry for what happened earlier. I know there's something special going on between you two, I can tell. You sort this out with him and I will sort out Matt. He is tough our Matt, and I'm sure he will survive."

She was stunned by the conviction in Mick's voice, and amazed that he knew anything was going on. Then she looked suspiciously at him.

"Matt told me how he felt about you and that he was going to tell you. Believe me Dan, I did warn him not to, but you know him, he has to learn the hard way… As for Panos, he explained what happened this morning. He is very sorry and is quite besotted with you, my girl. What have you got, Dan? What is it about you that makes you have men falling at your feet?" he laughed reassuringly, his arm still around her.

"It must be true. You are the second person to say that to me," she confessed recalling her last conversation with Stuart by the pool.

"Well then Dan, stay and talk to him. He really does like you, he told me so himself."

That was why she loved this man so much. Deep down under his flamboyancy and arrogance, lived a sweet caring sensitive man. She nodded in agreement as he kissed her on the nose and stood up. "That's my girl," he said as he walked away.

Danielle played with her half empty glass whilst waiting for Panos to come back to the bar. There were many guests in the lounge and the room was full of people talking about their experiences in Skiathos. Panos was talking to a couple who were sitting by the television, when he noticed that Danielle was alone at the bar. He quickly finished the conversation and hurried back behind the bar. He began to wash up the glasses and looked at her and smiled. She returned the gesture and smiled back at him.

"Has Michael gone up to the room?" he asked, his eyes transfixed on hers.

"Yes," she replied shyly, not able to look away.

"Panos why did you behave like that earlier?" Her voice was soft, and her eyes pleaded with his for a reply. He hesitated and thought carefully about what he was going to say.

"I am sorry, but I get very jealous when Matt is around you."

There he had said it. He couldn't believe his honesty.

"I have to ask you, is there something between the two of you? Please I have to know." He broke their eye contact by looking down at the bar, embarrassed by his curiosity.

"Panos, Matt is my friend like I told you before, and that is all we will ever be," she replied putting her hand on his arm.

That explains it, he is jealous, she thought to herself. Now it all made sense to her.

"It is you that I like," she said stroking his arm. He looked up and smiled at her, relieved at what she had said.

"That is good my beautiful Danielle, I am a very happy man again. Thank you for coming to my hotel."

The warmth she felt from his voice wrapped itself around her like a blanket, causing her to believe every word he said. She had never seen so much happiness in someone's eyes before and could have cried with joy. Once again, she secretly questioned what it was about this man that had completely swept her off her feet.

As she pondered these things and treasured them in her heart, they were interrupted by his father coming up behind him. He was saying something she did not understand and realised he had noticed the contact between them. Panos swiftly replied to his father's command. Apologising he said, "I am sorry Danielle, but I have to go. There is something I need to do. This is one of the downfalls of managing a hotel," he explained rolling his eyes.

"Will you sit with me later and then we can talk? I have a lot of things I want to say." His eyes smiled at her and she nodded. He kissed her hand and then walked away. His eyes stayed on her until he disappeared out of sight. He was so disappointed that he had to leave her.

Suddenly a warm feeling crept through her body and she could not help smiling to herself. This whole situation seemed so surreal. She was not expecting anything like this, and it had taken her totally by surprise, and she felt she could never be happier. She left her drink on the bar and floated on cloud nine up the stairs. *This sort of thing doesn't happen to me,* she thought, a cheeky grin covering her face.

When she entered the room, she could hear the men talking outside on the balcony. Celine Dion was playing so she went out to join them. She had never taken any notice of the lyrics before, but this time the song caught her attention. She sat and listened to the words.

'Falling into you, this dream could come true and it feels so good falling into you.'

The words flew out of the walk-man and straight into her heart. She thought it was going to stop as she closed her eyes and thought of Panos. *Am I falling into you?* she thought to herself, still overwhelmed by the events of the day.

The three friends sat in silence. Matt was now regretting that he had opened his heart to Danielle and wished he had listened to Mick. He had told her it was alright but, in all honesty, he felt very hurt by her rejection. Mick did his best to console him but nothing anyone could say would make him feel better.

I will be OK tomorrow, he tried to reassure himself. *A few more of these will help me forget*, he thought, staring at the large glass of vodka and orange in his hand.

Mick also looked at the drink, and for the first time he felt disgusted with himself. He knew deep down he drank too much. The talk he had with Matt had brought his own feelings to the surface. The pain evident in Matt's eyes was like a reflection of his own, and no amount of vodka was going to take it away. This revelation made him see what a lonely old man he was becoming. Right on cue the picture of Tracey emerged in his mind. He closed his eyes and she became real. She was smiling at him with her beautiful face, the one he had fallen in love with. Then her face began to change, and she started to laugh. At first, he thought she was laughing because she was happy, but then he realised she was laughing at him; the sad little man she wanted to divorce. He blinked his eyes open, took another look at the full glass in his hand, and drunk it down in one go.

This will make her go away, he convinced himself. Then he got up to pour himself another one.

"Right, I am going to drink this then jump in the shower. Who is up for going into town?" Mick asked, safely putting Tracey back where she belonged, to the back of his mind. Both Matt and Danielle agreed to the plan; Danielle so she could speak to Stuart, and Matt so he could get completely wasted. They took it in turns to get ready, and then went down to the bar.

The three of them sat patiently at the bar waiting for their lift into town. Danielle was anxious to speak to Stuart and she felt confident he would listen to her and come back to the hotel and enjoy the rest of his holiday.

Mick was full of vodka, but he was being his usual comical self by making them laugh. Danielle noticed Matt was knocking back the drinks quite rapidly. She was drinking her first when he was on his third.

“Are you on a mission tonight Matt?” she asked, concerned for him. He had hardly spoken to her since they got back from the beach. “Don’t you think you should take it easy?”

He just glared at her, telling her to mind her own business.

“Sorry mate,” she said, shocked by his response, putting her hands in the air. He had never reacted to her like that before. She hoped they could salvage their friendship but thought it best to give him some space.

She looked over to Panos who was working profusely behind the bar. A big smile dominated his face while he worked, and every now and again he would look at her and wink. Danielle smiled as she watched him interact with the guests. She felt a twinge of pride because his professionalism shone out of him like a light in the darkness. She could not wait to get back and be with this awe- inspiring man. The taxi arrived, and they went into town. Panos watched her leave and began patiently waiting for her return.

They ate at a restaurant in the high street. Danielle was now relieved Matt was finally talking to her as if nothing had happened. He was slurring his words by now, but she understood why and did not judge him. Their friendship seemed to be back to how it was before their little talk earlier. They paid for their meals and then took a walk towards the harbour where Stuart was staying.

“Isn’t that Stuart?” asked Mick pointing as they noticed him sitting outside an English restaurant. They all looked over. To Danielle’s delight it was him and he was sitting on his own.

"You two stay here and I will go over and talk to him," Danielle said and rushed over to where he was sitting. The two men did not argue with her and watched her go towards him.

She approached him, but he did not see her walk up behind him. Then she put her hand on his shoulder.

"Hello Stu. How are you?" she said quietly. He spun around, and it looked like he had seen a ghost.

"Sorry honey, I didn't mean to scare you." He looked at her, his eyes glazed. It was as if he didn't recognize her.

"Stuart, it's me Danielle," she said softly. She was reminded of the time they had met him at the airport.

"Stuart, it's me Danielle," she repeated. He looked at her for a second and then a sign of recognition swept over his traumatized face.

"Oh, Danielle. Hello," he stuttered. Danielle felt more at ease because he had finally recognised her.

"Stuart, what has happened mate? Please tell me, I feel so bad and we have been so worried about you." She looked at him pleading for an explanation, but he just sat looking at her with a vacant look on his face.

"You can talk to me. We can sort this mess out once and for all. Please tell me what has upset you." Stuart was about to say something when he noticed Matt and Mick waiting in a shop window. Sheer terror gripped him, and he tried to get up.

"I don't want to talk to you," he slurred, his eyes fixed on the two men.

"I don't want to talk to you," he repeated, his voice quivering and his face still with fright.

"Ok, OK, I will come and see you tomorrow on my own," she said calmly. "I know where you are staying so I will see you in the morning, OK Stuart?" She stroked his back trying to reassure him she meant no harm. He simply nodded, and she walked away. She could not get the look on his face out of her head; he looked petrified!

She walked over to the two men who were anxious to find out what he had said.

"He is scared out of his wits. Something is seriously wrong," she said. The two men just looked at each other in astonishment.

"I am going to see him in the morning, so I can get to the bottom of this mess," she convinced them. They turned around to where Stuart was sitting but he was gone.

They carried on towards the Taverna at the harbour where they had become regular faces and were greeted with a friendly welcome. They sat in their familiar surroundings, waited on by familiar waiters who talked to them like long lost friends and who plied them with plenty of drinks and conversation.

Their worries about Stuart faded, and Danielle was the first to notice the time, it was nearly twelve o'clock. She was eager to get back to the hotel and didn't realise how late it was. Matt's mission was complete because he was now terribly drunk. Mick was also pretty drunk and did not care what he was doing or saying. Danielle felt merry but the thought of seeing Panos kept her feeling that way, rather than drunk.

They said their goodbyes and with Danielle in the middle they walked arm in arm to the taxi rank. They giggled all the way and Danielle felt the need to look after her two drunken friends. Matt continuously apologised to her for his behaviour, and she reassured him it had all been forgotten.

They arrived back at the hotel in one piece and walked into the hotel laughing.

Panos saw the drunken three walk in. He felt so relieved. At last his Danielle was back in his sight again. The four hours they had been gone had felt like six. All the time she was away he kept thinking about her and what she was doing. She was at the forefront of his mind all evening and now she was back he could relax. He put a smile back on his anxious face.

They walked over to the bar and Mick ordered their drinks. Panos enquired about their evening and Mick told him about their encounter with Stuart.

"Danielle, you will be going to see Stuart tomorrow then?" Panos said turning to face her. He could see Matt in the background and watched him fall down on the settee.

"Is Matt OK?" he asked quickly turning back to Mick.

"Yes Panos, me ol' mate he has just had a few too many ouzo's. Don't worry, he will be OK, my friend," Mick replied mindlessly. He picked Matt's drink up and took it over to him. Panos watched as Matt picked up his glass and continued to polish off the whole lot. Panos looked at the man in disgust, and then turned his attention back to Danielle.

"I am sorry Danielle. You were going to answer me?" he said shaking his head at Matt's drunken gluttony. He quickly forgot his repulsion and was once again captured by her enchanting emerald eyes. She answered him and told him about the conversation with Stuart.

In the background Yannis picked up the phone that was ringing. Everyone around was caught up in their own conversations, totally unaware of Yanni's phone call. Panos listened carefully to what Danielle had to say but was disturbed by one of the guests waiting at the bar. He assured her they would get plenty of time to themselves very soon and continued to serve his customer. She picked up her drink and sat down next to Mick. Mick soon gave up on talking to Matt who had passed out on the sofa and was relieved to have Danielle to talk to.

Panos noticed Yannis was a long time on the phone. He looked over to his brother and could see the distress in his face. Once Yannis had replaced the receiver he began to walk over to where Mick and Danielle were chatting. Panos detected something was very wrong, so he also walked over to join them.

"Michael, what really happened with Stuart tonight?" Yannis asked with a severe look on his face. His question stopped Mick in mid- sentence and he and Danielle looked at each other confused.

"What do you mean, Yannis?" asked Mick half-heartedly. Panos was also intrigued by his brother's question.

"I have just had the police sergeant on the phone. He informed me Stuart was there at the police station and afraid for his life!" Silence fell as he continued.

"Stuart said he saw you all in the high street and you, Danielle, came up to him and said you knew where he was staying, and you would send Michael and Matt around in the morning to kill him. What is going on?" His ruthless words hit them like a sledge hammer.

"The police are taking his accusations very seriously Michael, he is refusing to leave the building."

Why does he keep referring to me? It was Danielle who went up to him, thought Mick.

Danielle very slowly went through every moment of the reunion at the restaurant. She kept looking over to Panos, insistent that she was telling the truth. Mick tried his hardest to think if there was anything he had said to Stuart before he left, which could have been taken the wrong way, but could not think of anything.

Panos turned and said goodnight to the last of the guests and was relieved to know they were now alone in the bar. All Mick could say in his defence was that it wasn't true, and they would have to take his word for it. He felt totally helpless.

"Michael, the police wanted to come and arrest you all now. I managed to delay him, but only for an hour or so," continued Yannis looking him in the eye.

Mick felt physically sick; he did not want to eat prison food and wouldn't be able to get a beer or vodka. His imagination went into overdrive as the prospect of being arrested became apparent to him. He shook Matt for some support but had no joy as he was still unconscious. Mick realised he felt extremely sober.

"I want to go and see him Panos. This is ridiculous, we have done nothing wrong. I need to sort this mess out. Please get me a taxi, we cannot get arrested," said Danielle beginning to feel really scared.

"It is OK Danielle. I will drive you down in my father's car. You cannot go down there alone," Panos interrupted. He glanced over to his brother and Yannis nodded his approval.

"I will meet you out the front OK Danielle."

Panos wanted to see what Stuart had to say for himself; if this got out it could be very bad for business. At least he would be alone with Danielle. This wasn't exactly how he had planned it! Stuart had once again ruined his night with her. Panos said something to Yannis and walked out of the room. Yannis responded by nodding and went to make himself a strong black coffee. *This could turn into a long night,* he thought.

"Michael, would you like a cup of coffee?" asked Yannis, holding up a small china cup.

"Are you crazy, Yannis? I will have a large vodka and orange. When the police come to take me away for attempted murder I want to be completely wasted!" answered Mick putting his hands on his head.

"Don't be such a drama queen Mick, it's not that bad," Danielle said sternly.

"The police are taking Stuart very seriously. If they think he is telling the truth you could all be in a lot of trouble," Yannis said, sipping his coffee.

You are not helping Yannis, she thought.

Panos sounded his horn at the front of the hotel, so she got up to leave. "Don't worry Mick, I will be back before you know it, and it will be sorted out," she said, trying to convince him as she walked out of the door. She walked down the steps to a black Mercedes waiting for her. Walking towards it she forgot herself and tried to get in the driver's side. She was overcome with embarrassment her when she realised her mistake. She got into the passenger side and smiled shyly at Panos. He started the car and they began to make their way down into town. He couldn't believe he had finally got her on her own, even though the circumstances were not quite what he had been hoping for.

"I will put on some music for you beautiful Danielle. Danielle," he began singing her name as he got a tape out.

"Danielle, Danielle. What a pretty name." She felt the blood rush to her cheeks as he sung looking at her, and she reassuringly smiled. He found a tape and put it in the cassette player.

"I am sorry, but I haven't got any English music, so I will play this beautiful Greek love song for you." The sound of the woman singing filled the car. Danielle thought she would have to take Panos's word for it, if it was a love song, because the woman could have been singing about a rusty old roof for all she knew.

He began to sing along to the song and kept glancing at her smiling. She felt strangely at ease with him and knew she would soon have this whole situation with Stuart sorted out. She couldn't help but smile at this gorgeous man. He put his hand on her leg as he drove down the steep hill. He turned the music down, but the words could still be heard in the background.

"Are you OK? Do not worry, it will all be over soon. I am sure there is a plausible explanation for all this," he said, slowly stroking her knee. His touch was soothing to her skin.

She went through the events of the meeting with Stuart again in her mind. His irrational behaviour had completely taken her by surprise, and she tried to make sense of it, but couldn't. They came to the top of the high street and continued down the hill. Panos parked the car outside a building and they both got out. Danielle looked up at the tall structure and found it hard to believe this run down, pile of bricks was a police station.

They walked to the front door and Panos pushed the buzzer. A deep Greek voice answered and Panos spoke into the intercom. They waited there for a few minutes and then the door clicked. Panos pushed it open and they began to walk up a steep flight of stairs. They came to another door and it was opened by a tall man in a police uniform. He ushered them in, saying something in Greek to Panos, shaking his hand. The officer did not even look at Danielle as they entered the main room. There, they were confronted by Stuart, who was walking to and fro.

"Hello Stuart," Danielle said calmly. She did not want to alarm him again. He just looked at her and glared. Not the frightened look he wore earlier. His eyes were burning red and his usual swept back hair was all over the place.

"Stuart, can we please talk and sort this whole misunderstanding out. You have got us all so worried mate." She could not believe he looked such a mess.

"You are not my mate!" he growled. "You want me dead I heard you all talking about it." He pointed at her when he spoke, saliva coming uncontrollably from his mouth.

"You were going to throw me over the balcony! I am not deaf. I heard you all!" He raised his voice until this unfamiliar tone was bellowing around the room.

He sounds like a mad man, she thought, and his distorted voice sent shivers down her spine. She took her eyes off him for a moment and saw the police officer looking unsympathetically at her.

She turned to Panos willing him to believe her, when Stuart suddenly lunged at her, trying to scratch at her face. Panos first reaction was to protect her, so he stood in front of her. Fortunately, the officer was quick and had managed to pull Stuart back before he had done some serious damage. The officer looked at Stuart, confused. He had not shown any sign of violence before now, so he shouted up the stairs for assistance, and his colleague came down into the room offering his support.

"And tell your friends not to talk to me, I know you are all out to get me," shouted Stuart. Danielle was reminded of what Mick had said about the couple who had seen him in the town.

They must be the ones he spoke about, she thought and shook her head in disbelief.

"What has happened to you, Stuart?" she said almost under her breath.

"And you Panos, you, my pretty Panos, I know your father and brother are outside waiting to shoot me when I leave. I know they have got a gun!" said Stuart mimicking a woman's voice.

He has totally lost his mind, she thought completely dumbfounded.

From that moment on, Panos knew Stuart was lying and so did the police officers. He had apparently made the whole thing up. Panos and his family were a well-respected part of the community and there was no way this crazy Englishman was going to change that.

The first police officer took hold of Stuart's arm and forced him to walk to the cell upstairs. "Oh ducky, I like you," Stuart said in a camp voice, stumbling up the first step. "Oh, I do like it rough," he continued, soon disappearing out of sight.

"Panos, I am so sorry he brought you and your family into it. He has completely lost his mind. This is so unbelievable," said Danielle still in shock. Panos walked up her and put his arm around her. Then the sergeant came back down shaking his head.

"I think he is very drunk, so we will keep him here

overnight. I am sorry he has caused you this trouble miss. I know now he was lying, so no further action will be taken."

He shook Panos's hand, saying something in Greek, and Panos patted him on the back.

The two of them walked down to the car, Panos's arm still tight around her. Danielle was trying to take in what had just happened, but she was totally taken aback by the recent events. She found it hard to believe that was the same man who had come away with them only a few days before. *It is inconceivable that he has changed*, she thought as she began to shake.

"Here, you are, take my coat," said Panos as his thoughts went on to his father.

My father will go mad about this. Nothing like this has ever happened before.

Pushing his father out of his mind, Panos took off his jacket and put it around Danielle's shoulders. He impulsively held her in his arms and she began to cry. The tears rolled down her face and Panos felt so comfortable holding her. He felt fury towards Stuart for upsetting this precious lady. They stood there for a few minutes unable to speak. Then she looked up at him with her big watery eyes, which sparkled in the moonlight as the pain showed in her tear stained face. He lifted his hand to her face and wiped away her tears. She looked into his eyes and tenderness radiated from them. She realised she had never felt so safe in anyone's arms before. Then she quickly looked down, afraid of what could happen. He lifted her chin and started to kiss her damp cheeks, then slowly kissed every part of her face. She found she could not move as his soft lips reached hers. He gently kissed her mouth. She did not want to respond but all her will power had vanished. She parted her lips slightly and he touched them with his tongue. She could not resist as her tongue quickly met his, unleashing a flood of emotions as they passionately kissed.

Unfamiliar sensations flowed through their bodies as they held each other tight, both frightened to let the other one go. Feelings of confusion arose. With the ache of wanting each other so badly flooding their hearts, she had to pull herself away. He drew her close to his chest and held her there, afraid of the feelings the kiss had conjured up. Danielle could hear his heart beating fast in his chest and concentrated on its soothing rhythm, taking deep breaths to synchronise her speeding heart rate to his.

The same feeling of familiarity swept through her body, a deep sense that this was what she had been waiting for all her life. She had only known this man for a few days, but she felt she had known him forever. *If only I could bottle up this feeling,* she thought.

The same thoughts and feelings were going through Panos's mind. He didn't ever want to let her go and held her tighter. It was if he had waited for an eternity just for this moment. He wanted to savour every minute as he breathed in this wonderful lady, but cruel reality kicked in when Danielle interrupted the moment.

"We should get back, everyone will be wondering where we are," she said smiling, looking into his deep brown eyes. For a moment he was mesmerised and kissed her again, this time even more passionately than before. Their hearts fluttered, and both felt a deep aching for the other. It took all her strength to pull herself away. Otherwise she would have been lost in him forever.

"Come on, Panos," she said gently, "we need to get back." He knew she was right, so reluctantly took her hand and led her back to the car.

Back at the hotel Mick was going out of his mind with worry. He had convinced himself he was going to be locked up for a long time and they were going to throw away the key. Matt had finally come around and was drinking a strong cup of coffee, nursing a very bad headache. Mick had explained to him what was going on, so they both waited patiently for Danielle and Panos to get back.

He was pacing the floor because he could not sit still, and this was making both Matt and Yannis very nervous. The minutes turned into over an hour and he kept going over Stuart's false allegations. Finally, they heard a car pull up outside, and moments later Panos and Danielle walked back into the hotel.

"It's about time," Mick said looking at his watch. Danielle took her time and explained what had happened at the police station. No one could believe their ears when she described the way Stuart had acted towards her. Yannis was astounded that even his family had been brought into it, and Mick had never felt so relieved. "This calls for a celebration," he said, looking at Yannis behind the bar. "If you would be so kind as to get us some drinks, please Yannis."

Matt declined; he just wanted to get to bed so he said good night and wandered up to his room. Yannis agreed with Matt, so he left Panos to pour the drinks. Danielle ordered a coke as she would be going up soon too. The evening had taken its toll on her, and she yawned. Panos went over to the bar as she and Mick sat down on the settee and she went through the whole police station saga again. They could not believe the craziness of their so-called friend. Panos brought the drinks over and sat next to Danielle. He put his arm behind her and started to caress her back.

"I see you two have sorted out your differences then," Mick said winking at Panos, aware of his arm behind her. They looked at each other and laughed and Panos kissed her cheek.

"Yes, you could say that my friend," he replied, smiling at his new- found love, kissing her again. He felt so happy, he could have shouted out his feelings from the rooftop of his hotel.

"Well, this causes for a double celebration." Mick raised his glass. The two of them followed suit and Mick said a toast. Panos took hold of Danielle's hand and squeezed it tight.

"Michael, I want to thank you."

Mick looked at his Greek friend bemused. "Thank me, for what my friend?"

Danielle looked at Panos suspiciously and wondered what he was going to say.

"Thank you for bringing this gorgeous lady to me." He took hold of her hand and gently kissed the back of it. Danielle could have died from embarrassment, and her cheeks went bright red. Panos could not imagine being happier. He was with two of his favourite people and was enjoying every minute of it. They sat and talked for half an hour. Then Danielle insisted she needed her bed. They stood up and Panos shook Mick's hand.

"Thank you again Michael for bringing her to my hotel. She is so incredible, my friend," Panos said smiling. He pulled him close and gave him a hug.

Mick felt embarrassed by the embrace and quickly pulled away. Panos laughed and kissed Danielle gently on the lips to say good night.

"I will see you soon, my darling Danielle," he said happily. Then he watched them walk away.

She could have burst with joy as she danced up the stairs and felt so thankful. Mick had never seen her so blissfully happy and he felt proud that he was responsible for her joy. She asked him not to mention it to Matt. She would tell him in her own time and he promised mum was the word!

When they entered the room, Matt was snoring very loudly. Mick shook him and told him to shut up. Danielle skipped into the bathroom to get ready for bed. When she came out Mick was also sound asleep, snoring. She nudged him and to her relief he went quiet.

She turned off the light and got into bed. She was so tired, but she couldn't sleep. Panos was on her mind and she could not wait to see him again. Her whole body ached for his touch; he had been so gentle with her.

He is a true gentleman, a rarity in my life, she thought happily. His face was vivid in her mind and she finally slipped into a light sleep. She was suddenly woken up by a strange sound. She opened her eyes and realised it was coming from Mick. She leant over and shook him. He quietened for a minute but then he started again, so she put her head under the pillow to drown out the hideous noise, and eventually drifted back to sleep.

CHAPTER

TEN

DANIELLE WAS AWOKEN BY THE sound of clinking plates. She opened her eyes to see where the strange noise was coming from and was confronted with a tray that Matt was putting down beside her.

"Good morning and happy birthday, Danielle. You didn't think you could get away with missing your special day, did you?" he said smiling.

She looked at the tray and could have cried. Along with the breakfast was a single red rose, and a handful of birthday cards. She picked up the cards and frowned.

"How did you know it was my birthday? I wanted to forget about being thirty-one. They say it's downhill from here!"

She opened the first card and let out a cry of joy. "Oh, my goodness it's from my babies! That's how you knew, what a lovely surprise." She could just make out the words as her eyes had filled up with tears. When she had finished reading tears were streaming down her face. She recognised Marie's hand writing. She wished her a great day and explained how they would give her presents when she came home. They hoped she was enjoying her holiday, they loved her and were missing her loads. As Danielle read the words, she suddenly felt extremely home sick. She longed to see her children again and a rush of guilt sailed through her body.

Matt sat down next to her and put his arm around her. He did not say a word but watched as her tears fell from her face down onto the card, smudging the sentimental words that had been written. They sat in silence. Danielle repeatedly read her daughter's words and could not control her emotions as the tears flowed freely. She had locked all her guilty feelings in the back of her mind, as all the time she was away it was too distressing for her to think about. But this birthday card in her hand stained with her tears was the key to unlock these emotions. The tears continued to flow, and Matt began to wonder whether he had done the right thing.

Marie had called him on the eve of their departure asking him to pick up the cards. He agreed and picked them up from Louise and Tony's house as promised. Marie had asked him to look after their mother and it was his responsibility to ensure she would have a birthday to remember. He felt quite put out that Danielle hadn't mentioned it would be her birthday whilst they were away, but guessed, that knowing her, she did not want them to make a fuss. He thought back to that day, remembering the sadness in Marie's eyes. He had reassured her he would make sure her wishes were carried out.

Things had been different then, he had a glimmer of hope that Danielle could be his, but now those dreams had been shattered. As he watched her cry, he felt helpless. He suddenly realised he did still want her in his life, even if only as a friend. She was still very special to him and he did not want to lose the closeness they once shared. Seeing her made him realise he had come to terms with this fact, and he would keep his promise to Marie and make this day a very special one.

She took her eyes off the card and looked into Matt's eyes. Her escaped emotions had stopped her ability to talk, so she just smiled. He returned the gesture and they sat in silence. Mick was still sleeping. Then he squealed like a pig, startling them both and they both burst out laughing at the same time.

"That's better Dan, you shouldn't cry on your birthday. Now open the rest of your cards." He picked them up and gave them to her. As she began to open them, he poured them both a cup of coffee. She read the cards, one from everyone at the King's Head, from her mother and sister in law, and a lump formed in her throat as she read their kind words. She also had a card from Matt and Mick; these brought a smile back to her face. She put them on the dressing table and began tucking into her breakfast. She decided to try to phone her mum again when they went into town later on that morning.

Mick woke up from his noisy sleep and wondered what was going on. He looked at the cards displayed, and it took a few moments for it to register that it was her birthday. He soon gathered his thoughts and sluggishly wished her a happy birthday. Then he joined them in their breakfast. He remembered they had planned a surprise evening and began to get excited about their special night. She was going to have a birthday to remember.

Danielle felt much better as they walked down to the lobby. It was full of guests waiting to go to town, and the room was literally buzzing with happy holiday makers. Panos was busy accommodating his guests but still found time to come over to Danielle and wish her a happy birthday. He took her hand, kissed it and she felt her face glowing with jubilation.

Matt felt a pang of jealousy rise up from his stomach as he watched this man, and a weird feeling slowly emerged. He sensed something strange happen between them as their eyes met. He quickly dismissed this silly feeling, just putting it down to paranoia, and forced a smile when Panos looked at him.

"Good morning Matt, Danielle looks very happy, doesn't she?" commented Panos, putting her hand down. Matt just nodded. He did not like the look in this Greek man's eyes. Mick soon joined them.

"Panos, I am feeling on top of the world and I know I am going to have a good day," said Danielle looking deep into his eyes.

"Mick, I need to talk to you outside mate," said Matt turning around to Mick, missing the eye contact between them. Mick just winked, and the two men went out onto the terrace to plan her special day.

"I know you will have a lovely birthday, my beautiful Danielle," said Panos, stroking her hand.

"Now I have to work but I will be opening the pool bar this afternoon. That way I will be close to you while you soak up this glorious Greek sunshine," he said gently squeezing it.

"Then we can be together." He kissed her cheek and walked away. Her heart melted as her eyes followed him across the room, and they stayed on him until he disappeared into the restaurant.

Panos's father stood at the reception, his eyes transfixed on the couple. He had seen his eldest son with girls before, but as he watched them together, he felt this one, he had to keep a close eye on. He had a very bad feeling about her.

Mick and Matt were discussing their course of action for the day. They wanted to go into town and buy Danielle something nice. Mick suggested they send her back to the hotel on her own, so they could look around the shops. He was sure she would not protest as she would be able to spend a few hours alone with Panos. Matt agreed, and when she joined them, he told her of their plans. She was delighted, as it fitted in nicely with her own plans. They decided to go into town for some lunch, and then she would get the bus back without them.

They went into town and walked along the harbour and Danielle breathed in the friendly atmosphere. She spoke to her mother on the phone and was overwhelmed by the voice from home. Christine filled her in on what was happening and assured her all her children were fine. They were missing their mum but were coping without her. She did promise to phone again to speak to Billy, who was now at school. When she hung up the phone, she took in a deep breath to stop her home sick tears in their tracks and returned to the two men. The three of them talked incessantly and Stuart wasn't mentioned at all.

She soon left them and walked up the high street to meet the bus to take her back up to the hotel. She felt a longing to be back with Panos and could not wait to see him again. This whole holiday had turned out to be something she could never have imagined. Apart from the fiasco with Stuart, she loved every minute of it.

The couple from Birmingham were also on the bus. They befriended her and took the time to talk to her on the ride back to the hotel. They explained that they were on their honeymoon. They were deeply in love and made physical contact at every opportunity. She was very taken by the couple and found she really liked them. When they reached the hotel, they asked if she would like to spend the afternoon with them. She agreed, so they arranged to meet by the pool.

When She entered the hotel, Yannis was behind the bar talking to Anna. It was one of the rare occasions she had seen the couple together because Anna was always in the kitchen helping her future mother in-law. They both greeted her with a smile, and she noticed how beautifully clear Anna's skin was. Her face was clear of makeup and her natural long brown curly hair was tied back in a ponytail: she was a natural beauty.

The hustle and bustle that filled the room earlier had disappeared and now peace and tranquillity hung in the air. Danielle smiled back and walked up to her room to get changed. She unlocked the door and crossed the threshold. She scanned the room for her bikini and couldn't help noticing how messy it was. She chose to ignore the clutter, found what she was looking for and went into the bathroom to get changed. She was walking out tying her sarong around her waist when the phone began to ring. She was taken aback by the unusual tone and hesitated before finally answering it. The voice on the other end startled her.

"Hello, my beautiful Danielle." It took her a few moments to realise who was speaking.

"You are alone, no?" the soft hypnotic voice asked.

"P-Panos, no I mean, yes I am alone," she replied, her heart pounding in her chest.

"Can I come up to your room for a minute please? I have some time to spare, so would like for us to talk. Is that alright?"

She tried to reply but her voice failed her, and she just squeaked. She felt so embarrassed and could feel her mouth drying up. She swallowed and cleared her throat, which did not help much, and let out a pathetic "yes." The phone went dead, and sheer panic shot though her body. *Oh dear*, she thought, *he is actually coming up here.*

She began to furiously pick up the clothes scattered over the floor, throwing them into a suitcase which she hurled into the bathroom, quickly shutting the door securely behind her. Her heart had now entered into her throat, and she thought at any minute it was going to jump out onto the white marble floor. She leaned up against the door, willing herself to calm down. She tried desperately to catch her breath when there was a faint tap on the door. She shot three feet into the air and was convinced she was going to have a heart attack. So, she took a very deep breath and pulled the handle down. She opened the door and Panos was standing there smiling, looking incredibly handsome. He came in, shutting the door behind him, and once again they were surrounded by silence. He could not help himself, but had to look down at her gorgeous, tanned body and suddenly understood what Mick had meant by "she will knock your socks off!"

He smiled and stared into her green eyes. He could not control himself so acted on impulse, taking her in his arms and kissing her. She could not resist as he took her breath away, and she kissed him back. They pulled each other closer and carried on kissing and the feelings that surfaced got stronger with every touch. Their embrace lasted for what seemed like an eternity and both of them could not hold back the passion that had been ignited between them. It was as if a smouldering fire had at last got the oxygen it craved to feed it.

Panos reluctantly pulled away from her, his head spinning. He did not want to let this woman go. Danielle's eyes were still closed, and her head automatically found its way to his chest. She felt so secure in his arms and for the first time, felt the true meaning of passion. It was like it had materialised and slapped her right across the face. Panos was breathing hard, not sure what to do next. He wanted her so much but the little voice in his head persuaded him otherwise. Danielle took his hand and led him over to the bed where they sat down.

"Panos," she said almost whispering. "I don't know what's going on here, but it is really scaring me."

She could not believe how honest she was being; her words had come out so naturally. It was as if they had been locked away and freed just for this moment. He understood totally and reached down and held her hand. He felt so confused, yet in complete awe of this lady beside him. He glided his finger up her slender arm and it felt as if fireworks were going off under her skin. Then he reached her shoulder and began to gently caress her skin. She felt a stirring as he touched her. She did not want him to stop but had to tell him to.

"Panos, I am not that kind of girl, I am feeling very uncomfortable," she said looking down. He carried on and with his other hand lifted up her chin, tenderly kissing her.

"I know, Danielle. I have never been in this situation before either, but it is OK, I am happy just to hold you. I want to spend every spare moment just holding you. I want nothing else, my beautiful Danielle," he said, softly kissing her again.

He could not believe what he was saying, but he knew he meant it from the bottom of his heart. She wasn't sure of his sincerity but decided to give him the benefit of the doubt anyway.

"I, too, do not know why this is happening," he said proudly holding on to the next sentence. "And- and it scares me too, Danielle." There, he had said it. He had gone against the grain of his heart and let a bit of how he felt escape.

"Let us see what happens, yes? I like you and you like me, so we will enjoy each other while you are here at my hotel, OK?" He knew he had to be realistic because she would soon be going home. She understood him and nodded.

It's not as if we will fall in love with each other, is it? she thought. He held her close and the thought of her leaving flooded his mind. He was suddenly overcome by a wave of sadness, but consciously pushed these unwanted feelings away. He looked at his watch.

"I have to go now and get the pool bar ready. I will see you down there OK, and then we will be close to each other." He kissed her again and got up to walk towards the door. He turned around and blew her a kiss as he walked out of the room. Danielle was left with all kinds of feelings swimming around in her head. She felt alienated from them as they whirled around. She was both baffled and excited by them. She felt like she was in a dream and did not want to ever wake up.

She got up and pressed play on the walkman and Celine filled the air. 'Falling into you this dream can come true and it feels so good falling into you.' She lay down and closed her eyes miming to the words envisioning Panos in her mind. She was definitely having the birthday of a life time! A smile stained her face as she lost herself in the song, feeling fully content with how she felt inside. The song finished, so she got up, gathered her things for the pool and walked downstairs to meet her new friends.

As Danielle walked along the pool side, she saw Panos opening up the shutters of the bar. He stopped as she walked towards him and willed her to sit on the lounger closest to him. She noticed the lounger was empty, so she went and claimed it. He smiled at her, pleased with her choice, and began to sing while he continued with his work. She placed her towel over the white plastic lounger and took off her sarong. He could not take his eyes off her as she lay on her back.

Ben and Lucy soon made an entrance and came and sat down next to her. They talked for a while. Lucy could not help noticing how Panos kept looking over at Danielle with a big smile across his face. She also caught her looking at him with the same look, and she grinned. They were both good looking and she thought they made a lovely couple. They continued sharing about their lives as Panos prepared the bar, and every so often their eyes would meet. He would wink, and she looked shyly away, aware of the obvious feelings showing for all to see. Lucy thought it was rather sweet and told Danielle so, and wished her luck with her Greek man. The attraction between them was obvious and Danielle felt very special as he was acting so openly.

Danielle spoke about her children and Lucy was surprised to hear she had three. *She certainly didn't have a figure that had borne three babies,* she thought. They also discussed Stuart and the peculiar way in which he had changed. Danielle wondered what he was doing now and just hoped he was alright.

Between their conversations Danielle went to swim in the pool to cool off. She swam over to the end nearest the bar to lean on the edge, watching Panos working, splashing her legs. The sun was inviting on her skin and she could not imagine leaving this wonderful place. Panos was singing and a smile had become a permanent resident on his face. He watched Danielle swim and longed to touch her again. The sooner the bar was ready, the sooner she could be in his reach, and everyday could be spent together.

He soon recognised Mick's voice from the terrace and realised they were back from town. Danielle pulled herself out of the pool. Panos felt the same explosive feeling emerge as droplets of water glistened on her sun kissed skin. Even Ben her new friend could not help but watch this sexy woman walk over to the lounger.

Mick and Matt were walking towards her holding something she could not make out. Then they began to sing happy birthday. She soon realised it was a cake Mick was holding. Matt was behind him with a tray and a bottle of champagne with glasses, and Danielle sat up blushing. She quickly glanced over at Panos, who had stopped what he was doing and was looking over at her, still smiling. He blew her a kiss and Matt put the tray down on the table.

"Happy birthday, Dan," said Matt leaning over to kiss her on the cheek. Panos was still watching and a pang of jealousy flipped his heart, so he quickly returned back to his work.

"Oh, thank you, Matt. This is a nice surprise," she said not knowing what else to say as he handed her a glass. Matt filled the glasses and handed them around.

"Here is to you and I wish you lots of happiness to come." They all lifted their glasses and toasted their special friend. She thanked them for making this a birthday she would never forget, and they spent the afternoon polishing off the champagne and cake. Mick informed her they were going to a club later, stating she could drink whatever she wanted. The vision of her first night when she arrived popped up in her head, and she literally cringed, at the thought.

"Anything but ouzo though Dan, it doesn't agree with you," said Matt aware of the colour rising in her cheeks. They all laughed at her expense and that night was soon forgotten. Danielle invited Lucy and Ben to the club later and they happily accepted.

It would be nice to be with a woman for a change, Danielle thought cheerfully.

Panos went inside to join his family for dinner. It was still difficult to watch Matt around Danielle because it brought out feelings of jealousy. He was finding them really hard to control, so he decided that what he could not see, could not hurt him. He had arranged to meet Mick at the club at twelve, so he had to make do with seeing her then.

The second bottle was now empty and all that was left of the cake were the crumbs. Danielle felt it was time to go and get showered and changed before she got too drunk. She was feeling a little bit tipsy now and kept giggling. She was so glad the events of the last few days had not spoilt the holiday and was happy to find things had returned to normal. The three friends had put it behind them and were enjoying each other's company again. They agreed to meet Lucy and Ben in the bar, so they could all travel down altogether. Then they made their way back to their rooms laughing all the way.

When they entered the room, Mick went straight over to the walkman. He switched it on and Celine's voice filled the air. Danielle was reminded of her time spent with Panos earlier and a deep yearning for him returned. Matt was the first to enter the bathroom and guilt overtook her when he questioned the suitcase lying on the floor. She acted the innocent and blamed it on the maids. He thought no more of it and put it back into the room and got into the shower.

Mick poured himself a large vodka and orange and went to sit on the balcony.

'Falling into you this dream can come true.' These words reeled around in her head and Panos re-emerged into her thoughts. She lay on the bed, rewound her mind to when he knocked on the door, and relived every moment spent with him over again. "And it feels so good falling into you." Danielle mimed the words.

If I am not careful, I could fall for him, she thought.

Oh, Panos, why did I have to meet you here? Why did you have to be Greek and not English? The song soon faded, and she joined Mick out on the balcony.

CHAPTER

ELEVEN

THE THREE FRIENDS APPEARED IN the bar an hour and a half later. Danielle looked as stunning as ever in a short mustard coloured dress. The colour complimented her tanned skin well, and once again heads turned when she entered the room. Panos was back behind the bar, and when his eyes fell on this beautiful lady, her beauty took his breath away. He could not wait to be with her again.

Mick ordered their drinks and they waited for their new friends. They sat at the bar and Panos tried his utmost to keep his eyes off her. All his attempts failed once again, captured by her splendour. He complimented her on her dress and took her hand to kiss it. She gingerly thanked him, and secretly wished he was coming with them.

"Panos is joining us later at the Borzoi club," stated Mick uncannily, taking a big gulp of his beer. Matt was talking to Yannis when he caught what Mick had said.

"Oh," said Matt perplexed.

He turned to look at Danielle and saw her face light up and was rather put out that Mick had invited Panos without consulting him first. He had seen how Panos had been looking at her and was beginning to like this man less and less. He knew there could be no future between them but did not trust this Greek man.

Surely she did not like this man, he thought and quickly dismissed his suspicions. He was relieved to see Lucy and Ben come into the bar. They would be going out soon, so he enjoyed a drink with them before going into town.

They all enjoyed a hearty meal and Danielle loved being the centre of attention. They laughed and joked, and all had a wonderful time together. They paid the bill and walked along to the Borzoi club which was situated just off the high street. She looked at her watch, it was a quarter to twelve. She would be seeing Panos soon and was very eager to see him.

They walked into the dimly lit room and the sound of Tom Jones's Sex Bomb greeted them. The room was filled with drunken holidaymakers gyrating to his raunchy words, and Danielle breathed in the rapturous atmosphere. Then she noticed him sitting with his back to her at the end of the bar. The vodka she consumed along with the champagne gave her the courage to go over to him. She acted on instinct and put her arm around him, kissing him on the cheek. He hastily turned to her, his face stern. It soon softened when he realised who had disturbed him. "Ah Danielle, it is my Danielle."

His face lit up as he spoke.

"Where is Michael?" She pointed down the bar. Mick saw

him and waved saying something Panos could not hear and waved back.

"And where is Matt?" he questioned scanning the room, his face hardening again.

"He should be with Mick somewhere. Come on, come and join us," she said excitedly, oblivious to his hostile look. He picked up his drink and they walked over to join the others. He said hello and noticed they were all very drunk. He swallowed his drink down and ordered another. He spent most of the night talking to Mick and Ben, as Danielle and Lucy ruled the dance floor. He was glad to be there, but Matt was starting to make him feel very uncomfortable. Each time he looked at him, his eyes were full of loathing. He also noticed how fast he was drinking so chose to ignore him.

He looked at his watch and realised it was getting very late. He wanted to spend some time alone with Danielle, so managed to steal her away from the dance floor and suggested they went somewhere else, just the two of them. She quickly jumped at the chance and agreed. She had been waiting all night to be with him. All of her secrecy to protect Matt vanished, as they said their goodbyes and left the club.

"I knew it," said Matt under his breath as he watched them leave, and then proceeded to drink down his newly bought drink. Mick was unaware of their departure as he smooched with a drunken blonde on the dance floor.

Panos took her hand and led her to his car. "Where are we going?" she giggled feeling very drunk.

"Somewhere we can be alone," he replied looking deep into her eyes. She stared back and put all her trust in him. He kissed her and all her feelings of wanting to be with him pushed her drunkenness aside as she responded to his embrace. Once again, she was overwhelmed by the force of Panos's charm and she got lost in his arms.

They drove past the hotel entrance and carried on down a winding road. Greek music filled the car. He sung to her, content to have her in his grasp at last. He now felt relaxed in her company away from everyone else. They travelled down a dirt track and came to a halt. They got out of the car and she soon realised they were at the beach. He took her hand and led her down onto the soft white sand. The atmosphere was calm and the only sound to be heard was the waves lapping the shore. The moon was nearly full, and stars flickered like little trinkets of hope in the sky. She became engrossed in the power of the darkness and stood there listening to the sea. She became aware that the nervousness she usually felt around him had gone. Quite objectively she noticed instead she was feeling very calm.

He came up behind her and put his arms around her waist. She could feel his warm breath on her neck as he lifted up her hair and began to gently kiss her velvety skin. His breathing became heavier and she closed her eyes, concentrating on his tender kisses caressing her neck. Her breathing followed his as his mouth kissed her shoulders. She could feel his tongue as a wave of desire careered through her body. She turned her head and kissed his dark brown hair and the smell of fresh shampoo danced up her nostrils. She took a deep breath and breathed in this gorgeous man.

Suddenly her heart began to panic when he turned her around. Sparks flew as he held her face and he kissed her. This time the emotion was too strong to control as the feelings erupted from their sleeping hearts. His hand clasped the back of her neck and his finger trailed down her spine very slowly, feeling every vertebra as it went. This made her shudder as his finger retraced its tracks back to the zip of her dress. She could feel the gentle touch of his hand and wanted to tell him to stop, but the raw emotion raised from her soul had masterfully overruled her urge to control the situation. So, she gave into the night and let herself be submerged into the power of his desire. He slowly began to undo the zip as they kissed, summoning the hidden passion that had been long forgotten. Then his hand rubbed against her uncovered flesh with a slight pressure being forced. She gasped as he slipped one of her dress straps off her shoulder. She could feel his teeth when he bit her skin, then slowly kissed it better. She felt a slight pain when he repeated the act, but it was a pain that excited her. She gasped again as he kissed her shoulder. His hand slipped off the other strap, her dress falling freely to the sand.

Panos stopped and looked at Danielle standing in front of him. He controlled his breathing and stared at her. He could not believe she was real and was once again in complete awe of this woman. Then the same frightening feeling claimed his heart, a feeling of a secret power she had projected which pulled at him and put him under her invisible spell. A woman had never scared him before, but as unpredictable as everything else he had felt since she came into his life, she did scare him. Being in the same room with her was hard enough to deal with but now she was in his reach, he did not want to push her into something she did not want. He held her face in his hand and hesitated, looking deep into her eyes.

Every part of her body was telling her to receive this man, but she just couldn't. "I am so sorry Panos, but I can't," she said, her eyes filling with tears.

He nodded slightly, respecting her wishes. He wanted her so much, every part of him ached for her but he knew it wasn't right. He pulled her to him and just held her, slowly controlling his breathing. His head was whirling, and he couldn't believe how close he had come to having her but did not want to jeopardise what was obviously flourishing between them. He loved feeling her body against his and he pictured her in his mind's eye. She smelt so lovely and for a split second, he wanted to be with her forever. He looked down at her and she could see the reflection of the moon in his eyes, he was so handsome. She could not believe she was here with him. She pulled away, aware of her nakedness, looking down at her dress at her feet. She felt an awkwardness, which surprised her. He had seen her topless many times at the pool, but she felt the need to put her dress back on. He watched her in silence and wondered what it was about her that made him be a different man around her.

She turned around and he willingly zipped up her dress. He took her hand and they sat down on a nearby lounger. Danielle looked out to sea and realised she felt completely sober. Doubts suddenly ruled her mind and she convinced herself all he wanted from her was sex, she could have kicked herself for getting into this situation.

Why did I drink so much? she thought. Her heart suddenly sunk to her feet as she looked down at the white sand.

Panos detected her regret and lifted her chin up. "Danielle, please do not be sad, I told you before I do not want you for your body. I would say I am sorry for what has happened, but I am not. I love being with you, everything about you I love. I just want you to be happy because it's what makes me happy.

I know I have only known you for a short time, but it is like I have known you forever."

He was shocked by his own honesty, but he needed to tell her to reassure her that his intentions were valid.

"If you do not want to make love, then it is OK. I mean it, Danielle I really do." He held her to him again, his mind filled with what he wanted to say to her.

"I want to hold you, be near you whenever possible…" he hesitated, frightened of what he wanted to say.

"Please believe what I say," he said, keeping his unfamiliar feelings to himself.

Danielle was touched by his sincerity and had to admit she felt exactly the same way about him. She loved being with him too and to her surprise, felt she could trust him. She nodded, listening to the rhythm of his heart and marvelled at the fact that she felt so safe in his arms.

"Do you feel the same way as me?" He could not help himself but had to ask. His heart began to beat faster as he waited for a reply, frightened the answer would be no. She just nodded, afraid to let the words come from her lips, and her heart began to bubble with anticipation.

Panos was overcome by pure joy, turned her around, picked her up and spun her around. They both laughed at his motivated act and she told him to put her down. He stopped to kiss her, and she felt helpless in his embrace. They kissed for a long time, when he finally stopped, a big smile was spread across his face.

"Come on, my beautiful lady. Let's go back to the hotel." He kissed her again and they walked hand in hand back to the car.

They arrived at the hotel and the place was quiet. They both presumed everyone was sleeping and walked into the lounge. Danielle thanked him for making her birthday complete and kissed him good night. Then a look of disappointment washed over his face.

"I would like very much for you to come and sleep in my bed with me," he said, looking down at the floor. He wanted to ask her before and found he couldn't, but the thought of her leaving him prompted his boldness. He wanted to hold her close to him when she slept, he did not want to be alone.

"I am sorry Danielle, but I like you very much, no," the words he wanted to say earlier had got stuck in his throat.

"I think I am falling in love with you."

His eyes searched hers looking for a response to his daring statement. He could not help the way he felt, and he knew he had to tell her.

She felt the back of her eyes sting with tears as his words rolled around in her head. He had taken her completely by surprise; she had not seen this coming.

"But Panos, I will be going home in a week and then you will soon forget all about me," she said, willing him to agree, but he didn't. Instead he shook his head and held her hand.

"I will never forget you, beautiful Danielle," he said, placing his other hand over his heart. "You will always be in here."

Danielle found his words hard to believe and this became apparent by the expression on her face.

"I do not lie," he said sternly, offended by the look on her face.

"You are different from all the other girls I have met, and

I knew that when I first saw you. My words are the truth and what I feel inside when I am with you, I cannot hide."

She thought he sounded sincere but doubt still lingered in her mind.

"I am sorry Panos but I find it hard to trust something that is so hard to believe. I have never experienced anything like this before and I do not want to get hurt."

She was troubled by her own honesty and felt she had let her barrier down, giving a small piece of herself away.

"Then that is, how do you say, a first for both of us then."

He smiled at her, unsure whether he had done the right thing by letting her into his heart, but something told him deep down it was alright.

"I would not hurt you," he said, kissing her gently. But they both knew in the back of their minds they were going to get hurt when the dreaded time came, and she had to leave.

"Ok then, we will spend as much time together, enjoy each other and make the most of everyday. What about that?"

He wasn't sure who he was trying to convince but it seemed a perfect idea. She nodded, overwhelmed by this gorgeous man. She thought what the hell and agreed to spend the night with him. Then he took her hand and led her to his room. She fell asleep in his arms and peace claimed her, her dreams filling her mind.

He could not sleep, so he lay awake all night just watching her breathe. His love for her became more prominent with every breath she took. He knew she had come into his life for a reason, but he did not know why. He squeezed her even tighter and wished he could lock this moment away forever.

CHAPTER

TWELVE

MATT WOKE UP WITH A START and his eyes quickly looked over to Danielle's bed. To his disappointment it was empty. He had hoped last night had been a terrible nightmare, but harsh reality soon set in as he stared at the deserted bed. An unbearable pain clenched his heart, as his irrepressible tears began to fall. All the love he felt for her filled his tears, and all the pain and hurt that erupted accompanied them. He put his head in his hands and prayed the pain would go away. He sat there and the vision of the two of them left him haunted, unable to control the feelings that escaped from his heart. After a few minutes he wiped away the tears and looked at the time. He had an overpowering need to get away from the hotel. Danielle could walk in any minute and he felt he didn't have the strength to face her, so he quickly showered and got dressed, deciding to go for a very long walk to clear his head. Mixed emotions flowed through him and he needed time to be on his own. Mick was still asleep, totally oblivious to his best friend's heartache.

As he left the room a smile fell on Mick's lips as he and Tracey made love on the pure white sands. He called out her name when the moment of passion came to an end, and the sound of his voice brought him out of his dream. It took him a few seconds to realise it was all a dream. An empty feeling overcame him, and he longed to be with his wife again. Oh, how he wanted to touch her, for her to touch him like she used to, to feel her body beneath his and be a part of her life again. It suddenly dawned on him he was alone in the room and he tried desperately to gather his thoughts.

The antics of the night before came flooding back and the blonde woman he had been with pushed Tracey to the back of his mind. He wished he had not been as drunk because he could have had his wicked way with her. "She was all over me," he convinced himself, and hoped he would see her again. He tried to recollect their conversation before she had left the club, racking his brains for talk of another meeting, but his mind was blank. He suddenly felt relieved he was alone as he reached for the vodka bottle and poured himself a stiff drink, "For medicinal purposes, of course," he reassured himself.

Danielle was awoken by a hand gently stroking her arm. As she turned over, she was greeted by Panos's gorgeous smile. No words were spoken as he welcomed her with his eyes and kissed her. She closed her eyes and breathed in the memory of their conversation the night before. He held her tight and she felt so secure in his presence. He moved closer from behind her and his body fitted so perfectly into hers. He kissed her shoulders and the now familiar feelings escaped through his lips. As he held her perfect body, he was forced to use all his strength to control himself from making love to her. She turned to look at him and she could see the compulsive look in his eyes. It took all her strength not to let him, as she dared to kiss him. They got lost in each other and the world outside was soon forgotten. He pulled himself away and just stared into her eyes stroking her sexy curves.

"I love you," he mouthed, and all his power of restraint vanished. She started to say something but, he put his finger on her mouth, stopping her from speaking. He just stared at her and smiled.

"You are so perfect," he said, watching his hand go up her tanned body. He did not want to leave her, but he was aware of the time; he had work to do. Then the phone started ringing bringing them both back to reality. He leaned across her to answer it. He began to speak Greek and she listened to the alien language, thinking how sexy his accent was. She began to kiss his bare chest and as he spoke his voice became quite agitated. Then he abruptly put the receiver down.

"That was my brother. I'm sorry but I have to leave you now and get to work." His eyes filled with regret and he kissed her firmly on the lips. He reluctantly got out of the bed and got dressed. As he put on his clothes his eyes never left hers as she watched him cover up his masculine body.

"I will see you in the bar soon, no?" he said, still looking at her.

"You will see me in the bar, yes." Her voice was soft as she answered him. His beautiful Greek accent was enough for her to drag him back into bed, but she refrained. He kissed her again and her eyes followed him to the door, eye contact lost when the door closed.

She lay there smiling, trying desperately to work out what was happening to her. She soon chose to give up as she could not figure it out. She picked up her dress and put it on, the smell of Panos was all over the material. She took a deep breath, breathing the memory of him in, and glided back to her room, her thoughts dominated by the lovely Panos.

Matt found himself walking along the beach and only a handful of people occupied the sun loungers. He walked past them oblivious to their presence. He knew he had no chance of being with the woman of his dreams, but this did not take away the pain that gripped hold of his heart. He suddenly came to a standstill and soon realised he was in the same spot where he had expressed his feelings for her. Various emotions swam around, as he recalled those fateful words, tears welling up behind his eyes. He took a deep breath to keep them at bay. He sat on the warm sand and held his head in his hands.

How could I have let this happen? he thought to himself.

Why did I let myself get so close to her? Why did I let false hope rule my heart? He knew that she had always told him she only wanted to be friends, but secretly he hoped she might change her mind. But now he knew the truth, last night had confirmed it. Instead she wanted that Greek bastard! Suddenly rage erupted as he envisioned them together and was convinced Panos only wanted her for one thing. He was sure it would end in tears for her.

Well I am not going to be there to pick up the pieces, he thought. Those thoughts bred a surge of strength in him and he started to laugh uncontrollably. The realisation of the outcome of the situation was welcomed into his heart. He gathered his positive thoughts together and laughed away the tears. "You can have her Panos," he said out loud. Then he made himself a promise to never let another woman near his heart again.

Danielle opened the door and walked into the unoccupied room.

"Dan is that you?" shouted Mick from the bathroom.

"Yes, it is me. Where's Matt?" asked Danielle flippantly. She walked over to the walkman and put the music on.

"He was gone when I woke up. I thought he was with you," said Mick walking out of the bathroom with only a towel around his waist. Danielle was lying on the bed with her eyes closed as Celine's voice dominated the room. "Falling into you this dream could come true." The words travelled through Danielle's body as she remembered the night spent with Panos. Then Mick noticed she still had the dress on she was wearing last night.

"Did you have a good night Dan?" She opened her eyes and looked at Mick and had a big grin across her face.

"Well I guess that look on your face answers my question," said Mick smirking. He picked up his clothes and went back into the bathroom.

Her thoughts went straight back to Panos. Half an hour later they made their way down to the bar. Mick was slightly concerned about Matt; he had no idea why he would go missing like this and just hoped he was alright. Suddenly Stuart popped up in his mind and he was taken back to when he went missing. He shook his head.

No, Matt wouldn't do anything like that to us, he thought quickly, forcing such thoughts out of his mind.

As they entered the lounge Panos was serving behind the bar. When his eyes fell on her, his face lit up with sheer happiness. Mick noticed his beaming expression, and this brought a smile to his face. He felt so happy for them and had to admit they did look good together.

"Good morning Panos and how are you this fine morning,

my friend?" asked Mick, looking straight at Panos smirking.

"Michael, I am feeling very happy thank you my friend," Panos replied, happily smiling back at him. Then he turned his attention to Danielle.

"Good morning my beautiful Danielle and how are you my darling?" He took hold of her hand and kissed the back of it. Her heart fluttered, and she gently squeezed his hand.

"I am very happy thank you, ecstatically happy," she replied staring into his brown eyes.

"If I could just tear you two love birds apart for a few minutes, I would like a drink please, Panos."

Mick ordered a beer and Danielle chose to have a cup of coffee. Panos poured Mick's beer and his eyes never left hers. No words were spoken, but silent communication was obvious between them. He had waited patiently for her to be in his reach and felt a sense of relief when she walked into the room. As soon as he had left her this morning his heart had ached for her. She was constantly in his thoughts and he could not wait to be with his beautiful Danielle again. He wanted to spend as much time with her as he could, before she would be leaving his life as quickly as she had entered it. His heart sank when he thought about the day she would be going back to England. He took a deep breath and quickly put the dreaded thought to the back of his mind. When Danielle walked in, all he felt was happiness and all of these untainted feelings for her escaped through his smile.

"I would like for you to have lunch with me this afternoon," he said placing her coffee down in front of her.

"A good friend of mine has got a restaurant," he continued, "and I would very much like him to meet you." Panos's father was at the reception and the quietness of the room made it possible for him to hear his son's conversation. He had never known his son to invite a girl to meet Nicos before. The look on Panos's face and the tone of his voice unnerved him. He did not like this English girl, something had to be said. Then Yannis walked up behind his father and noticed the harsh look on his face.

"Yannis what is happening between Panos and.... and that English girl?" he asked, his eyes still on the couple.

"I do not like the look on your brother's face. I hope he is not serious about her." He turned around and looked at Yannis, his eyes boring into him like hot pokers.

"Papa, they are just friends." Yannis said, confused at his father's aggression. His father had never questioned his brother's affairs before. "Danielle is ..." he began to explain but his father cut him dead.

"I do not care what she is, and I do not care what her name is. I will not allow her to get into my son's heart!"

His distinct words caused Yannis to take a step back, shocked by the tone in which they were spoken. Then the phone rang, causing Panos to look over. Yannis answered it and his father quickly left the room. Yannis lifted up the receiver, indicating the call was for Panos.

"Please excuse me I have a telephone call," he said. He walked over to his brother as Danielle's eyes followed him across the room.

"You can't take your eyes off him, it must be love," Mick teased.

"Don't be silly, how can I fall in love with him? We will be going home soon," she stated dismissively.

The words repeated themselves in her head but every time

she looked at him another spark lit up in her heart. She could not afford to fall in love with him, but every glance between them was mysteriously bringing them closer together, and it was harder for her to control her state of heart. She was determined to keep her emotions to herself. She had a little box vacant in her mind so that when she stepped onto the plane to go home, she would put all her thoughts and feelings neatly away, closing the lid forever. She sighed deeply at the hardness she tried to cultivate when Panos returned.

"That was the police sergeant informing me Stuart has been asked to leave the island. He is going back to England today. He was very drunk, and he has been causing trouble in the town. He was shouting and swearing at everybody, so he has been told to leave," said Panos sadly.

"Blimey Panos, that's a bit harsh. He definitely did lose the plot," Mick laughed.

Danielle was speechless and still could not get over the sudden change in him. She just hoped he would be alright on the plane journey. She soon convinced herself that when he was at home, he could get the help he needed. After all the trouble he had caused them, they decided not to mention him again during the rest of their holiday.

"So, Danielle I have to work down at the pool bar now, are you coming with me?" Panos said, his eyes pleading with her to be near him. She turned and looked at Mick.

"Do not worry about me Dan. I'll go into town on my own."

She wasn't sure whether she could detect sarcasm in his voice.

"You never know, I might bump into my mysterious blond.

I will also look for Matt. I will probably have more chance of finding him." Mick gulped down his drink. The bus would be leaving soon, and he did not want to miss it.

"I will see you two later," he said contently, getting up and walking out to the bus. Panos said something to his brother and walked around to Danielle.

"We will go to the pool now, OK?" he said, taking her hand, and they made their way to the poolside. On the way, he told her about his good friend Nicos and how much he wanted her to meet him. He told her the story of their first meeting and she hung on to his every word as he shared his account, mesmerised by his Greek accent. She had to remind herself a few times not to get too engrossed by this man, but it was now nigh on impossible for her not to.

As they walked down the steps only a handful of guests occupied the loungers around the pool. All the guests said good morning to them and Danielle felt extremely special because of the attention she received by being with this man. He led her to the vacant lounger nearest the bar and kissed her. Then he left her to get on with opening the bar. He turned to face her as she was taking off her clothes, revealing her slim tanned body that he had held that morning. He had an overwhelming urge to walk back over to her and take her back into his arms, and it took all his strength not to. He felt so proud to be with her. Watching her brought the same unfamiliar feelings to the surface, the same emotions which had emerged from his heart the night before. He wanted to say so much to her, but he knew he couldn't. He had never felt so confused. He had always been in control; that was what his success was built on. But looking at Danielle and being with her had materialised another side of him he didn't know existed. It both excited and scared him. He recalled the conversation from the night before and decided he would have to try and control this wonderful situation.

Danielle lay on the lounger and looked over at Panos, who was staring at her. He smiled, and her heart skipped a beat as she impulsively smiled back. She closed her eyes and took in a deep breath. *I have got to be dreaming,* she thought. *This cannot be happening.* She put her hand down the side of her body and pinched herself. She jumped when a sharp pain went through her leg. *No,* she thought, *this is real.*

She opened her eyes and remembered she had put Mick's walkman in her bag, so she sat up and got it out, placing the ear plugs in her ears. Panos watched her every move, ignoring the guest ordering some food in front of him. Danielle pressed play and then lay down again. Celine's voice echoed through her head, 'Everything you are everything you'll be touches the current of love so deep in me.'

She closed her eyes as Celine's voice drifted her back to the memory of being in his arms. 'Your most innocent kiss your sweetest caress, seduces me.' The memories empowered by the song brought goose bumps to the surface of her skin. A single tear formed in the corner of her eye as she listened to the words, recapturing all the feelings he provoked.

Panos busied himself preparing the bar for the day ahead. More guests frequented the pool in the afternoons and he had to make sure it was ready for their demands of hunger. He found himself singing while he worked, and feelings of happiness escaped through his words. Every so often he was stopped in his tracks as Danielle got up and swam in the pool. He waited patiently for her to be close to him, keeping a close eye on his watch.

CHAPTER

THIRTEEN

MICK WANDERED DOWN THE HIGH street and noticed that a new bar had just opened. The craving for alcohol was too strong for him to ignore, so he decided it was a good excuse to try it. As he walked in, he was surprised at how small the bar was. Only a few bar stools lined the room and there were only three at the bar. A man and a young girl were talking behind the wooden counter; they both looked at him as he sat on one of the stools. He felt welcomed by their smiles and the young girl asked him politely what he wanted to drink. He ordered a beer, then the man said something in Greek to the girl and proceeded to walk out.

"He is my boss and he is very bossy," the girl said, rolling her eyes. "That's six hundred Drachma please." Mick fumbled around in his pocket and handed her the money, noticing she was very young and pretty. She had shoulder length dark brown hair and stunning chocolate brown eyes.

I am going to enjoy it here, he thought to himself as the blond girl from the previous night quickly vanished from his mind. Mick spent the afternoon talking to the young girl. She was very bubbly, and she enjoyed her conversation with this English man. She listened intently to him when he talked about his wife and could not help feeling sorry for him. The day drifted by as did many people, and Mick had no intention of returning to the hotel in a hurry. He daren't look at his watch because he did not want to be reminded of the time. He was very happy just sitting at the bar, drinking his drink while watching this gorgeous Greek girl work.

Panos's work load had been reduced and he could now at last, spend some precious time with Danielle. He asked his brother to take over from the bar while he went out for an hour or so. Yannis felt obligated to tell Panos about what their father had said, but the glowing look that lit up his face made him keep quiet. He would tell him eventually of his father's harsh words, but only when the time was right. He had the utmost respect for his father but felt, that this time he was wrong.

Panos walked over to Danielle indicating it was time to go, so she got dressed and they made their way to the car. They travelled down the winding road to the town, Greek music prominent in the air as he sung to her. She looked out over the calm blue sea, and once again the same familiar feeling flowed through her body.

"It is a beautiful place, no?" he asked her.

"Yes," she whispered.

The diminutive word escaped her lips, as she was consumed by this man and her surroundings. They entered the top of the high street and he parked the car. As Danielle got out, she suddenly realised they were outside the police station. The vision of Stuart's twisted face appeared before her and the memory of that dark night replayed in her mind. She still felt bad for what happened to him, but there was nothing anyone could do, because he was now on his way home. Panos looked at her and she caught his glance.

"He will be OK, Danielle." It was as if he could read her mind. He put his arm around her and looked lovingly into her eyes. She felt so safe and protected in his arms and believed he was right. He gently kissed her, and all her worries and fears rapidly dissolved in his kiss. They continued to walk down the high street towards the harbour. The usual hustle and bustle of the Greek way of life surrounded them as they walked.

They were interrupted many times by the Greek shop owners who came up to Panos and greeted him with a hand shake. They talked for a few minutes and then proceeded down the high street. She felt in complete awe of this man as she watched him speak. She noticed the respect these men had for him in their faces and felt very proud to be on his arm. Each man would look at her and smile. Greek words were spoken as they took her hand and kissed it. She was intrigued by the alien conversation, hearing her name mentioned. This was starting to annoy Panos because each man complimented him on his lovely English lady. He didn't have much time and all he wanted to do was get to the restaurant, to be with his gorgeous Danielle. It didn't escape him all the attention she received as they walked past the people scattered about.

He did feel proud to be the one with her, but jealousy played a strong part in the back of his mind. His fears were starting to become reality when he saw men's faces as she passed by them.

The fear of losing the one person who had brought him happiness in a long time, fed the fear that he would have to let her go, to another man to claim her heart. An overwhelming sadness consumed him when they reached the restaurant.

Danielle had been unaware of what was going on around her, and all she could think about was how happy she was with Panos.

A smile had become a permanent fixture on her face, and the constant flutter of butterflies reminded her of the joy that filled the empty space in her heart. When she was with him the thought of her home back in England was forgotten. The realisation she was three thousand miles away from her world was not evident when his arms were wrapped around her. All her control and keeping one step ahead of the situation which she had promised herself earlier, had secretly abandoned her when she was with his amazing man.

They entered the restaurant and Panos scanned the room looking for his friend. The room was filled with many people, and to his disappointment Nicos was nowhere to be seen. They walked up to the bar and he ordered their drinks. Danielle looked around the busy room and couldn't help noticing just how posh it looked. He looked at her as her big green eyes sparkled with fascination. The happiness they projected made him feel good, and the sorrow he felt earlier disappeared. He now felt calm inside and could not take his eyes off her gleaming face. He instinctively kissed her cheek.

"What was that for?" she asked looking into his eyes. He shook his head slightly, not able to explain the feelings that emerged. They stood locked in each other's stare, neither of them hearing the barman putting down their drinks.

"Panos!" The sound of the voice of a Greek man from across the room startled them. They both looked around as a tall man was coming towards them. He was saying something in Greek and had his arms stretched open.

"Nicos!" Exclaimed Panos as he put his arms out and the two men embraced. Danielle watched them greet each other and started to feel very nervous. She had listened to Panos talking about his special friend and suddenly felt on edge. Nicos looked at her and continued to speak in Greek.

"Nicos please, you have to speak in English," said Panos patting his friend on the back.

"Oh, I am sorry, you must be Danielle!"

Panos had spoken to Nicos the previous day telling him about the beautiful girl who had come into his life. Nicos thought he was exaggerating, but when his eyes met hers, he realised his friend had been telling the truth. He took her hand and gently kissed it.

"It is so good to meet you Danielle. Panos has told me all about you."

Nicos slyly glanced at Panos and a big smile erupted across his face. Panos proudly returned his gaze, as if to say I told you so! Then he protectively put his arm around her. She felt honoured to know Panos had told his friend about her. She was also flattered that he told him to speak in English. He had not seemed bothered when all the other men he had spoken to were using their native language. She took this as a show of respect and it shocked her. She could not help wondering whether the feelings of love he had displayed were actually genuine.

"Come with me and I will show you to your table," said

Nicos as he led them over to a table overlooking the sea.

"Sit down here and order your food, I will join you shortly."

Nicos pulled out a chair and Danielle sat down. Panos sat down next to her and then Nicos walked away.

"The food here is very good," said Panos looking through the menu. Danielle looked across the sparkling sea and couldn't believe how lucky she was. Watching a fishing boat glide across the still water, she wished she could stay here in Greece forever. This place was what her dreams were made of. She couldn't believe she was actually living her wonderful dream. She looked at him and smiled. *He is a part of this dream,* she thought, and as she gazed at him, she suddenly realised she was falling in love with him.

He looked up from the menu, aware her eyes were on him. He put the menu down and took her hand in his. He smiled back at her and gently kissed her soft hand. "I am so glad you are here with me, it makes me so happy," he whispered.

She nodded and sighed, the feel of his breath on her slightly trembling hand made her quiver inside. This was not how she wanted it to go. She wanted to be in control, but her guard was rapidly going down. She squeezed his hand and kissed him firmly on the lips.

"Oh, Panos," she sighed. "This is crazy. You make me feel so good. Nobody has ever made me feel this way before. I feel totally out of my depth here." The sound of her vulnerability made him want her more than ever.

He had to agree this was crazy. He hadn't experienced anything like this before either. He looked at his watch, time was running out.

"We must order," he said, turning around to catch the

waiter's eye. The waiter scurried over to take their order, and suddenly Nicos reappeared. Cassia was with him, and they both sat down at the table with Panos and Danielle.

"Danielle, this is Cassia," said Nicos. Danielle looked at the attractive Greek girl and smiled. Cassia half-heartedly smiled back, and her eyes shot back to Nicos. "S-she is my girlfriend," continued Nicos noticing the stern look on Cassia's face.

"It is nice to meet you," said Cassia after Nico backtracked and did the introduction that she approved of! Her face softened slightly as she continued to speak. They talked as they waited for their food to arrive. Nicos was intrigued by this English girl and wanted to know all about her. Danielle told him all about her life back home and about her three children. Panos noticed the way her expression changed when she spoke about them. Pride seeped from her words and to his surprise this made him love her more.

Cassia listened to the English girl and did not like the way Panos hung on her every word. She noticed the look on his face and did not recognise it. She had never seen him like this before and it disturbed her. It was a well-known fact that Greek men were not interested in women who had children, especially if they were foreign, and especially not Panos.

This was the first time she had met any of the girl's that Panos liked. She had known about them as he would boast to her about his conquests, but that was all they were, women he conquered, holidaymakers that were out for a good time. The two of them had become good friends over the past year and had grown close. She was thankful for their friendship. It was because of him she met Nicos. She had never felt threatened before, but to her the English girl sitting across from her posed a great threat. A pang of jealousy seethed through her when she looked down at him holding Danielle's hand, caressing it with his fingers. *Something is not right about this girl, she thought*. She decided she did not like her.

Nicos loved English people. They were his favourite customers and he loved to hear about their country and way of life. His dream was to go there one day and to see it for himself. They always came across as so open and friendly. He also liked the way they spoke their language and the tone of it fascinated him. Listening to Danielle confirmed that fact.

He had also never met any of Panos's so called girlfriends before, so when he had phoned him wanting him to meet her, he was pleasantly surprised. He was not sure how he would feel meeting her, especially because Panos spoke very highly of his new-found love. But looking at her and hearing her speak, he knew instinctively why she was so special to his friend. He felt very honoured that Panos wanted him to meet this lovely English lady.

The meals finally arrived, and Danielle felt comfortable in the presence of Panos's friends. The two men and Danielle chatted while they ate their food. Cassia on the other hand just sat and listened. She could not wait to get out of the restaurant and get back to work because she felt very uneasy about it all. She had booked a two hour lunch break, but after the meal she made her excuses and got up to go. Nicos was disappointed she had to leave so soon, and was somewhat surprised, but did not question her actions. She kissed Panos on the cheek and quickly said goodbye to Danielle. Nicos got up and embraced her, promising he would see her later. She kissed him and left the restaurant.

Danielle did not notice the coldness in Cassia's voice but

Panos did. It was unusual for Cassia to act in such a way. She was normally so friendly, so put it down to the women's first meeting and dismissed it. They carried on their conversation and Nicos asked about Mick. Panos filled him in on his crazy friend. Danielle lost all track of time as she interacted with the two men and found she liked Nicos very much. The fact she was from a different world did not get in the way of their laughter. The language barrier was down when she talked and listened to her new acquaintance. Panos was relieved Nicos was getting on with her and vice versa. He was having a great time, until he looked at his watch.

"I am sorry Nicos but we have to go. I have to get back to the hotel." He was over three quarters of an hour late.

"Thank you for your company and for a lovely meal," said Panos, putting his hand in his pocket searching for his wallet.

"No, no, this is on me," Nicos said cheerfully, taking hold of Panos' hand and shaking it.

"If you are sure that's OK?" Panos replied, embracing his friend.

"It is my pleasure," Nicos squeaked because Panos hugged him so hard he found it hard to breathe. Nicos laughed and pulled himself away.

Danielle stood up; he took her hand and kissed it. "I hope to see you again Danielle," he said optimistically.

"I hope so too. I have had a great time, thank you Nicos."

Danielle was sorry she had to go back but was hopeful she would see him again. They said their farewells and the lovestruck couple walked back to the car.

CHAPTER

FOURTEEN

MATT LOOKED OUT ACROSS THE sea and decided to take a swim. His eyes felt puffy from the tears he had shed earlier. He had an overwhelming urge to wash away the tiny remains of Danielle and the pain she had induced. He had been so engrossed in his anguish, that he hadn't noticed the happy holidaymakers filling the beach.

He looked around and became aware of how busy it had become. The time spent there had felt like only minutes, but when he looked at his watch, he realised he had been sitting there for over an hour. He took off his shorts and t-shirt and walked the short distance to the edge of the shore. He stood there for a few minutes watching the waves lap over his feet. The water felt cool against his skin and he slowly stepped into its calmness. The sun was beating down on his back as he got deeper into its power. Then he dived under the crystal blue water, letting it envelop his body. The coolness of the sea was cleansing against his warm skin, and he began to swim furiously. He let the water splash over his face, ridding him of the traces of tears which had fallen there earlier. He pounded the surface with his hands letting all his anger out, cutting through the salty water.

Suddenly he found himself at the rocky end of the beach, so he stopped and looked up at the clear blue sky. He closed his eyes and let the sun beat down on his face. He had swum so hard he was finding it hard to breathe, but the warming of its rays relaxed him as he claimed back his breath. With his breathing returning back to normal he realised he felt a little bit better. He felt invigorated by his swim and at last felt calm inside. He laughed at his stupidity; at what a fool he had been and felt he had finally been cleansed of Danielle. The love and the hate he had felt for her had miraculously been dispersed into the sea. He laughed again feeling a lot better and took a slow swim back to where his clothes were. He strolled out of the sea and walked over to his belongings, took a cigarette out of his trouser pocket and lit it. Then he lay down on the sun lounger letting the sun dry his damp skin. He shut his eyes and inhaled his cigarette. He heard his stomach rumbling and realised he was hungry. He had no intentions of going back to the hotel; he wanted to stay away from there as long as possible, so decided to take a slow walk into town to get something to eat.

Panos spent the car journey back to the hotel asking Danielle about her family. He explained that he wanted to know everything about them. He could not understand why such a beautiful lady should be left alone to bring up three children. This deeply concerned him because given the choice he would not have let her slip through his fingers. He shared his concerns, saying the woman you fall in love with and the mother of your children should be loved and cherished no matter what happened. She told him that it wasn't that simple, explaining, the situation between her and her ex-husband.

Panos was shocked. He said he was sorry but could not understand why a man would choose to leave his family, especially for another one. He knew times could be hard. This made him think about his own mother and father and the heartache they had endured in the early days of building up the hotel, but they made it through. It was all worth it in the end. "There is nothing more important than family," he exclaimed. "Your husband is not a man, he is a fool!"

The thought of this man he had never met who was responsible for hurting this precious lady enraged him. "I am sorry but as I said I do not understand that man! Greek men are not like that," he said, his face stiffening as he spoke.

Danielle was totally taken by surprise at his reaction. She looked out of the window and recalled the mess her husband had left behind. Panos glanced over to her and recognised the sadness in her face. Her beautiful smile had faded and had been replaced by sorrow.

"Greek men are very romantic," he said, his tone softening. Then he put his hand under her chin and gently turned her face to his.

"I am very romantic, and I will show you what you deserve." He smiled at her willing her to smile back, and somehow because she believed him, she did. The way he had reacted around her all day made her trust him even more. Something from deep within her was telling her she was making a huge mistake, but at this moment in time she just didn't care. A big smile escaped from her lips, and Panos was relieved to have his beautiful Danielle by his side again.

They arrived back at the hotel and Panos wondered what his father would say to him for being late. He felt so happy in himself though, that his father could have said anything he liked, and the words would just bounce right off of him.

"I will meet you at the pool and then we can finish off our little talk..." he paused, looking into her big green eyes.

"I have so much I want to say to you. You deserve to be treated properly, like a lady should be treated." He closed his eyes and kissed her, all his feelings rushing up to the surface of his heart. He took a deep breath and said something in Greek. She was too afraid to ask him what he had said. She was frightened of what it could have been.

Oh dear, she thought. *I am falling for him. This is crazy.*

"I will not be long my beauty," he said. Reluctantly they both got out of the car and went in different directions.

Panos went up the steps to the entrance of the hotel, and as he walked in, he saw his father standing behind the bar. No guests were to be seen, and as he walked towards his father the smile dropped from his face. His father had heard his son pull up in the car and was waiting for him. He glared at Panos and intently watched him walk across the room. Panos's heart began to beat faster as he got nearer to his father's scolding stare.

"You were only meant to be out for an hour, you have been gone nearly two!" his father bellowed across the quiet stricken room.

"I am sorry papa, but I was..."

"I do not care where you were or what you were doing. You need to be here to help your brother. You cannot go out for hours and leave everything down to Yannis. Panos I must tell you the truth, you can do what you want, but it must not, I say must not, interfere with the running of the hotel. I want you to stay away from that English girl, she is bad news and she will hurt you. Listen to your father; she is only after your money." His father's honesty shocked them both.

"But papa she is not like that. She is a nice girl. I am not stupid, and I would know if she just wanted my money," Panos pleaded with his father to listen. He had never witnessed his father react this way before, as he had never questioned him.

What is going on? he thought.

"Panos, you are a good hardworking boy," his voice mellowed.

"Just do not be taken in by this girl," he said, emphasizing the last part of the sentence.

"But papa I like her." Panos's voice was shaking from the unpredictable way his father was behaving.

"Well I do not! You can take my advice, or you can ignore it, but she will hurt you." Then his father slammed down a glass and walked out of the room.

Panos just stood there trying to understand what his father had just said. His ears were ringing. He had never seen him lose his temper like that over a girl, and this was the girl he was falling in love with. It just did not make sense to him. As if it wasn't all confusing enough feeling this way about Danielle, and now his father's irrational behaviour, this was a very worrying situation.

His father's brutal words rattled around in his head. *How can he not like her?* he thought. *He doesn't even know her.*

Then tears began to well up in his eyes when his mother

walked in to the room. She had been in the restaurant laying the tables and had heard everything. She had strategically waited for her husband to leave before approaching her son. She studied Panos's face and could see the look of despair written all over it. Her heart went out to her firstborn son, recognising the pain in his eyes. Her husband's harsh words had not surprised her and she understood the reasoning behind them. It was not often she had seen him scared, but she knew he was worried for their son's welfare, and anxious for the hotel as well, which had taken a lot of sweat and tears to build. The unfamiliar look of anguish on her son's face shocked her, and she soon began to realise the feelings he had for this English girl.

"I can see you like this girl very much," she said, taking hold of his hand.

Panos looked into his mother's eyes and a single tear rolled down his cheek. He simply nodded, aware of his emotions escaping through his tears. His heart now not only ached for Danielle but for his father's approval. Panos had never witnessed this behaviour in his father before and was in complete shock.

His mother had seen the difference in him since Danielle had been in the hotel and it had lifted her heart to see her son happy again. She knew Sophia had hurt him immensely and felt let down it ended the way it had. She thought he had dealt with the breakup harshly, but he was his father's son, her husband's pig-headed streak was prominent in Panos's makeup.

She had secretly watched her son's conduct with other girls at the hotel and was worried he was throwing his life away. It hurt her to see him use these women; it seemed the only way he knew how to get his own back on Sophia for the pain she had caused him. When she saw him with Danielle it was like another light shone out of him, a positive light was guiding him in the right direction. She knew they could have no future together, but if she made her son happy then that was good enough for her.

"I like it that she makes you happy son, but you know you will have to eventually marry a Greek girl, don't you? Your father only wants what's right for you. You do understand he is only saying those things out of love for you," she said her voice calm and serene. Panos could see the words from his mother were heartfelt.

"I know mother, but I cannot help the way I feel. I love being with her and I really do like her and yes, she makes me very happy. We both know it won't be long before she goes home, so I want to make the most of being with her before she is gone. I just wish papa would have let me explain. She does not want my money, she is a sincere and genuine lady."

The openness he shared made his mother's heart bleed.

"I do not want to fall out with papa, I just want his blessing," he said, his voice pleading for his mother's support.

"Do not worry, I will talk to your father. He will come around when I explain." A reassuring smile formed on her face and she kissed him on the cheek.

"Now, go and tell your brother to come inside to tend the bar, then you can be with Danielle. She will be wondering where you are…" she paused.

"I understand what is going on in your heart and I will make your father understand also." The gentle sound of his mother's voice was welcoming to him and he had faith in her words, trusting the sincerity in which they were spoken.

"Now put that handsome smile back on your face and go and fetch your brother." Panos followed his mother's command and walked down to the pool.

When he walked down the steps, he was aware it was quite busy. A boy's laughter could be heard as he played with his father in the pool, and the sound of the guests talking was prominent in the air. As he followed the steps down, they stopped their conversations to say hello. Their glowing smiles were silently thanking him for this wonderful place, and a sense of pride overwhelmed him.

Then his eyes fell on her. Danielle was lying on her back inviting the sun to gently enrich her slender body. She had her eyes closed and her lips were moving slightly. He noticed thin wires coming from her ears and smiled, realising she was miming to a song.

That was why she did not see me, he thought. *She is preoccupied with her music.* His smile widened when he looked up and down her exquisite body. Oh, how much he wanted to be with her, to make her happy and to give her his all. He sighed as he recalled his mother's words. He knew what was expected of him. Seeing however this captivating lady before him, made him wish the unwritten rules were different. He had so much love to give her, his heart felt like it would burst. *How did this lady get into my most inner place?* he thought. His stomach bubbled with anticipation as he just looked at her. He thought she was the most beautiful person he had ever laid his eyes on. The vision of her soon put his doubts and worries to the back of his mind.

'Falling into you, this dream could come true.' Danielle could not stop listening to this song. It reminded her of Panos and all of the feelings she felt towards him accompanied the memory.

"I was afraid to let you in here now I have learned that love can't be made in fear. The walls begin to tumble down, and I can't even see the ground." She mimed the words and all the feelings of love she tried to deny rushed to her heart.

The sun was warm on her body and she felt it was only shining on her. It felt like it was personally wrapping itself around her, holding her like a blanket of light, engulfing her very being. She imagined it was Panos holding her, his arms inviting her into his world, his touch promising her she was safe from harm, protecting her so no one could ever hurt her. Suddenly her thoughts were interrupted, and she had the overwhelming urge to open her eyes. Her eyelids lifted and as if by an invisible force her view was stolen by the same person that had dominated her thoughts. She took the ear phones from her ears and put her hand up to block out the sun.

"H-hello Panos, I was just thinking about you," she grinned at the thoughts going through her mind. He reached down and tenderly stroked her face. She instinctively closed her eyes as a tingling sensation sailed through her body.

"Are you alright my beautiful Danielle?" His soft voice enthralled her and the feel of him touching her face rocked her soul. She nodded and began to caress his arm. The feel of her hand on his skin excited him, provoking an uncontrollable desire to pick her up and take her as far away as possible. He managed to stop himself, knowing he had to relieve his brother from the bar.

"I must tear myself away from you as I have got to work," he said sighing, regret washing over his face. He delicately kissed her mouth and walked over to the bar. Danielle shut her eyes and could still feel his warm touch on her skin. She took a deep breath and held on to that thought until it slowly dissolved from her mind.

Danielle spent the next two hours in Panos's sight. He watched her as she sunbathed, and his eyes never strayed from her even when she went for a swim. He was constantly interrupted by his guests but could always see her out of the corner of his eye. He was mesmerised by her, and as he watched her slender body glide through the clear water his heart pumped liquid love through his veins. She swum to the side of the pool and pulled herself up the three steps to the edge. His eyes never left her as she walked over to her lounger. She glistened as small beads of water travelled down her darkened body, and he felt a stirring in the pit of his stomach as he watched the droplets slide over her breasts. He could contain himself no more; he needed to touch her. She looked at him when she tied back her hair and he looked at her, willing her to come over to him. She sensed his request, put her bikini top back on and walked over to the bar. It was like his smile was an unseen force pulling her to his side.

"I am sorry, but I cannot stand you being so far away from me. I would really like you to be close to me."

She leaned on the cold bar and he took her hand and held it. She squeezed his hand and he kissed her firmly on the lips. He knew the other guests were aware of his actions, but for once in his life he did not care. He wanted them to know she was with him, and something very special was happening between them.

"You are so beautiful," he whispered. "And you deserve to be loved by a real man. I know I should not say this, but I cannot help the way I feel…"

He hesitated, and it was if he was looking deep into her soul.

"I have fallen deeply in love with you. The more I see you, the stronger my feelings become."

His eyes shone as he spoke, but he quickly looked down, instantly regretting his true words. He had desperately tried to keep his feelings from her, but his heart had reached his lips before his brain had time to control it. The same passionate feelings erupted inside her. She pulled his chin up to her face and kissed him.

"I-I think I am falling in love with you too Panos. I too cannot hide my feelings. I have tried, believe me I have, but I am fighting a losing battle. I know I will probably regret this, but I have decided to give in to my heart." *That's it*," she thought. *I have said it. There is no going back now.*

He searched her face for some sign of a joke, and his heart skipped a beat when he realised, she was being serious. Unable to stop himself, he ran from behind the bar and picked her up. He held her tight and his joy spewed over as he spun her around laughing. His laugh was contagious, and she laughed uncontrollably. They were both unaware that they had caught everyone's attention, and the poolside fell silent. They kissed as they rotated, caught up in each other's arms. Then they were stopped in their tracks as the sound of cheering became evident. Still holding her, Panos became aware the cheering was aimed at them, and a feeling of embarrassment swept over him. He put her down gently and turned to the onlookers with a bow. Danielle was now laughing out loud trying to cover up her humility. Laughter erupted, and clapping followed it, until their audience soon dispersed and carried on with what they were doing.

He looked at Danielle as tears of joy and embarrassment flowed down her cheeks. "I love you, I love you, I love you," he said, enjoying the freedom of being able to say these words, and kissed her. All their barriers were down; they wanted to spend all their time together and make the most of the precious time that was left. They spent the rest of the afternoon talking and laughing. Considering they came from two different cultures they found they shared the same sense of humour. He held her at every opportunity and was overjoyed with the new-found freedom he displayed. The earlier lecture from his father lingered in the back of his mind, but he trusted that his mother could persuade his father to reconsider the opinion he had formed earlier.

Panos's mother finished laying the tables in the restaurant. She could not get Panos out of her thoughts and knew she would have to talk to her husband carefully. She knew him inside out and would have to approach the situation with kid gloves. She loved her husband very much and was proud of him for the life he had built for her and her son's, but she knew how stubborn he could be when he put his mind to it.

She was aware he was in his office looking through the books, so decided now was a good opportunity to speak to him. She finished her chores and walked into the kitchen to make him something to eat. She made him a sandwich and a cup of coffee and then made her way to the office. She gently knocked on the door and walked into the large room. He was sitting at his desk talking on the phone, and she placed his sandwich down. His eyes stayed fixed on the figures in front of him, not acknowledging his wife's presence. She waited patiently for him to finish his conversation and looked out of the window. As she stared at the sparkling blue sea she thought even after all these years the view still took her breath away. She sighed at its magnificence and turned her attention back to her husband. His conversation had come to an end and he was tucking into his sandwich.

"Thank you, this is good. What have I done to deserve this?" He took another bite and sipped his coffee. She walked behind him and began to rub his shoulders.

"Ah, that feels nice," he said, as she kissed his head. "Shouldn't you be downstairs doing something?" he asked, suspicious of his wife's behaviour towards him. He finished his sandwich and picked up a pen.

"Yes, but it can wait. Can I talk to you please?" she asked him. "It will not take long."

He proceeded to carry on with his work half-heartedly listening to her. "Why are you being so hard on Panos? He seems to have found some happiness at last. He has not stopped smiling since he met Danielle."

His ears pricked up when she mentioned their son, and winced as she said Danielle's name, provoking a stern expression.

I was right to get suspicious, he thought. He turned to look at her, his eyes boring into hers, but this harsh look did not deter her, and she continued.

"I think you are being very unfair to the boy, he seems to care about Danielle very much. After the pain he has endured, I think he deserves this little bit of happiness. He likes her very much, and I can see she is a lovely girl," she said in a softly spoken voice. Her eyes searched his for a glimmer of hope, looking for the sensitive husband that she knew existed deep down inside.

"How can he really like her?" he said laughing sarcastically. "He has only just met her. That's ridiculous, woman. He cannot afford to fall in love with her, in case you haven't noticed, she is English! It is not right. I will never let that happen," he said, his face becoming red with rage.

"I know where she comes from," she said, choosing to ignore his sarcasm. "But can't you just let him make the most of the time that's left with her. She is going back to England in a few days and then things will get back to normal. You have to let him do things his own way. He is a grown man and he has to make his own mistakes." Her tone did not change as she spoke.

He thought about his son and how proud he usually made him feel. The possibility of this affair fizzling out was high, in fact he knew it was an inevitable outcome, and this pleased him. He had noticed his son was happier since the girl had been there, but this did not make him want to make himself, like her.

"I do not approve of this situation, and I will have nothing to do with her, but I will turn a blind eye for now. I do love my son and want only the best for him. You must tell him it must stop as soon as she leaves the hotel to go home," he continued. "There are plenty of beautiful Greek girls he can choose from. He must not disgrace his family, nor will I allow him to take his heritage for granted. Now I must work and so must you," he said dismissing his wife as he turned back to his duties. She kissed her husband's head and walked out of the room.

She knew in the long term the affair had no future, but she just wanted Panos to realise he could love again, and Danielle could be holding the key to open his heart. She realised he had to find a Greek girl and settle down, but she found herself thinking they did make a lovely couple. For some strange reason she liked her, but even she knew Panos could not fight against his Greek family values, which were engrained into his soul.

CHAPTER

FIFTEEN

MATT TOOK A SLOW WALK INTO town and soon found himself at the top of the high street. He felt a lot better now as the walk had done him the world of good. He quickly put Danielle and Panos to the back of his mind, and all he could think of was food. His stomach was being stung by hunger pangs and he could no longer ignore the need for something to eat. He recognised the sound of familiar English music coming from a bar he had not seen before, and read the big sign outside advertising food, so decided to go in. When he neared the building, the echo of a familiar laugh could be heard over the music.

Mick was propping up the bar and was intrigued by this young Greek barmaid. He had found out her name was Demi and she had come over from the mainland looking for work. The owner knew her family and he had offered her a job and a place to stay. Mick sat there mesmerised by her conversation. He had lost count of how many beers he had drunk, but knew by the unsteadiness of his balance as he got up to use the toilet, that he had had quite a few. The nervousness and the shaking had left him as a result, and now he felt totally at ease talking to Demi. He felt there was a bond forming between them as they swapped details of their lives.

I think she likes me, he convinced himself, realising he felt very happy. A computer was behind the bar which had a built-in juke box, and he was content listening to the tunes he requested. To his surprise she knew the songs well and they both sung along to the words. He found she understood him well and he could easily make her laugh. He loved to make people laugh and knew he had a talent for it. Seeing her face light up made him feel very good about himself, a feeling he had not known in a long time.

Demi was pouring him another beer, when she looked towards the door. Mick's eyes followed hers and he soon made out the figure walking towards him.

Matt walked into the bar and was pleased to see his best friend sitting there. He hadn't realised how alone he had felt earlier so was relieved to see a friendly face.

"Matt, I am so pleased to see you," said Mick getting up and putting his arm around his shoulders.

"What are you having mate?" he asked patting his friend's back.

"I will have one of the same," Matt replied, pointing at the beer that was put down in front of Mick.

"Could I also have a sandwich? I am starving." Demi obliged and after giving him his drink she went out to the kitchen.

"Isn't she gorgeous, Matt? I think I've pulled here," said Mick proudly.

He continued to tell him about Demi and by the way he talked, she was the best thing since sliced bread. Matt felt a pang of jealousy as he listened to his best friend, and with no control of his thoughts, Danielle became immersed in his mind. Mick sensed something was wrong so stopped in mid-sentence.

"Are you alright mate? You look like you have lost fifty quid and found a pound."

Matt had to laugh at Mick's blatancy. Then he aired his thoughts about Danielle and Panos. Mick listened intently and could not help feeling a little bit guilty. He loved Matt like a brother and cared a lot for him. He also liked Panos and felt slightly responsible for what happened between him and Danielle.

"So, I have decided to forget about her," he continued.

"As far as I am concerned, he can have her, she is not worth the hassle." His words were genuine as he took a big swig of his beer.

"That's the way forward mate. Just let them get on with it. You never know Demi might have a friend."

They both laughed just as Demi returned with a plate full of sandwiches, putting them down in front of Matt.

"Demi," Mick said eyeing up the food. "Can I ask you something?"

A pattern developed for the following days. Danielle spent most of her time with Panos and shared his bed at night. His mother had told him what his father had said, and he was relieved he could now relax and enjoy being with Danielle. He tried his best to stay out of his father's way when he was with her, and just concentrated on making her happy.

Mick and Matt spent most of their days at the bar with Demi when she was working, and the rest of the time at the beach. Matt started to enjoy himself again and loved being around Mick, who seemed to have the knack of making him forget all about his worries as he amused him with his humorous nature. The two men still sat down and ate their breakfast with Danielle, which Matt found very hard at first. The atmosphere between them lay thick in the air, making them feel uncomfortable around each other and Mick was the one to do all the talking. But this did not last for long, much to Mick's relief, as it was hard work trying to keep the peace.

The day of their departure was near, and no one mentioned that in two days they would be going home. Matt was the only one who was looking forward to it and could not wait to be on home ground again. He secretly regretted what had happened between him and Danielle, but it made him look at his life from a different perspective. The strength he found from within made him more determined to make something of his life. He thought about her and missed the friendship they had lost over the past days. At least when they got home, they should be able to salvage some of what they used to have. It would never be the same, but he still wanted to be a part of her children's life. He had done a lot of soul searching over the past few days, and he found he had finally got his head around the situation. He did not blame her anymore and understood why she had fallen for this charming Greek man, who had obviously swept her off her feet. He was simply jealous she did not want to be with him, and his pride had been badly dented. He still found it hard to talk to her when Panos was around, but he knew that back on English soil she would be different.

Mick loved being around Demi and spent all the time he

could with her. Since he met her, he hardly thought about Tracey. He wanted to push their friendship and take her out, but he did not have the nerve. Demi had never mentioned a boyfriend and he could kick himself for losing the courage to ask. Even if nothing did happen between them, he would have great pleasure in telling his estranged wife about his Greek girlfriend, even if he was stretching the truth slightly. He would show her he still had it with the ladies and did not need her anymore.

Danielle's heart was beginning to ache as the final day in Skiathos loomed. It had seemed like she had been there forever, and she was enjoying every minute spent with Panos. He treated her like a queen; he was always complimenting her, taking every opportunity to touch her. He was so romantic, and she thought she could easily get used to being treated this way. No man had ever made her feel so special and so wanted, and a pain flipped her heart when she thought about the dreaded day she would be going home. She knew she had to be realistic and convince herself she was able to leave the man of her dreams.

She had spoken to her children on the phone and she knew by the excitement in their voices that they could not wait for their mother's return. She was filled with mixed emotions; she missed being with her children and could not wait to see them, but she felt so strongly for Panos and knew it would be hard to get back to normality. She was aware there was no future for them and once back at home she could get on with her life. She had experienced a slice of pure happiness whilst being with him, and he would always be in her memories. Although it was a struggle, she managed to convince herself she was strong enough, to leave all this behind. She was sure she was prepared to go back to her world. She put all of these feelings aside for the time being, as she decided to treasure every moment left with him.

The morning before their departure Danielle was woken up by Panos gently stroking her hair. He had been awake for a while and just watched his beautiful Danielle sleeping. She looked so peaceful lying there, and he wondered if he would ever be graced by such a special lady again. He found it hard to imagine her not being there beside him. A deep sadness consumed him when his thoughts wandered to that day, and a single tear formed in the corner of his eyes. The pain of losing her tugged at his heart as he stroked her soft auburn hair. He looked up and down her luscious body and he could not believe he hadn't made love to this adorable lady. He so wanted to, but it wasn't the most important thing on his mind. He just wanted to make her happy and feel like the woman she deserved to be. He could not take is eyes off her and continued to stroke her hair.

He did understand his father's reasoning and had always believed in keeping in his own culture, but that was before Danielle had stepped into his life and he could have cursed his heritage. The past two weeks had taken him completely by surprise and he wouldn't have wanted it to be any different. This lady in his reach had brought a new meaning to his life, and for that he would be eternally grateful. He thought that after the pain Sophia had caused him, he would never be able to love again, but he was wrong. Danielle made him feel worthy again, a piece of himself he thought Sophia had taken away. He closed his eyes as he breathed in this liberating moment. He knew that he would never, forget this lovely lady.

As Danielle opened her eyes, he opened his and smiled lovingly at her. She returned the gesture, and her heart sank when she realised, she only had one night left in this man's arms. He began to stroke her forehead and kissed her passionately on the mouth.

"We must not be sad," he said thoughtfully, recognising her pain.

"I am so grateful you have come into my life." He gently caressed her golden body loving the silky feeling of her skin beneath his fingertips.

The need for words escaped from the room as they held each other tight. Danielle could feel the tears sting the back of her eyes and it took all her strength not to let them fall.

I don't want to go home, she thought but knew fate was out of their hands. This was unfortunately the way it had to be.

CHAPTER

SIXTEEN

PANOS SOON LEFT TO GO TO work and when he walked out of the room a single tear rolled down Danielle's face. She took a deep breath and swallowed the pain that was desperately trying to escape. She had felt so happy, but now she felt so sad, going from one extreme to the other in a matter of minutes. She decided to take her mind off things and got into the shower. The water rinsed over her, she grabbed the shower gel and began to wash herself. As she touched her silky-smooth skin, she closed her eyes and imagined his hands caressing her body. She shuddered as the image conjured up deep feelings of desire and she yearned for his touch. She wondered what it would be like making love to him, pulling up deep rooted emotions that had long been forgotten. Her body began to quiver as the long-lost feelings began to take her over.

How can he make me feel like this? she thought feeling shame

"I must be strong," she said out loud, quickly dismissing the sensual feelings that had been aroused. She got out of the shower, dried herself, and then got dressed. As it had become her habit to spend the night with Panos in his room, she had moved many of her things there including her suitcase. At first it was mostly because she struggled to sleep with all the snoring that went on between Mick and Matt. As time however became so precious with Panos, it seemed to be the natural thing to do. They cherished every moment together and tried to make the most of what was becoming an intolerable situation.

Desperately trying to pull herself together, she walked downstairs hoping that Mick and Matt were still in the restaurant. She felt relieved to see them sitting down eating their breakfast and planning their last day on the island. They were heading into town and she was pleased because she wanted to go into town to buy some presents. She asked if she could go with them and they agreed it would be OK. They decided to take the next bus down. Panos came out of the kitchen and walked across the room. He smiled at her when he walked by and proceeded to go into the lounge.

"I won't be a minute," she informed the two men, getting up to follow Panos out of the room. He walked behind the bar and could feel her presence behind him. An overwhelming joy consumed him as he turned around and was confronted by her looking stunning, in a white strapless top, and black shorts. His heart melted at the sight of his beautiful Danielle. He took her hand and kissed it, looking deep into her eyes.

"I am going into town with Mick to do some shopping. Where will you be when I get back?" she said kissing him on his lips. Then a look of horror careered across his face. He wanted her to be with him.

"I will take you," he said harshly, not realising his tone. The thought of her being away felt like he had been shot in the heart. His quick reaction startled her.

"I am sorry," he said immediately realising his mistake.

"It's just that I want to spend all of my time with you near me. You can be with them when you are back in England."

His sorrowful eyes pleaded with her to stay with him.

"I have to go into town soon for my father, so you can go then. I was going to ask you to come with me." He looked into her eyes and his heart wanted to explode with the longing he felt for her.

"Please, my beautiful darling. I love you and I cannot bear the thought of you being apart from me. It is bad enough I have to let you go tomorrow, but that I cannot change. I want to be able to touch you, to feel you near me, to smell you."

No one had ever spoken to her like that, and Danielle could feel herself weakening as he said those tender loving words. She felt he could have easily reduced her to tears. She wanted to be with him too, she could not deny that and wanted everything he suggested. His sudden outburst persuaded her to stay with him, not that she needed much persuading.

"OK, I will come with you," she replied, as a big smile appeared across her face. "You are right…" she hesitated, looking deep into his eyes. "I am going to really miss you." Then he quickly put his finger to her lips.

"Shush, we will face tomorrow when you get on the plane. Today we will be happy," he said, mimicking a bad English accent causing her to laugh.

"You make a bad English man, but you make a brilliant Greek," she teased as she continued kissing him firmly on the lips.

Oh, if only things were different, she thought, completely captivated by this man.

Mick walked out of the restaurant, followed closely by Matt, who had noticed Panos holding Danielle's hand, and carried on walking out of the hotel. Mick headed towards the bar.

"I will meet you at the bus," Mick shouted to Matt.

"Panos my friend, how are you on this fine day?" he asked, standing next to Danielle.

"I feel I am going to have a good day today," Mick continued, not letting Panos answer his question.

"I am going to spend the day with Demi. I know she will not be able to resist my English charm. I can outrun you Greeks by a mile." He felt surprisingly happy considering it was their last day. He had a gut feeling that today would be the day of hot passion with the gorgeous Demi. *What a way to end my holiday,* he thought.

"Are you ready then Dan?" he asked already knowing what her answer would be.

"I am going to go into town with Panos. We want to spend as much time together as we can, sorry mate." Her words filled Panos with pride.

Mick put his fingers in his mouth pretending to be sick, and Danielle gently slapped him across the back.

"Easy Bert, there is no need for that you, big bully!" he said, nearly throwing himself to the ground.

"OK then. You two love birds have a good day. I know I will," he said, walking out of the hotel.

"Michael is a funny man, no?" Panos said laughing. *I am going to miss him too,* he thought.

"We will go out shortly but first I must do something. Do you want a cup of coffee before we go?"

She nodded and watched him make her drink. She felt she was dreaming and the feelings he had induced simply could not be ignored. Once again, she felt in complete awe of this man and could not imagine being without him. She tried to remember how it had got this far but could not place the exact moment she had fallen in love with him. It felt like she had known him all her life. Panos put her coffee down on the bar and kissed her.

"I will not be long, do not go anywhere!"

She shook her head and watched him leave the room. She was the only person in the lounge and it was eerily quiet. Most of the other guests had gone into town and the remainder she guessed, were by the pool. Her eyes scanned the perfect room and she imagined being a part of its perfection.

I could easily get used to this way of life, she thought, letting her mind run away with her wishful thinking.

The beautiful Greek sunshine and the laid-back way of life, sharing it all with the man of my dreams, yes this could be for me.

It definitely was a dream. Her heart suddenly felt like it was made of stone at the realization that her dream would be coming to an end very soon. Her depressing thoughts were interrupted by the sound of footsteps coming towards her and she was pleased to see Panos again. She drank her coffee and the two of them walked hand in hand to the car.

"Where's Dan? Is she not coming?" asked Matt half-heartedly already knowing the answer.

"No Matt, Panos is taking her down there instead. Don't let it bother you, there are plenty more fish in the sea; big Greek beauties," said Mick cupping his hands to his chest. He had organised a big surprise for Matt. He had asked Demi to bring a friend for Matt and she said she had the perfect one for him. It was all arranged that they would all meet at the bar and then take it from there.

For the first time, Matt realized seeing Danielle with Panos hadn't bothered him at all. This made him smile and pleased him. At last, he had felt no pain this time and he liked it.

"What are you talking about Mick?" he asked wondering what he meant by his strange statement. Mick put his finger up to his nose, gently tapping it.

"That is for me to know and for you to find out," he said, grinning from ear to ear. Matt wondered what Mick was up to.

Knowing Mick, I am sure I will soon find out, he thought.

When they got into town the bar was still closed. It didn't open for another half an hour, so they used this time to buy some gifts for their friends back home. Mick got out a list from his wallet. Most of the requests were for cigarettes. The list was quite long, and the names written down made him think of home. He wondered what they were doing in the pub now and whether they missed his jokes and mischief. He wondered whether Stuart had been in telling everyone they had tried to kill him and couldn't help but laugh.

They wouldn't believe him. I still don't believe it, the silly sod, he thought.

Then for the first time in days, he thought about Tracey and wondered what she was doing and whether she missed him. Suddenly he had an overpowering need for a beer. "I don't care what she thinks," he reassured himself. "I am on a promise tonight. Come on Matt, let's hurry up and get this shopping out of the way, I am in need of a swift half," Mick said enthusiastically.

"A swift half!" Matt stated, nearly choking on his words. "You wouldn't know what a half pint glass looked like. I have heard it all now Mick, you don't do anything by half."

Mick felt hurt by his friends comment but played the game.

I certainly won't be tonight. I have a cunning plan, he thought.

Panos parked at the top of the high street. They both stepped out of the car and the road was teeming with happy holidaymakers. The island was a lot busier now and Danielle noticed quite a few of the foreigners were still looking very white in colour. She felt a pang of jealousy and envied the fact they were about to start their holiday when hers was just about to come to an end.

Panos told her he needed to go to the bank and then she could buy what she needed. He held her hand and pulled her close to his side as they walked through the crowds of people. This time, when they passed the shops, only a few shop owners greeted him by waving. Panos was courteous and returned the gesture. They came to a building Danielle presumed was the bank and walked in. The room was quiet. Danielle was relieved by the cool air circulating, cutting through the heat like a hot knife through butter.

He walked up to the smartly dressed lady behind the counter, and speaking in Greek, pulled out a bundle of money from his pocket. Danielle's eyes widened as she eyed up what looked like a wad of monopoly money.

There must be thousands of pounds there, she thought.

It wasn't until this point she realised how much money he must be worth. She remembered Mick mentioning he was a millionaire, but she hadn't taken any notice of what he had said at the time.

Panos did not come across as being flash. He was very down to earth, one of the qualities she loved about him. He was always smartly dressed, and she adored him in his uniform. She was taken aback at their first meeting and remembered how handsome he had looked then. She would never have guessed then in a million years that she would fall for him and smiled at the memory. The bank teller continued to count the money, then handed him a piece of paper which he signed. She said something to him and he thanked her, putting another piece of paper in his pocket.

"We can go now," he said smiling as they walked out of the door.

They went into a couple of shops and Danielle became excited about buying gifts for her children. Panos watched her as she eagerly picked out some presents. He was overjoyed by the glowing look on her face as she paid for them. He also felt a twinge of regret because he would never meet her three children, who she obviously adored. He looked at his watch, aware that time was passing, but for once he did not care if he was going to be late getting back to the hotel. It was, after all, the last whole day he would be able to spend with her. If his father was not happy then he had the strength to deal with his wrath.

Danielle was happy with her gifts so walked back over

to Panos. He smiled at her and took her hand in his as they walked out of the shop into the brilliant sunshine. He suggested they stop for a coffee before getting back to the hotel. She nodded in agreement and they went to the nearest Taverna. He pulled out a chair, willing her to sit down, and went in to order their drinks. When she watched him walk over to the bar she took in a deep breath of joy. As he waited for their drinks, he suddenly had an overwhelming need to go and buy something for her. He wanted her to have something to remember him by. He knew exactly what the perfect gift would be. Taking the drinks over to the table he placed them down. He didn't take his seat but kept standing until there was a look of confusion sweep over her face.

"I will not be long my beautiful Danielle. There is something I need to do," he said kissing her on the mouth.

"Do not go anywhere." Then he walked away leaving her wondering what he could possibly need to do, and what he was up to.

Mick was overcome by a sense of relief when he saw the door of the bar open. He rushed in pulling Matt by his arm. He was glad to see Demi cleaning an ashtray and walked over to the bar.

"Good morning, young Demi and how are you today?" he said, grinning from ear to ear.

"Good morning Mick, I am very happy, thank you," she replied, kissing his cheek. He felt his face go bright red, taken aback by her kind gesture. He quickly looked to Matt for an approving response, but he was busy looking at the drinks menu, totally unaware of the kiss she had given him. Mick's heart beat with regret as his moment of pride was lost.

"Can we have two beers please me lovely?" Mick asked Demi.

She nodded and started to pour the drinks. He noticed Matt was still engrossed with the menu, so he touched her arm.

"Is your friend going to be joining us?" he whispered to her, a boyish grin staining his face.

She nodded, putting his drink down in front of him. "She will be here very soon," she whispered touching his arm.

I knew she liked me, he thought, as a wave of expectancy flowed through his body.

Demi was very taken by Mick. She loved him being around while she was working as he always made her laugh. She noticed he was always flashing his money about and guessed he must have a lot of it. Even though he was old enough to be her father, she was aware she couldn't help flirting with him. She knew she was attractive, so set her goal on getting what she could out of him before he went home. She had her eye on a gold chain which was way out of her price range. She instinctively knew by the end of the day she would have persuaded him to buy it for her. She had told her friend Angel about him and they laughed at his expense. She also told her he had a friend, who was also 'loaded' and wanted her to meet him. The two girls smiled at the prospect of letting these two English men spoil them rotten. It was for only one day and they would never have to see them again. Angel was tall and blonde and a complete contrast to Demi. She was up for anything apparently! Demi was sure Matt would like her voluptuous friend, so arranged for her to come down to the bar at lunchtime.

While Demi worked, she listened to the two men talking, keeping a close eye on the door. It was nearly one o'clock. Angel was due to walk in any minute now, and she could not wait to see their faces when they laid their eyes on her sexy friend.

Angel was right on cue, dead on one o'clock. She boldly walked in wearing a tight, black low-cut top revealing her ample breasts, and short pink hot pants showing off her long, tanned legs. She proudly walked up to Demi and kissed her friend on the cheek. Mick took one look at her and spat out a mouthful of his drink.

"Blimey Demi, is that your mate?" he said, wiping the beer off his chin.

"Yes," she answered simply.

"Angel this is Mick, and this is Matt, the two men from England I told you about."

"Boys, this is my good friend Angel."

Mick looked at the blonde girl and his eyes instinctively went down to her chest. He suddenly felt envious that she was there to meet Matt. It was just his luck he had got the busty one.

Matt just stood there with his mouth open at the sight of this curvy girl who shook his hand. She noticed the look in their eyes and smiled to herself. *They will be putty in our hands,* she thought confidently.

The two men simultaneously offered her a drink as they clumsily took out their wallets. Angel said "yes," and Matt was the first to pull out his money and pay for a large vodka and coke. He thought he had won the lottery when she leaned over to him and kissed him on the cheek.

Mick could not help eye up, her toned bottom. With great difficulty he managed to tear his eyes away and rubbed his hands together. "Right, who's up for some music?" he asked giving Demi some money to put on the juke box. She happily obliged, as they shouted out their requests.

Danielle was sitting anxiously waiting for Panos to return. He had been gone for fifteen minutes. She began to panic when the thought of him abandoning her entered her mind. She sipped her coffee and looked around. Everyone seemed to be very happy, talking and laughing amongst themselves. She smiled at a couple who were staring into each other's eyes, holding hands across the table. She felt a pang of resentment and was once again reminded of how little time she had left on the island. She looked at her watch again, agitated by her wait. Eventually to her relief Panos walked in holding what looked like a small bag. He hurried over to her and kissed her on the lips.

"Sorry I took so long my darling," he said panting. He had been rushing, so he sat down to catch his breath.

"Here, this is for you," he said handing her the bag. Her heart stopped as she reluctantly took it. She could feel her face burn with embarrassment; she did not like surprises. She suddenly felt nervous when she opened the bag, reaching in to see what it was. He just looked at her smiling, secretly hoping she would like his present. Slowly she pulled out a small blue box and held it in her hand. She was afraid to open it and just sat there looking at it, her heart beating hard in her chest.

"Go on then Danielle open it," he encouraged her.

She took a deep breath and lifted up the lid and was confronted with a sparkling diamond ring. She thought her heart was going to stop, taken aback by its beauty.

"Well do you like it?" He suddenly felt the blood drain from his face, noticing the expressionless look on her face. "I can take it back if you don't like it…"

"No," she interrupted. "No, it's gorgeous Panos, you shouldn't have," she said completely stunned by his generosity. She took the ring out of the box and laid it in the palm of her hand staring at it.

"I wanted to get you something to remind you of me and our special time together. You are worth it my beautiful lady." He picked the ring up and held her trembling hand. Then he slid it onto her finger; it fitted perfectly. She lifted up her hand and just gazed at the diamond.

"Oh, Panos thank you. Thank you. You are such a lovely man," she said in awe of this generous man. A huge smile erupted across her face and her heart seemed to expand with excitement. He was overcome with joy as pure happiness beamed across her face. She managed to look away from her hand and leant over to kiss him on the mouth.

"Thank you, I will never forget you, never. I love you so much." She kissed him again and his heart melted as he kissed her back.

"I love you too, special lady, from the bottom of my heart," he said reluctantly looking at his watch.

"Now my pretty one, we have to go." He got up and took her hand, walking slowly back to the car. He held her close as they went. His head was held high, proud to show off his lovely English lady, feeling very satisfied with himself.

Mick and Matt had lost all track of time as they talked to Demi and Angel. The drinks were flowing, the songs were playing, and they laughed at Mick's stories from back home. Matt was now feeling very happy; Angel was paying him a lot of attention and his former dented ego was now fully intact again. They had decided when Demi finished work that they would all go somewhere else to eat, and then go to a club.

Mick felt very pleased with himself because Demi was showing a lot of interest in him. He felt confident his earlier intentions had a good chance of becoming a reality. He looked at Matt and felt extremely good about his wise choice of asking Demi to bring a friend along. He hadn't seen Matt enjoy himself so much in a long time, and this made him smile. *This is what a holiday is about,* he thought. *Beer and two gorgeous girls, it doesn't get any better than that.*

Back at the hotel Danielle left Panos in the bar and went up to the room to change into her bikini. Her heart was racing, and her appetite had faded. She kept looking at the ring on her finger and an air of happiness radiated from her. She quickly changed and went down to the pool to be near him. When she neared the pool side, she realised the place was packed with guests. Her heart sank when she looked around at the occupied loungers and envisioned herself having to lie on the floor. She stopped and strained her eyes, and to her relief her usual spot was vacant. She couldn't believe no one had sat there and felt very honoured that they hadn't. She proudly walked over and put her things down. Panos was behind the pool bar serving when she arrived, and his heart seeped out liquid love for her. He called her over to be with him. She obliged, walked over to the bar and everyone she passed greeted her and smiled.

When Panos got back to the hotel, thankfully there was no sign of his father and he was overcome by a great sense of relief. He had expected to have the third degree for being so long and was pleased nothing was going to upset his otherwise perfect day.

He sung as he walked down to the pool and was oblivious

to his observer. His mother had been in the restaurant when her son entered the hotel. By his singing she guessed he was having a good day. She had noticed he was gone for a long time and hoped her husband hadn't. To her delight her husband had been busy in the office. Her son's singing had infectiously made her smile and she was overjoyed to see him so happy. Then she went about her chores, reassured and pleased about her son's cheerful attitude.

Panos and Danielle spent the afternoon absorbed in one another, both interacting with the other guests. Danielle felt totally at home, so when the bar got busy, she helped him serve behind it. Panos noticed the way she related naturally to the thirsty customers and felt a pang of sadness as he imagined her working back in England. She was bubbling over with confidence. The thought of her doing it away from him provoked a disturbing wave of jealousy. He slowly controlled these abnormal feelings as she looked at him and smiled. She looked like she belonged there, and he had to force himself back into reality. He wanted so much for her to stay with him forever but knew it would never be, and once again cursed his heritage. When she finished serving, he asked her about her work, and she took great pleasure in telling him all about her life at the Kings Head.

Panos's father watched Danielle from the window of his office and he was enraged by her conduct behind his bar. He could not wait until tomorrow when she was on the plane and safely out of his hotel. He knew that when she had gone, he was going to have to have a long talk with his eldest son. He needed to persuade him to meet a good Greek girl. He did not want to have to go through this ordeal again. He felt confident that Panos would listen to him and would finally come to his senses. He sat down at his desk, unable to continue to watch his son make a fool out of him. He was glad to get on and finish doing his work.

CHAPTER SEVENTEEN

MICK FELT VERY CONFIDENT AS the alcohol flowed through his veins. Matt was in deep conversation with Angel, so he took Demi's arm and pulled her towards him. He kissed her and let out a sigh of relief when she kissed him back. His head began to whirl as her tongue darted in and out of his mouth. She induced a sudden rush of passion he thought had been lost forever. He came up for air and she walked away, smiling. He picked up his drink and started to gulp it down. His strained heart was beating so fast, he thought it was going to stop any minute! He collected his thoughts and took in deep breaths to control his unusual heart rate. *If she does that to me with a kiss? What is she going to do to me when we have sex? She is going to kill me!* he thought again, wondering whether she was worth it. He calmed himself down and realised he was being silly. Of-course she won't kill me. *When I get her in the sack, I will have her begging me for more*, he reassured himself smirking at the image in his mind.

Demi looked at the clock and was pleased her working day was was at last over. She had hoped Mick would make a move on her and was relieved when he kissed her. Letting him believe she liked him boosted her confidence; everything was going to plan. She looked across the room to Angel, who was resourcefully pulling Matt in to her clutches. She laughed as she imagined chains being tied around his wrists and Angel holding them tight in her hands. She got her bag and told them she was ready to go. They finished off their drinks and followed her out in to the high street. They stood outside, and Mick put his arms around her as they discussed where to go next. Matt's self-confidence was high, so he put his arm around Angel. She took a quick glance at Demi and winked.

"I know a great place. It's a bit expensive but the food there is brilliant. It is on the harbour," she said frankly.

"I don't care about the expense, girls. Money is no object with me around," Mick reassured them. "Let's go."

Demi felt a wave of hope go through her and realised she had done the right thing by kissing Mick. The two couples started to walk towards the harbour, singing at the top of their voices, causing everyone they passed to look at them. Mick and Matt were oblivious to their stares, they were just happy to be with these two gorgeous girls. *Tonight, is going to be a night of love, if it's good enough for Danielle, then it is good enough for me,* thought Matt leaving all of his inhibitions behind him.

They walked along the harbour and the girls led them up an alley to the front steps of a Taverna. Mick suddenly felt familiar in his surroundings, when he remembered being there before with Tracey and Panos.

"I know where we are, I have been here before with Panos

and my..." he stopped mid-sentence and looked at Demi, aware of what he was going to say. "Err... With Panos and my friend," he continued, not wanting to put her off, by admitting he had been there with his wife.

"Yeah Panos's friend Nicos owns this place. He's a good friend of mine, too," he finished. Demi was impressed, he knew one of the wealthiest men on the island, and she could not help smiling to herself. They walked happily up the steps when Mick became aware of the big burly man in a tuxedo standing by the door.

"Blimey he's a lump," he said trying to speak under his breath, not aware it was clearly heard by the giant man. The man put his hand out to stop Mick from entering. Mick couldn't remember Nicos having bouncers before and was surprised he needed one.

"Have you got a reservation, sir?" the man asked calmly, in a deep Greek voice.

"N-no but I know Nicos, he is a friend of mine," Mick stuttered.

The man looked him up and down noting that he was drunk. He had seen men like him before and was under strict instructions not to let the lower class people in, especially if they were drunk. There had been a lot of trouble last year and Nicos was adamant it wouldn't happen again this year. That was why people had to make reservations first.

"I am sorry sir, but no reservation means no entry. Those are the rules," the man said firmly, keeping his hand on Mick's chest. Matt looked at the man's arm across Mick and decided to walk up to him. He was very protective of Mick and had an impulsive urge to punch this man on the nose.

"It's OK, Matt," Mick said calmly, sensing his friend's hostility.

"I will sort this out… I know Nicos, like I said, he is a very good friend of mine. Do you know Panos? He owns the Oasis hotel and he is also my friend." Then Mick became aware of the two girls with him and felt his face go red with embarrassment.

This is not good, he thought.

"I said no reservations no entry." The man raised his voice and was getting rather agitated by this English man. Mick looked through the door and saw Nicos sitting at a table. He began to wave his arms around trying to get his attention, but the man got hold of Mick's arm and forcibly pushed it down.

"Oi mate, get your big filthy hands off him!" shouted Matt, lunging himself at the door man, finding it hard to control his anger.

Nicos was sitting talking to Cassia when he noticed a commotion going on outside and got up to see what was occurring. When he opened the door, he could see his security man was pushing a man down to the ground, while trying to protect himself from a second man who was trying to hit him.

"Hey what is going on?" he shouted, instantly stopping the disturbance.

"M-Michael, is that you?" he said, looking down on the floor.

"H-hello Nicos me ol' mate, is there any chance of a drink?" Mick asked smiling cheekily.

"Yes, yes, of course there is," Nicos replied helping him up from the floor.

"Come inside the first drink is on me." He quickly gave the burly man a distinct look.

"I am so sorry, Michael." he apologised. Mick stood up and walked past the door man smirking.

"Blimey Nicos, your staff are a bit heavy handed. He could have really hurt me," he said brazenly. They all walked in laughing and Demi felt like a big weight had been lifted. She had begun to get quite worried when she saw her gold chain disappear out of her reach. When Mick was trying to get into the Taverna she suddenly had a bad feeling he was just another loser. She thought she could detect one from a mile away because she had met so many on the island, and she could have kicked herself for her misjudgement. She soon felt a wave of relief when Nicos came out and recognised him, and her doubts quickly disappeared from her shallow mind. She felt at ease again, her gold chain back in her reach. She looked at her wrist and imagined it wrapped expensively around it. She put on a self-assured smile and took Mick's hand, walking with her head held high.

Nicos showed the four friends to a table. He told them he would send a waiter over to them shortly and promised to join them as he walked over to the bar. Mick felt sure of himself and puffed up with pride just because he knew this man. The four talked and laughed while waiting for their drinks to arrive.

Panos looked at his watch and noticed it was getting late. To his relief all of the guests had left the poolside and were busy getting ready for the night ahead of them. Danielle helped him clear the bar and he pulled down the shutters. He had enjoyed her working with him immensely and thought they made a good team. It was early evening and he was feeling very hungry. He usually ate with his family but tonight he wanted to be with Danielle. He told her to go up, get ready and meet him in the bar afterwards, because he had something to sort out with his brother. She agreed, and he walked her to the stairs. She kissed him and went upstairs to take a shower. He hated her leaving him and as soon as she got out of his sight, he began to miss her.

For once in his life he hoped the guests would be dining elsewhere tonight so he could take her out to dinner. He wanted to shower her with his love and be able to give her his undivided attention.

He walked into the lounge, which was now empty of guests, and saw Yannis behind the bar. He asked him if he would take care of things there while he took Danielle out to Nicos's. Yannis said he didn't mind as long as they weren't inundated with guests. Panos thanked his brother and shook his hand.

"You are a kind brother and I love you very much," he said, pulling Yannis to him, embracing him. Yannis felt flattered by this unusual show of affection, and secretly thanked Danielle for his brother's loving attitude.

"I love you too brother. It is so nice to see you so happy. It makes my heart smile to see you in such high spirits. Danielle is very good for you," he said, smiling.

"Do not worry Panos, if papa comes in, I will cover for you."

Yannis's heart pumped admiration for his older sibling. He had not seen him act this way since Sophia, and the thought of what she did to him, enraged him. He hoped he would never see her again for the pain she had caused his family. He patted Panos on the back and they walked through to the restaurant where Anna and their mother were busily setting the tables.

An hour later, Danielle emerged back into his sight looking as beautiful as ever. He told her so as he poured her a drink. He gave the full glass to her and kissed her on her alluring lips. His heart pumped with pride when the guests began to trickle into the bar commenting on how lovely she was. Even the women congratulated him on this beautiful lady. They also said they made a good team, which confirmed how he had felt earlier, and this made his smile widen.

He told her he wanted to take her back to Nicos's later for something to eat because he wanted to make her last night there a memorable one. She laughed and explained she would remember the whole two weeks for the rest of her life, then thanked him with a long hard kiss. He smiled and furtively congratulated himself for completing his mission in making her a very happy lady. He became quite busy when the guests wanted drinks before they headed into town. He was pleased no one had asked what was on the menu for dinner.

Lucy and Ben walked in holding hands and Danielle felt a rush of joy because she hadn't spoken to them since her birthday. She took this opportunity to sit down with them while Panos was working, so they could catch up on their adventures of the past few days. Panos felt relieved Danielle had someone to talk to. He hated the thought of her being left on her own. The hotel soon quietened down and the happy holidaymakers, Lucy and Ben, left to take the bus into town.

"I will not be long my love, I am just going to get showered and changed and then we can go out. Yannis will look after you, I will be as quick as I can." He turned to his brother for approval and Yannis nodded. Then he ran up to his room.

As he went up the stairs, he could not believe his fortune, everyone had left the hotel. It had never happened before. He stopped halfway up the stairs, looked up and said, "thank you," into the air. He knew it was fate that had intervened and was overcome with joy that God was on his side.

Danielle felt rather awkward sitting at the bar as Yannis cleaned it. She couldn't stop looking at the gorgeous ring on her finger. She hoped Panos would not be long. The telephone started to ring and Yannis left the bar, walked across the room and answered it.

Right on cue Panos's mother came out of the kitchen into the restaurant, and noticed Danielle sitting at the bar on her own. She stopped and looked at her innocently sitting there and had an overpowering urge to go and talk to her. She acted on impulse and went over to the bar. "Hello, Danielle," she said, approaching the bar making Danielle jump because her thoughts were consumed with Panos.

"I am sorry. I did not mean to startle you," she said softly, sitting down next to her.

"T-that's OK, my mind was elsewhere," Danielle said, beginning to feel very nervous in the presence of this woman.

"Danielle. That is a pretty name for such a pretty lady."

Danielle felt her cheeks blush at her kind words, and guessed it was from her, Panos had inherited his charm. Danielle looked at her and smiled, her eyes sparkling. His mother saw why her son was so smitten by this English lady.

"Thank you," his mother said taking a deep breath.

Danielle looked at her dubiously.

"Thank you for making my son a very happy man. It is so refreshing for me to see him like that. It lifts my heart to see him always smiling and you, my dear, are the one responsible," she continued.

Her words were heart-felt, and she just had to say them. Danielle could not believe what she was hearing, and tears welled up in her eyes. *Now she tells me, and to add salt to the wound, on the eve of me going home*, she thought.

"He has been very hurt in the past and I thought he had given up on love, but since you have come into his life, my old Panos has resurfaced again. Thank you," she said touching Danielle's arm before getting up to walk away. Danielle was left sitting there ready to burst out crying. She swallowed her emotions back down and wondered what had happened to Panos in the past that could have made him so unhappy.

She looked at her hand again, at the splendid ring on her finger, and felt a horrible empty feeling rise in the pit of her stomach. She lit up a cigarette and took a sip of her drink. She felt a heaviness fill her heart, making her want to cry. *Why is this happening to me?* she thought, once again, fighting back her tears. She heard the sound of familiar footsteps as Panos came back into the room. He had never showered and changed so fast. He just wanted to be with his sweetheart, because being without her for ten minutes was beginning to be unbearable.

"There, I said I wouldn't be long," he said excitedly. He kissed her and noticed the solemn look on her face.

"Are you alright, my darling? Has someone upset you?" he asked stroking her face. His heart dropped at the thought of someone causing her pain.

"No, no, it's quite the opposite," she answered. He

questioned her with his eyes.

"I- I was just thinking about tomorrow," she continued her eyes starting to water.

"Like I said before, my beautiful Danielle, we will cross that bridge tomorrow. Now we must be happy and cherish every moment spent together, yes?" he asked, willing for her to smile at him.

"OK Panos I am sorry," she apologised, a smile slowly forming on her face.

"You do not have to be sorry. I feel the same way, but we must be happy." He adoringly stared into her dark green eyes.

"I love you," he continued, kissing her passionately on her mouth.

"Now we must go."

He took her by the hand, said goodbye to Yannis and they walked out of the hotel. Yannis smiled at the handsome couple and hoped Panos would be alright when Danielle went home, back to England.

Mick ordered a bottle of champagne and then said a toast to his new Greek lady friends and they all joined in. Nicos joined them at their table accompanied by Cassia. Cassia had met Demi before and was pleased to see her again because she liked her very much. They all drank plenty of champagne and enjoyed being in each other's company. Angel was all over Matt and kissed him at every opportunity, and he soaked up all the interest she showed him. They all laughed and enjoyed themselves. The thought of them leaving tomorrow was put safely to the back of his mind. The bar was busy and Nicos was so pleased Mick had come to see him. They talked like long lost friends and Mick shared what had happened between him and his wife. Nicos listened carefully and his heart went out to this unfortunate man.

"But all that is in the past my friend," said Mick holding up Demi's hand. "Here is to my future."

He lifted up his glass and took a mouthful of champagne. "Well, for tonight anyway," he whispered to Nicos winking slyly at him. Nicos gestured with his hand to the barman and the familiar music filled the room.

"Oh, I love this song," Angel said, silently willing Demi to get up and dance with her. Demi obliged and pulled Cassia up also. The three girls started to move on the small dance floor. Matt managed to take his eyes off Angel for a second and looked over to Mick.

"Thanks mate, you are a diamond," he said to him lifting up his glass.

He watched Angel as she gyrated provocatively. She professionally moved her sexy body, dancing in time with the music and Matt had a sneaky feeling his night was going to end very well.

"You are so welcome, me ol' pal, you are so very welcome," Mick said grinning, drinking down the rest of his drink.

I like it here, he thought, as he watched Angel and Demi dance. They were doing it so provocatively he thought he was going to witness a girl on girl any minute. He felt a stirring in his loins as the treat conjured up a vision of them in his mind. *If Tracey could see me now,* he thought smiling to himself.

Nicos was unaware of the floor show and went over to the bar to get another round of drinks. He turned around as the song finished just as the girls sat down. He felt unusually happy tonight. Putting his hand in his pocket he felt the little box as euphoria rushed though him. He tried his best to contain his excitement because he did not want to spoil the surprise. He knew Panos was on his way with Danielle, and he wanted his good friend to be there when he dropped the bombshell. He looked at his watch, secretly hurrying his future best man along. He smiled when right on cue Panos and Danielle walked up the steps. Panos shook the burly tuxedoed man's hand and proceeded to walk in.

Danielle felt like royalty when she was with Panos; wherever he went he had everyone's attention. This made her heart jump with joy, loving him more. They walked into the bar and were met by Nicos, who was waiting for them. The two men embraced and Nicos took Danielle's hand, gently kissing it.

"Welcome you two handsome people, come and join us."

Panos smiled at his friend's cheerful face and was glad he was not the only one who was overcome with joy. He detected a twinkle in Nicos's eyes that he had not seen before, and he wondered what was going on in his friend's mind. Nicos had not told anyone about his intended proposal and was very proud of himself for keeping such a big secret. He could not wait to see the look on Cassia's face when he gave her the ring. He knew they had not been seeing each other for long but believed she was the right girl for him. Nicos led them over to the table, and Panos and Danielle were surprised to see Mick and Matt sitting there.

Danielle was more than surprised when she saw a blond girl with her tongue down Matt's throat that she nearly walked into the chair. She also noticed a very young, dark haired girl rubbing Mick's leg up and down. The two girls looked very drunk and she wondered what had been going on. *Ha! This is what happens when you leave two rampant forty-year olds, to fend for themselves,* she thought laughing to herself.

"Ah Danielle," Mick said getting up. "Welcome to the party… This is Demi, you know the girl I mentioned from the bar... I think I am in love." He took hold of Demi's hand and kissed it. Danielle nodded slightly at the girl and turned her attention to Matt.

"And who is that attached to your face Matt?" she asked laughing as he pushed Angel away just for a minute.

"Oh, hello Dan, this is Angel my new friend. Angel, this is Danielle, my old friend," he said laughing, wiping his mouth. Danielle did not like the look in her eyes as Angel gave her a self-satisfied look and carried on kissing him. She felt something was not right and took an instant disliking to her. She soon forgot these thoughts when Panos pulled out a chair and she sat down. He sat next to her and felt happy that Matt had found such a charming little girl. Angel was now sitting on Matt's lap, running her fingers through his greying hair. Panos simply laughed and looked at his sophisticated Danielle and felt proud to have met such a classy lady. Then he leant over to her and kissed her on her cheek.

"I love you," he whispered in her ear. Her whole body shook inside as he said these loving words.

"I love you too, Panos," she said, kissing him back.

Cassia watched the couple and thought she was going to be sick. Then Nicos stole her attention by handing her a fresh glass of champagne. He proceeded to get down on one knee and took hold of her left hand. Cassia blushed at his unprovoked gesture. She noticed the music had stopped and everyone was looking at her. She was lost for words as he put his hand in his pocket and pulled out the small box.

"Cassia," he hesitated, getting the large diamond solitaire ring out of the box.

"Cassia, I know we have only known each other for a short while, but I love you very much... So, will you marry me?" He looked deep into her brown eyes, waiting for her reply as he put the ring on her finger. Cassia looked at the ring and then at Nicos in a daze. The room had gone deadly silent. Everyone was eagerly waiting for her answer. The corners of her mouth lifted, and she began to nod her head slightly, completely thrown by Nicos's proposal.

"Y-yes Nicos, yes, I would love to marry you," she said, as a big smile erupted across her face. Nicos got up and pulled her into his arms. Then he kissed her and the whole room exploded with cheering and clapping.

"This calls for a celebration!" Panos said getting up to raise his glass. "Here is to Nicos and his future wife, Cassia." Everyone followed suit picking up their glasses to toast the happy couple.

Panos had no idea Nicos was going to ask Cassia to marry him. His heart filled with pride when he saw the sheer look of joy dominate his friend's face. He went over to embrace Nicos and noticed the tears in his eyes.

"I am sure you will be very happy my friend, Cassia is a lovely girl."

Panos's words were genuine and he kissed Cassia on the cheek.

Danielle looked down at her new ring. She secretly wished it was an engagement ring on her hand and could not help but feel a little bit envious of Cassia. For a split second, she wished she was Greek too as she eyed up her own diamond.

Matt looked at her and wondered what she was looking at, then saw the sparkling diamond that was a new addition to her jewellery collection.

"Dan is that a new ring on your finger?" he said loudly, rubbing Angel's long leg.

"No, no, Matt it isn't." She wasn't aware he had been looking at her, so quickly hid her hand. She did not want to steal Cassia's lime light so continued to shake her head. Panos noticed her sensitivity and smiled. *That is why I love her so much,* he thought and kissed her.

They all sat at the table and shared their opinions on weddings, and Cassia welcomed the attention she was getting. As Danielle spoke to her, Cassia realised she was a sweet lady. She felt a twinge of regret for the way she had been with her the other day. She did not know if it was due to the excitement or the champagne, but she quickly grew to like this English girl. She had to admit she and Panos did look good together.

Demi and Angel got up to dance and got lost in the music, gyrating to the song. Danielle looked at her two pathetic friends. They were watching the girls dance and she laughed. She thought any minute now they would be drooling all over the floor.

Panos took no notice of the two girls, who were dancing like tarts. He only had eyes for Danielle and smiled to himself. They were the sort of girls he would usually end up in bed with and cringed at the thought. He had now been spoiled by the most beautiful woman in the world and could never go back to that. He held Danielle's hand and fondled her ring. Danielle felt extremely happy. Then she suddenly felt a need to go to the toilet, so made her excuses and went to find the ladies. When she closed the door to the cubicle, she heard giggling. The door to the main toilet opened and she heard two female voices. She instinctively knew who they belonged to but ignored the girlish laughter and went about her business.

"That Mick I've got him eating out of my hand," one of the voices said laughing. Danielle's ears pricked up at the mention of Mick's name.

"Did you see all the money he had? It will be all mine tonight, and his Rolex watch," Demi laughed. "That stupid English bastard, as if I would really fancy an old man like that."

Danielle kept quiet, trying her hardest to stop the rage she felt, from bubbling over.

"And that Matt," said Angel sniggering as she joined in. "He is fat and ugly and so disgustingly drunk. He deserves to be robbed."

Danielle could not believe what she was hearing and could feel her face redden with anger as she listened to them bad mouthing her close friends. She froze on the spot and clenched her fists tight together.

"They are just stupid fools and we should get everything out of them that we can. Demi girl, you have an eye for suckers I give you that." Then they both burst out laughing.

Danielle knew she had a bad feeling when she met Angel and her female intuition had been right. She had to do something to protect her friends before it was too late! She had to think fast on her feet.

Should I tell Matt what I heard? she pondered.

But would he believe me? Right, that's it. I will have to say something to these girls myself!

She swung open the toilet door. Both girls were looking in the mirror, touching up their lipstick when Danielle confronted them. Their laughter soon stopped, and Danielle stood there staring at them, feeling furious! "So, you two slappers think you can take advantage of my two friends, do you?" she asked glaring at them and putting her hands on her hips. She eyed them up and down, feeling disgusted at being in the same room as them.

"I heard everything you said, and you are both a disgrace to the female race. You will have to get through me first and I warn you that will not be easy!"

Demi dropped her lipstick on the floor and as she bent down to pick it up Danielle noticed her hand was trembling. She acted on impulse and quickly put her foot on Demi's hand.

"If I were you lady, I would get my arse out of Nicos's and go home to mummy and daddy." She pushed her foot down harder then released it, and Demi picked up her lipstick and aimlessly put it in her bag.

"I am warning you. If you don't, I will go out there and tell them what I heard. Then you will have to deal with them yourselves," Danielle said her eyes still blazing. They quickly rushed out of the door, frightened at what she would do to them. Danielle followed close behind them just to make sure they left the Taverna. They did not even look over to the table as they pushed through the busy crowd at the bar. They left the building, and she watched them leave. She let out a sigh of relief because neither Matt nor Mick had seen them go.

She composed herself by taking in a deep breath and was

relieved to find her anger subsided as quickly as it had risen. She shook her head in disbelief walking back over to Panos and sat down.

"Are you alright, my darling?" he asked, taking her hand. He could feel it shaking.

"Yes Panos, I am fine. I just had to sort out something dirty," she replied kissing him on the mouth. "Now, where were we?" she asked.

She looked over at Mick and his eyes were searching the room for his play mate. Confusion swept over his face because Demi was nowhere to be seen, and he could not see Angel either.

"I think I just saw them leave Mick, they did rush out a bit hastily," she told him.

He will thank me in the morning, she thought to herself.

Mick was baffled so he got up and looked around the bar. Matt was very drunk and was singing at the top of his voice. Eventually Mick sat down and scratched his head feeling very confused.

"Oh well, best I have another drink then," he said, noticing his empty glass and a very pretty girl at the bar, so he went over to get himself a beer. Danielle laughed at Mick's flippancy.

They were right about one thing, they are fools… Men, what are they like? she thought.

They ate their food and after an hour Panos said they had better get back to the hotel. Danielle nodded, and they got up to say goodbye. She felt slightly guilty about leaving Matt and Mick but, was reassured when Nicos said he would make sure they got back safely.

They said their goodbyes and Nicos hugged Danielle, thanking her for coming and hoping she had a good trip home. She had forgotten that this time tomorrow she would be in her own house, and a pang of grief pricked her heart. She was quickly brought back to reality, and she did not like it. Nicos pulled Panos to him, embraced him and whispered he was there if he needed him. Panos simply nodded as the aroused bitter reminder penetrated his heart. He found it hard to imagine her not being there with him again. They both put on a brave face and walked out to the car.

Panos opened the door, but before she could go in, he pulled her close to him and kissed her. The same desperate feeling of wanting each other escaped through their lips as they held each other tight. They finally let go of one another and got in the car in silence, frightened to say anything. The music played as they travelled up to the hotel, and Panos found it difficult to sing to her. Danielle looked out into the darkness, aware of the sadness that filled the car, her heart heavy with sorrow. She thought about her home and being on her own again. He sensed her heartache and felt exactly the same way as he also thought about being alone again. He put his hand on her leg and started to gently stroke it. Tears began to form in his eyes. *If only things were different,* he thought.

All the strength to face their fears of what the following day would bring, had escaped them, as the realisation of their inevitable separation became an unwelcome reality. Momentarily caught up in their own thoughts, both fought the rising panic that threatened to overwhelm them in a sea of raw excruciating pain and utter helplessness. They reached the hotel and he stopped the car. He took the keys out but did not move. Instead he sighed heavily as he turned to look at her. Even though he could see the pain of leaving him in her eyes, she still looked absolutely stunning.

He took her hand, looked down at the ring on her finger and touched it. "I wish this was an engagement ring," he said softly. There is nothing more I would ever want than to be married to you my beautiful Danielle. I do love you, my heart tells me so and I will never forget you. Since you have been here you have made me feel complete, and when you go you will take a piece of me with you!"

He looked down aware of the emotions he had let go and sighed as his feelings escaped from his heart straight into hers. She put her hand under his chin lifted up his face and kissed him.

"I love you," she said, as those fateful desires rose up and overcame them.

"I love you too my darling," he responded fighting back the dormant tears.

They smiled at each other and got out of the car and walked up to the entrance of the hotel. As they went in, they were met by silence. He felt a wave of relief that no one was around.

"Come with me out onto the terrace," he said quietly.

She did not argue as he led her out through the French windows. There was a calm feel in the air and the warm atmospheric night enveloped them. He walked over to the edge and looked out across the sea. The moon was full, and it hung perfectly in the sky, radiating a heavenly power that stole Danielle's heart. She had never witnessed such a beautiful sight before and she thought it would swallow up the sky. They stood there mesmerised by its authority, and she thought if she put her hand out, she would be able to touch it, it was so big and imposing.

"I think God has brought you to me," he said suddenly in awe of its simplicity, his eyes reflecting its supremacy.

She was lost for words. He had not spoken about God before. She looked up into the heavens and sighed. She found his explanation hard to believe, because she was not a religious person.

"Yes, that has to be it. Otherwise, why are you here and why have you had such an effect on me. That must be what has happened," he said, his eyes still distracted by the moon's magnificence.

"But if that's so, why would he bring me here to find you and let me leave you?" She could not believe what she was saying; it was as if she was agreeing that God was real.

"I do not know the answer to that Danielle, but it is the only thing that makes sense to me." He had tried reasoning with his own logic but had come to no other conclusion. He had to make sense of it somehow.

"I thank him every day for bringing you here my darling."

He turned to her and smiled. "You are a gift from heaven and you will always be in here, locked away for me to remember," he said pointing to his chest, his voice thick with emotion. "I will never forget you." He shyly looked away, aware of tears stinging his eyes.

His words rolled around inside her head. They were caught up in silence. Danielle tried to reason with her own heart but to no avail. "When you are gone, I will look at this moon every night and I'll think of you, and I'll know somewhere in the world you will be looking at it, and you will think of me. I know this will bring me some comfort in the pain of losing you."

His heartfelt words shot into her hurting heart and she realised she would never meet a man like him again. He was right when he had said that Greek men were romantics. She had never met such a loving, kind man who made her feel so special.

"Thank you Panos, for showing me that I am worth loving, and showing me that not all men are the same. You are a wonderful man and I am so grateful to have met you."

Her love induced words made his heart pump so much love for her, he thought it would burst and all of his unexplained words would uncontrollably spill out. He put his arm around her and pulled her close to him. They looked out into the night sky, both consumed with the same thought, that of her leaving. She rested her head on his shoulder and breathed in this moment, capturing it in her heart forever. "Shall we go to bed my darling, it is late. I want to hold you in my arms for one more night and feel your body against mine. I will not sleep as I treasure every moment with you, my beautiful lady."

"I would like that Panos very much. I love you." She spoke softly, and the words rolled off her tongue.

He took her by the hand and they walked up to his room. When they came to the door of his room, he told her to shut her eyes. Suddenly she felt nervous when he opened the door, and blindly walked her over the threshold. She could hear him close the door behind her. When he gave her permission to open them, she gasped as she looked around. Held back tears began to fall as tiny candles flickered around the room, and there was a big bunch of flowers neatly placed in a vase on the table. He smiled proudly as she turned around and flung her arms around him, kissing him passionately on his lips.

Panos wiped away her tears with his kisses and picked her up. He took her over to the bed, still kissing her and laid her down. Mixed emotions swam around in his head as he controlled this sudden urge to make love to her. He was confused as to what to do, staring at her beautiful face. He mouthed those three loving words and she smiled, kissed him and held him tight. All her need to control the situation left her as she gently nodded her approval that he should carry on. Then she put her hands up behind her head and immersed herself in his caress. Hidden feelings and emotions were lost into the night as they made love in the candle light, unable to control the feelings that filled their hearts.

Nicos called Mick and Matt a taxi because he felt it was now time for them to go back to the hotel. He thanked Mick for a lovely evening and embraced him. "It was so good to see you Michael. Make sure you come and see us again if you come back to the island," he said patting him on the back. "And make sure your friend Matt, is OK." Mick reassured him he would on both counts and led a rather drunk Matt out to the road. He was also feeling drunk and they both fell into the taxi laughing. He felt a pang of regret that Demi had gone so soon, but he did get the phone number from the girl at the bar, whose name he could not for the life of him remember. A sudden wave of sadness washed over him when he thought about his flight home to England. *I'm going to miss everyone here. They are such a great bunch of people,* he thought.

He looked at his watch and realised how late it was, and hoped that someone would still be up to let them in. Their flight was at one o'clock, so he relished the thought of getting into his bed, even if it was only for a few hours. They pulled up to the hotel and were relieved to find the door was still unlocked. Stumbling into their room, they fell onto their beds and still in their clothes drifted off to sleep for the last time in Skiathos.

Panos lay next to Danielle stroking her face. Making love to her was even more intense than he had imagined, and he loved the exhilarating way she made him feel. She had completely stolen his heart and he wanted to hold on to this feeling for as long as he could. He took a long look at her then closed his eyes. She watched him and wondered what he was doing. His eyes were shut for ages and he was still stroking her face. Panos opened his eyes, unaware she was looking at him, and saw the strange look on her face.

"Do not look so worried pretty lady. I am taking a picture of you in my mind to keep." He laughed at this cheesy comment. She kissed him and once again they got lost in each other.

CHAPTER

EIGHTEEN

MICK WOKE UP TO A COCKEREL crowing outside and had an overwhelming urge to throw something at it. He soon thought better of it when the prospect of being put away for animal cruelty came into his mind. He sat up and touched his head, which was throbbing. He looked over at Matt, who was snoring very loudly.

"I bet I could get away with throwing something at him," he said under his breath. Then he scanned the room for the vodka bottle and found it was empty. His heart dropped to his stomach when he thought about the long wait he had to endure until his next drink.

He took his mind off his craving by reminiscing back over the past two weeks and was pleased it certainly hadn't been boring. He looked over to Danielle's empty bed and smiled.

She undoubtedly was the one who has had the best time, he thought. He wondered if two people could fall in love so quickly. It had taken him months to fall for Tracey. *Boy, did I regret that decision,* he thought.

Matt began to stir as he got up to take a shower. "Oh, my head hurts," complained Matt waking up with a severe hangover. He heard the shower and presumed Mick was in the bathroom.

"Mick what happened last night?" asked Matt. "It's all a blur," he admitted trying desperately to retrace his thoughts, to the previous night. He remembered being in the bar with Angel and then going to Nicos's. He had a vague memory of Nicos asking his girlfriend to marry him, and then his mind went blank. He did remember Angel being all over him, and had half expected her to be with him when he woke up. *This isn't right, its usually Mick who has the blackouts,* he thought.

"What happened to the girls, Mick?" he shouted and winced because it hurt his throbbing head.

Mick walked out of the bathroom with a towel around his waist.

"I don't know mate, they disappeared half way through the night without even saying goodbye," he replied. He picked up his trousers and proceeded to go through the pockets looking for any loose change.

"I think our English manliness must have scared them away."

He laughed half-heartedly, pulling out a screwed up, piece of paper. He looked suspiciously at it. There was a row of numbers written down, but he screwed it up and threw it in the bin.

I won't need that, he thought to himself, smiling proudly because he had got the phone number from the girl with no name.

"Come on Matt, we had better get packed. Not long now until our flight home. We have to meet Dan in the bar in half an hour," he lied, needing to get in a couple of beers before their flight.

Panos lay close to Danielle and he watched her while she slept. *She is so beautiful,* he thought, realising she would be leaving him very soon. He had not been able to sleep, so just lay there watching her breathe, unable to stop touching her. Suddenly Danielle opened her eyes and sat up disorientated as she dreamt of being back in her own bed. She was relieved to see Panos and touched his face. She could have cried, so he pulled her back down and kissed her distraught face.

"It is OK my darling, you are still with me."

He kissed her lips and they made love again, even more lovingly than before. She held on to him tight and tears began to fall down her face. She did not want to let him go. He kissed her tears away and found it hard not to let his fall too. They got lost in each other as their love flowed freely, making the most of every moment. They both gasped as it came to an end, and Danielle found she had been crying all the way through. Her heart ached with pain when she looked at the clock and realized she only had a few hours left with him. The irrepressible tears flowed as she held on to him so tight. He felt a lump rise up in his throat as he desperately held back on to his own sorrow. He hated seeing her in so much pain, and fought with all his might, not to make it worse for her.

"I am sorry Panos but I cannot help it. I wish this hadn't happened," she said looking away, unable to look into his eyes.

"But it has my darling, it has," he said quietly lifting her chin up. Then he gently kissed her tear stained face. "We cannot change what has happened."

She slowly nodded her head in agreement.

"Now I am going to get into the shower. You can get your things together and I will meet you downstairs, OK my darling?"

Danielle nodded again in silence and watched him walk into the bathroom. He shut the door behind him; she sat up and rubbed her eyes, took a deep breath and told herself to pull herself together. She found her suitcase under the bed and began to pack. She noticed that the usual sound of Panos singing was not heard, and this made her feel better. *He must be feeling just as sad as I do,* she thought.

He came out of the bathroom as she put the last of her clothes into the suitcase. He had a towel around him and she could not help looking at his gorgeous toned body. She came up behind him and began to kiss his back. He stopped what he was doing and concentrated on her tongue caressing his naked flesh. He was overtaken by a wave of desire and furiously tried to control his urge to make love to her. He turned around to face her and kissed her lips. Then he pulled himself away because he could so easily have been lost in her again.

"I am sorry, but I have to get downstairs. My father is probably angry with me for being away for so long last night," he said quickly, regretting his words, but he had to go.

"OK Panos I understand. I do not agree, but I do understand."

They both laughed, and he got dressed. Reluctantly he walked out of the room. When he shut the door, he stood still and leant up against the wall. He felt so sad and it was getting harder for him to contain his tears. He had to take a deep breath before he was able to continue down the stairs.

When he entered the lounge Yannis was the only person present. He said good morning to his brother and proceeded to go in the restaurant. The kitchen door opened, and his heart rose in his mouth as he half expected his father to come out. To his relief his mother walked through the door holding some cutlery.

"Good morning Panos," she said, laying the knives and forks down on the neatly made tables. He did not reply and just watched her doing her daily routine. She stopped in mid flow, aware of his silence. She placed the remaining cutlery down and walked over to him.

"Panos. What is wrong, my son?" He looked down to the ground and she took his hands in hers. Tears began to well up in his eyes as he squeezed them tight.

"Mother, I don't know what I am going to do when she is gone. I am feeling so much pain in my heart. I cannot get it to stop."

Her eyes began to water as she listened to his pain ridden words. She was lost for words and didn't know what to say, so she just held him to her now saddened chest. As she held him, he felt his heart give in to his emotions and tears began to flow freely. Then she heard a noise coming from the lounge. She quickly looked around, not wanting her tearful precious son to be seen. "Come on, Panos let us go into the kitchen, we can have some privacy in there."

He gently nodded, letting her lead him to where they could be alone. The door swung shut behind them and she again put her arms around her grief stricken son. She held him tight letting him release all of the deep felt hurt that was breaking his heart. They stood there for a few minutes, consumed by his pain.

"Panos my darling, I am so sorry, but you knew this time would come and your wonderful time with her would have to come to an end," she said sympathetically, aware that her words would cut through him like a knife.

"But I don't want it to, mother, I love her and cannot bear her being away from me!" His voice rose as he sobbed harder. She refrained from saying any more, not wanting to add to his anguish any more than she had to. She just held him tighter in the way only a mother can.

His father came down into the lounge seething with fury, as he began looking for his eldest son. He could not believe the insolence Panos had showed by leaving his brother for so long the night before. He felt his anger bubbling in his stomach at the sheer thought of him taking advantage, not only of his status as a manager, but also as a son. He stormed past Yannis ignoring him as he was greeted and walked into the restaurant. He stood still trying to calm his raging heart when he heard Panos's voice coming from the kitchen. He went closer to the door and soon realised his son was sobbing as he spoke. As he got nearer, he strained his ears to make out what Panos was saying. He was stopped in his tracks as he listened to his son speak about how he was feeling. He looked through the small window in the door and witnessed his son crying into his mother's arms. His eyes widened, and his heart softened when he saw his son's heart breaking before his eyes. A door that had long been shut, opened in his hardened heart, and he was taken back to thirty years ago. The memory of him appeared in his mind; he was also crying into his mother's arms, traumatised by an indescribable pain that tore at his heart. He felt a twinge of yesterday's pain fill him, induced by the memory of that agonizing day all those years ago, and the lid of his past was lifted.

He was twenty-five years old and working as a trainee manager in a local hotel back on the mainland. His heart and soul were filled with dreams of opening up his own hotel one day. He worked all hours to learn everything he could, so he could make his dream come true. He loved his work and meeting different people. He did everything in his power to make the guests happy. He was renowned for his workmanship, so was soon given the position of manager. His road was set for his future; he turned the hotel into a popular place for visitors to stay. He felt very proud of himself and was confident his dream was becoming closer. Then she walked into his life and he was totally swept off his feet. Elizabeth was from England and had come to stay at the hotel on a business trip. He was taken by her beauty the first time he laid eyes on her and they soon became friends. They would talk until the early hours, and their friendship soon flourished into a love he had never felt before. She left to go back to England, but they kept in touch regularly. The pain of their separation was so hard that she came back, but for a month this time. He was over the moon to have her in his sight again. He introduced her to his family, but his father took an instant dislike to her. He was very set in his ways, and the two men argued constantly about his future, or lack of it if he kept seeing her. His father dug his heels in and refused to accept her into his family. This began to put holes in his mother's and father's relationship. His mother tried her best to convince her husband to give the young couple a chance as they were so obviously in love, but her powers of persuasion failed miserably.

Her son was also very stubborn and ignored his father. He took matters into his own hands and asked her to marry him. Elizabeth happily accepted, aware of the circumstances. He planned to leave the family home, moving them into a small apartment near the hotel. He broke the news to his parents one day and left for work leaving his mother in tears and his father feeling very angry. He did not care about the consequences, he just wanted to be with the love of his life. He was due to leave the following morning and was very excited about his new life which was about to begin. He had just got in from the hotel and was packing his things together when his mother knocked on the door holding a letter in her hand. It was obvious that she was crying.

He took the letter, recognising the handwriting on the front. His heart began to beat faster as he reluctantly opened it, his hands shaking. He read the words and his heart dropped to the floor, consumed by so much pain he thought it would break. He read her words again, which explained that she could not be responsible for the breakup of his family. She admitted that this hurt her deeply, but she knew she was doing the right thing, and he would be grateful to her one day. She was apparently leaving that night to go home but would always love him. She finished by saying good bye.

He held the piece of paper in his hand and it felt like she had cut open his chest, pulled out his heart and stamped on it. He could not believe her cruel words, his pain escaping through his tears. *How could she do this to me? How could she want to cause me so much pain? I was going to give up everything for her,* he thought bitterly. He was in a complete state of shock. He turned to face his mother and she put out her hands to claim her broken-hearted son. He quickly went over to her and sobbed in to her loving arms.

"She has gone, hasn't she mother? My love has really gone," his tearful words shook her to the core.

"Yes, my darling," she replied, softly kissing his head. "She has."

The days turned into weeks and the weeks into months. He threw himself into his work and soon made himself forget the pain of Elizabeth.

He was at home one evening and his uncle had come over for a visit. When he walked out into the garden his father and uncle were talking, unaware he was coming towards them. He stopped when his father mentioned Elizabeth's name and listened to what he had to say. Then he heard him tell his uncle how easy it had been to convince her to leave his son.

"Love," he huffed. "She did not love him. Otherwise she wouldn't have gone without a fight. I knew the girl was a gold digger, a father knows these things. I have done the boy the biggest favour of his life."

Panos's father's mouth dropped open and his newly mended heart was crushed. From that day on he vowed never to get involved with anyone from another culture again. Elizabeth's name was never spoken again from his lips, and she was soon forgotten as he got on with his life. He had not even told his wife about her, and left her where she belonged, in the past. But seeing his son like this was a sad reminder of the love he had felt so long ago. He closed his eyes, sighed and began to wipe out the memory, quickly putting it safely to the back of his mind. He thought twice about telling Panos off for the night before but then decided instead to leave the two alone. He walked back to his office and could not help letting his softened heart go out to his eldest son.

Half an hour later, Mick and Matt were all packed and ready for their journey home. They picked up their suitcases and took the last short walk down to the bar. When they reached the reception, they were met by Yannis who was talking on the telephone. He smiled at them gesturing he would be with them in a minute. Mick looked around the quiet room looking for Panos and was disappointed to see no one was tending the bar. His need for a beer was getting stronger by the minute, and he became quite agitated by his wait. He took a long look around the hotel and a wave of unhappiness gripped his heart. He had really enjoyed his time here, and the thought of going back to his cold-hearted wife saddened him deeply.

"Good morning you two, are you all set for your return to England?" asked Yannis replacing the receiver.

"No not really my friend, but as they say all good things must come to an end," replied Mick. He pulled out his room key and gave it to Yannis who took it from him and proceeded to hang it up in its rightful place on the wall.

"Is there any chance of a farewell drink, Yannis? I need a beer to calm my nerves for the flight home." He felt his insides shaking and welcomed the thought of a nice cool beer. Yannis nodded and began to walk over to the bar, the two friends following close behind him. They got their drinks and decided to sit out on the terrace to wait for Danielle. He asked Yannis to tell her where they were going to be and went out of the French doors. The sun was very warm, and the two friends sat down to wait for her.

He looked at the pool looking for Kosta but he was nowhere to be seen. He suddenly realised he hadn't had the chance to throw him in the pool before he went home, because most of his time had been spent out of the hotel. His heart sank at the thought of breaking his usual tradition. Then Tracey invaded his thoughts. He wondered what sort of welcome he would get from her when he walked through his front door. He suddenly felt nervous at the prospect of going home, and not knowing the outcome of his return. He began to gulp down his beer.

Matt on the other hand was not feeling nostalgic at the thought of being back in his own house. He could not wait to get back on English soil and get back to his life. His holiday had not ended how he had planned, and he longed to be home again. He looked at his watch and wondered what was keeping Danielle. Then a picture of her and Panos came into his mind. *I can guess that's why she is taking so long. I can't wait to get out of here,* he thought taking a big mouthful of his drink. They shared small talk until the familiar sound of footsteps were heard coming from the hotel. Matt felt a sense of relief when Danielle walked out by herself, but he could not help noticing the desperately sad look on her face.

She got into the shower when Panos left and stood under the warm water. She let its cleansing power sprinkle over her, ridding her of any traces of tears that had flowed earlier. Her heart pumped pain as the thought of actually leaving this place became unbearably real. She knew she would have to be strong and managed to convince herself that once they were on the plane, she could make herself forget Panos. She was an expert at pushing her pain deep inside, as she had done it so often in the past. *This will be no different,* she thought as she sighed heavily and got dressed.

Coming out of the bathroom she walked over to pick up her suitcase, looking around the room. The thought of never being here again consumed her. She quickly walked out of the hotel room door, before she lost control and let her solemn feelings free again.

Taking a slow walk down to the lounge, she forced the excitement of seeing her children again, override her sadness. Yannis was alone in the room and her heart filled with disappointment at him not being Panos. He told her Mick was out on the terrace just as his father walked out of the restaurant. When he passed by her, he looked at her and a small smile escaped from his usually stiffened lips. She was taken aback by this unusual gesture, but soon convinced herself it was because she was going home. He had always displayed hostility around her. She had never seen him smile and was thankful she had not really seen him very often.

She asked Yannis if he knew where Panos was. He shrugged his shoulders but reassured her, he would tell him where he could find her. Taking a deep breath, she ordered herself a cup of coffee and then went out on to the terrace to meet the others. She walked over to them and sat down. Mick was talking about Demi and he couldn't understand why they had left Nicos's so soon. He had been convinced he was going to get lucky with her and couldn't get his head around her sudden change of mind. Danielle smiled as the picture of those two silly girls in the toilet replayed in her mind. She decided to put them out of their misery, so told them the story behind their quick disappearance. His jaw dropped when she explained. He could not believe what he was hearing.

"Blimey Dan that was close. Thanks mate," he said when she had finished. He found it hard to believe he had fallen for this Greek girl's charm and was grateful for his lucky escape. He looked at the beer in his hand and blamed his sheer stupidity on it.

If only I hadn't had so much to drink, then I wouldn't have gotten myself into such a situation, he thought.

He thought about cutting out the drink altogether and his heart skipped a beat at the thought of never drinking again. *Yes, that is what I will do, but not until I get home,* he thought.

Matt listened to what Danielle was saying and he was not surprised. He had let himself be taken in by another woman yet again and hated himself for being so gullible. Her explanation had confirmed the fact he would never get involved with another woman again as they were nothing but trouble, as far as he was concerned.

Panos left his mother in the kitchen and went out into the lounge. His heart ached so badly, and his eyes were sore. He quickly composed himself and spoke to his brother. Yannis told him Danielle was out on the terrace and noticed his brother's red eyes. He sensitively did not say anything, but the sight of his brother's obvious despair tugged at his heart. He watched him walk out of the door and sighed. He knew his brother was going to miss her and hoped he would soon come to terms with his loss. He told himself his brother was strong enough and would soon get back into his normal routine. He was sure he could cope without her.

As Panos walked through the lounge he saw Danielle's suitcase on the floor. He thought his heart was going to explode as the realisation of her leaving filled his confused mind. He did not want to say goodbye to her but forced a smile as he walked out onto the terrace. He stopped and looked over to where the three friends were sitting. He was instantly taken back to the first day he met her, and his heart grieved. That day seemed so long ago; then it felt like they had all the time in the world to spend together. But now, here he was only hours away from letting her go.

His thoughts went back to the previous night when he had made passionate love to her for the first time, and he wanted to cry. She had made him feel so loved, and the thought of him ever loving someone else this way was impossible! He smiled as he watched her talking. She was a vision of loveliness. Everything he ever wanted in a woman was there in front of him, and the thought of losing his dream hurt him so much inside. He stood there staring at his Danielle and wanted to reverse time and go back to that special moment when he first laid eyes on her. He sighed at the pleasant memory.

Mick was the first one to see him standing there and called him over. Danielle quickly looked up and her heart melted when she saw her handsome man. All her feelings for him rushed to her heart when he walked over. He kissed her and sat down next to her, taking hold of her hand and gently squeezing it. "We will have to go soon," he said unenthusiastically. "I will take you down in my car."

Danielle felt like everything was going in slow motion as his words bounced around in her head. The thought of being without him played heavily on her mind as she fought back her pain fuelled tears. They sat in silence for a few minutes. She looked at the ocean and remembered her last night with him. Her body ached for his touch and the memory of their lovemaking stole her thoughts. Her heart palpitated when she closed her eyes, imagining a world where she was back in his arms.

Matt looked at his watch and reminded them it was now time to go. He had seen the look in Danielle's eyes when Panos approached them and thought the sooner they were out of here the better. Panos got up and told them he would meet them at the hotel entrance in five minutes. His mind was racing with what he wanted to say to her as he walked back into the lounge. He was tempted to get her phone number; just so he could make sure she got home safely, but soon thought better of it. Hearing her voice so far away would only make things worse. He walked passed the bar and looked at the stool she had sat on to be near him. He imagined her sitting on it, her beautiful green eyes sparkling as she spoke to him. He couldn't help smiling at the memory until a wave of sadness flowed through him and the reality of her never sitting there again haunted him. Taking a deep breath to ease the pain, he grudgingly went to get his car keys from his room.

The three friends went back into the hotel and picked up their suitcases. Yannis was now at the bar with Anna and they said their goodbyes. Danielle started to walk towards the door when Panos's mother came out of the restaurant and called her over. She told Mick she would not be long and that she would meet them outside.

She walked over to Panos's mother who put out her arms and embraced her. Danielle felt a lump rise up in her throat, brought on by this kind gesture, and it took all her strength to stop herself from crying again. His mother's words were few. She thanked her from the bottom of her heart for being there. Then she kissed Danielle on the cheek and told her, her son really did love her. Danielle was totally lost for words, so just nodded. She quickly let go and practically ran out of the hotel. The older woman was left standing there with tears rolling down her face, and she feared her son would find it hard to get this lovely lady out of his heart.

Danielle stopped at the top of the front steps and could have wept. His mother's gratitude and loving words had totally thrown her, and the ache she felt inside grew. She suddenly felt the need to get out of there because the pain was just too much for her to cope with. She desperately tried to contain her tears and felt proud that only one single tear managed to escape. She pulled herself together and told the two men she was ready. At that point Panos came around in the car.

They proceeded to put their suitcases into the boot and Mick and Matt got in the back. Danielle took one last look at the hotel, took a deep breath and got in next to him. They journeyed down in silence, the Oasis hotel slowly disappearing behind them. It soon became a distant memory as he drove down the winding road. They reached the airport and he parked the car. Still in silence they all got out and began to walk towards the entrance. Panos put his arm around Danielle and they held each other tight. Few words were spoken as they walked over to the check-in desk. They quickly checked in but found they had about three quarters of an hour to spare.

Mick remembered that there was a Taverna outside, so suggested they should have a goodbye drink. Panos and Danielle were pleased they still had some time together and quickly agreed. Matt was slightly put out by the delay, but he went along any way.

They walked over to the Taverna, and Mick asked what everyone was having. Danielle was surprised Panos ordered a large vodka and tonic, he didn't usually drink during the day, and this made her heart ache even more. Mick went to the bar to get their drinks and Danielle began to feel nervous as the time to say goodbye was getting closer. They held hands neither of them wanting to let go of the other.

Mick soon came back carrying a tray of drinks. They sat there for half an hour idly chatting, and Panos could not take his eyes off her. He could feel his heart racing in his chest. The thought of her going played on his mind and made him panic. His palms felt sweaty in hers, and he did not want to let go. Suddenly he became overwhelmed by emotions as he began to panic. He quickly stood up abruptly.

"I am sorry, but I have got to go," he said sternly. He looked at his watch and realised they only had five minutes left. He just could not bear to watch her walk away from him.

"Well, goodbye Mick. It has been good to see you my friend," he said shaking his hand.

Then he proceeded to shake Matt's hand. "Goodbye Matt."

Matt just nodded, and Mick looked at Panos in amazement.

Then he turned to Danielle. She stood up and he embraced her. "Goodbye Danielle," was all he could say. He quickly pulled himself away from her, unable to look in her eyes. He did not want her to see his pain.

"Goodbye Panos," she said, willing him to look at her, but he didn't, and with that he walked away. She stood there frozen by his quick exit and slumped in the chair in complete shock.

He didn't even tell me he loves me, she thought brokenly as the unsaid words induced a gut-wrenching pain inside her.

"I don't believe it, he called me Mick. He has never called me Mick," he said, totally unaware of the torment Danielle felt inside.

"Oh, shut up you, stupid man!" shouted Danielle abruptly, desperately trying to hold back her tears.

Mick looked at her and was just about to say something when he noticed the deep sadness in her face. He put his arm around her and all he could say was how sorry he was.

Matt looked away and felt better that Panos had finally gone. A smug feeling rose up inside him; he had predicted he was just a Greek womaniser who was only out for a good time with a stupid naive foreign girl like Danielle. He secretly smiled. *I knew it would end in tears,* he thought downing his drink in victory.

"Are you going to be all right for a minute, Dan? I have got to use the little boy's room and then we can go," said Mick looking at his watch, taking his arm from around her shoulder. She nodded, and he kissed her head. He walked around the side of the building to the gents. He felt really sad for Danielle and couldn't believe the way Panos had left so abruptly. *Maybe he was only after one thing after all*, he thought.

He smiled proudly to himself because Panos had called him Mick, and without thinking looked out into the car park. He stopped and strained his eyes at a person sitting in a car. *It's Panos,* he thought, recognising his black Mercedes. Mick looked closer and saw him sitting there with his head in his hands. He watched as Panos got a tissue out of his pocket and began to wipe his eyes. *He is crying. The poor bloke is breaking his heart over there,* he thought.

He wondered if he should go over to him and looked at his watch. He realised they were pushed for time and he really needed to go to the toilet so decided not to. *His feelings for her must have been genuine*, he thought as he rushed into the cubicle.

Danielle and Matt sat in silence as they waited for Mick

to come back. He soon returned to Matt's relief, and they walked over to the airport. Danielle was in a daze. The way Panos left so abruptly pained her. She couldn't get over the sudden way he had gone, and the deep gruelling pain made her feel sick to the stomach. They continued to walk through the airport and she was oblivious to all the happy tanned holidaymakers going home. They went through customs without a hitch and carried on towards the conveyor belt that was by a huge window which was the height and length of the room.

Danielle just looked down as it began to move. She felt so ashamed for letting this man into her heart; he had obviously deceived her.

He is just like every other man I have met. What does his mother know? He obviously had her fooled too. Why did I let myself be taken in by this man? she thought. She could have kicked herself for her stupidity as she wrestled with her thoughts.

Mick was standing next to her. He peered out of the window to look at the plane which was going to take them home. His eyes squinted as he tried to focus them on a figure outside running towards them. Then he nudged Danielle to get her attention as it became clear to him who it was. She did not respond so he nudged her again, harder this time.

"What!" said Danielle angrily. "What are you doing that for Mick?" she shouted at him, giving him an irate look, but caught his eye as he looked at the window. She followed his stare as Panos came running up to the glass putting his hand up to it.

"I am sorry my beautiful Danielle, I should not have left you like that. I will never forget you my darling…" he hesitated. "I love you," he said walking with the conveyor belt.

He was still touching the glass, tears streaming down his face. She looked at him as he repeated those three words and she slowly put her hand up to the glass to meet his, in complete disbelief. His tears and heartfelt words were enough to open the flood gates, as her uncontrollable tears began to flow. All her love for him quashed her doubts as she told him she loved him too. They stared into each other's teary eyes and were locked together as their tears continued to fall. Then he came to a sudden stop when he was confronted with a fence. She tried to walk back not wanting to lose sight of him but found she couldn't as too many people were in her way. She became frustrated at the block but had to give in to the human obstacle in front of her. Inevitably she watched him fade away into the distance. Her heart felt like it was going to break when he disappeared out of sight.

She looked at Mick, who was now crying, and just fell into his arms and sobbed. Matt ignored the whole uncomfortable display of love and was rather angry that his earlier opinion was obviously wrong. He could not bear to watch, so disapprovingly looked away. They got to the end and Danielle tried desperately to compose herself. Everyone was looking at her and she felt like she just wanted to die. They walked to the boarding lounge, Mick's comforting arm still around her, and they were quickly ushered onto the plane. She stopped before embarking and closed her eyes envisioning Panos's face in her mind. She never wanted to lose the image for as long as she lived.

"Goodbye Panos," she whispered and reluctantly forced herself to step onto the plane.

Panos stood by the fence unable to move. His tears were still flowing, induced by a tormenting pain clenching his heart. He stood there distraught, until Danielle was no longer there. He wanted to run in there, pick her up and take her back to the hotel with him, where she would be by his side forever. He fought back this great urge when he heard the engines of the plane begin to rev up. His broken heart raced furiously as the plane began its short journey down the runway, getting faster as it went. He let out a tearful gasp and watched motionless as the plane began its ascent. As it went higher into the clear blue sky, his mind was consumed by an overwhelming fear that he would never see her again. This fuelled his sorrow, and he tried desperately to turn and run away, but was unable to. He watched the plane fly further into the distance, soon becoming a small dot on the horizon. Her name escaped from his quivering lips as he sobbed uncontrollably. He watched his Danielle disappear and then, in the blink of an eye, she was gone.

TO BE CONTINUED..........

ABOUT THE AUTHOR

Lisa Labon is an author who has had her fair share of hard times. She has however allowed her life experiences to shape her into becoming an inspiration to others as her passion for writing shines through, and can be seen in this novel, ***In The Blink Of An Eye,*** the first of a trilogy.

She is the mother of four children and lives in Kent.